THE SOOTHSAYER

BY THE SAME AUTHOR

The Unanointed
Voice of the Lord
Believe My Love
Marcus

For my father, Herbert Morell Chambers, whose character makes the Great Apostle seem real for me, comprehensible, and altogether human

And it came to pass, as we went to prayer, a certain slave girl possessed with a spirit of divination met us, which brought her owners much gain by soothsaying.

She followed Paul and us, and cried, saying, These men are the servants of the most high God, which shew unto us the way of salvation.

And this she did many days. But Paul, when he could bear it no longer, turned and said to the spirit, I command thee in the name of Jesus Christ to come out of her. And he came out the same hour.

And when her masters saw that the hope of their gains was gone, they caught Paul and Silas and drew them into the marketplace unto the rulers;

And brought them to the magistrates, saying, These men, being Jews, do exceedingly trouble our city,

And teach customs which are not lawful for us Romans to receive, neither to observe.

And the multitude rose up together against them: and the magistrates rent off their clothes and commanded to beat them.

—Acts 16:16–22

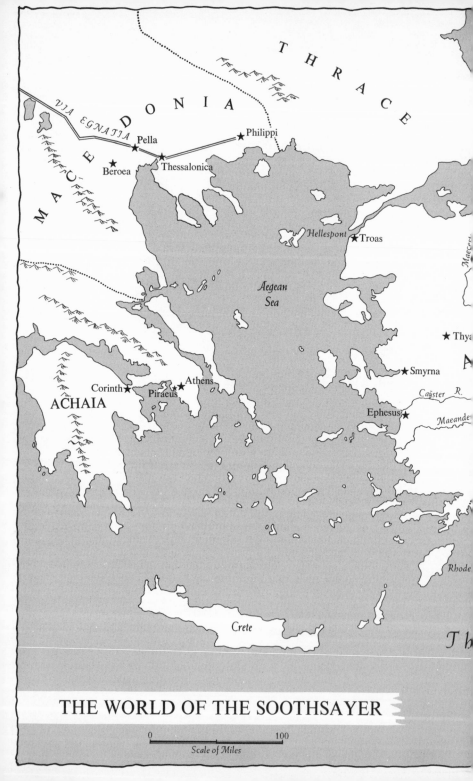

THE WORLD OF THE SOOTHSAYER

Scale of Miles

Euxine Sea
BITHYNIA
GALATIA
I A
CAPPODOCIA
Antioch
Iconium
Lystra
Derbe
ANTIOCHUS
Cilician Gates
TAURUS MTS.
SYRIA
PAMPHYLIA
CIA
Tarsus
Antioch
ner Sea
Cyprus

BOOK I
Lystra

I

EUNICE WATCHED them climb the hill, one hand shading her eyes against the slant of autumn sun. Timothy was talking. Lycon listened attentively, as one adult to another. Well, the boy was thirteen. It was time he was treated as a man, not as a scatterbrained youngster.

When Timothy talked every movement of his graceful body was animated, his restless hands expressive. Say what you like, Mother, thought Eunice, the mixture of Jew and Greek in that boy is charming.

The cottage door opened. Lois emerged, vigorous for all her twoscore years and twelve. She pushed back a heavy strand of graying hair. "He forgot the oil! Your son is not only uncircumcised, he is unreliable."

Eunice returned to her spinning, paying out the combed strands to the whirling spindle with swift competence. Lois continued, "Lycon is to blame. He's got no call to mix in our affairs."

"He has every right. He is Timothy's next of kin." Eunice stirred restlessly on the low stone seat under the oak. She looked out over the valley toward the walled city. Summer heat was passing, and autumn would be here all too soon. With the coming of the cold she would be spinning beside the courtyard fire, and another winter of bickering would begin. But while the pleasant weather held, surely she was entitled to quiet and peace here under the two oaks which fronted the fieldstone cottage.

Widowed almost a year, Lycon had been courting Eunice these past six months. For twelve years, she thought, indulging in a fit of rare self-pity, I have been lonely. Epaphras and I had our love for two little years, and that so long ago. Still, I know my duty. I cannot leave Mother to live alone on this hill, nor would I let Lycon make the sacrifice his brother made in coming to dwell in my mother's house, even if he were willing. Oh, if I felt for Lycon the ardent rapture—but that will never come again. Nor will I again endure with Mother what I endured as a giddy girl for the sake of my Greek lover. I am wiser now—or less courageous. I will live out the slow, compliant years, lonely, pitying myself, pitying also Mother because we have only ourselves and Timothy, and we find so little joy in one another.

The boy and the man were nearer now. Lycon was telling a story, one of the Greek tales of a time long, long ago, when the walled city of Lystra was only a mud village beside the river, and the gods came to visit in the guise of ragged wanderers. Eunice caught a flash of the blue eyes that gleamed so oddly in Timothy's dark, thin, Jewish face. The dancing eyes reflected the volatile spirit, the gaiety and charm which, with the blue eyes and the mop of yellow hair, were Epaphras' legacy to the son whose birth had occurred only half a year before his father died of an infection on the knee that no amount of poulticing would reduce. As they reached the house, Lycon nodded to the two women and concluded his story.

"This may be the hill they climbed, with village dogs yapping at their heels and village urchins flinging stones. Where your house stands the cottage of Baucis and Philemon may have stood on that summer day when the gods punished the churlish Lystrans and rewarded an elderly couple for kindness shown to strangers. These oaks which shade your portal might be the trees into which the souls of Baucis and Philemon entered after death to dwell forever side by side, their wind-stirred leaves murmuring companionably together."

Timothy's blue eyes twinkled. "Where is the miraculous pitcher Zeus gave to Baucis? Grandmother would like to set such a pitcher on our table."

Lycon took Eunice's busy hands in a warm clasp, while spindle and combed wool fell together into the yellowing grass. "It was a Greek pitcher and must be held in Greek hands. If I lived in this house, my love, your pitcher would never be empty." He kissed the thin, busy hands, then turned a gentle smile on the older woman.

Lois said tartly, "The pitcher would be filled then as now with milk from my goat." She turned toward the cottage, erect and angry. "So marry the girl! Give me more uncircumcised grandsons."

Humiliation tightened Timothy's lips. The vivid eyes were washed with quick tears. Lycon said kindly, "I would never forbid the circumcision of a son of mine if his mother desired it."

Eunice pleaded, "Please, Mother, let us be pleasant together."

Lois said grimly, "I take too much upon myself. Do what you like. You always have. I wash my hands of you." Then, furiously, "Timothy, I sent you this morning to bring oil. Here you are, late to return, and with no oil. A great boy like you, can you not perform one simple errand?"

Lycon said quietly, "I will walk down the hill with you, Timothy. I must get back to the loom." He bent to Eunice again. "If I had my way, dearest girl, you would never know a moment's anxiety." He turned again to

Lois. "My whole concern is for the well-being of all who dwell in this cottage. I cannot forbear from coming here, yet when I come I bring dissension. I wish my visits were happier occasions. Good day to you."

He and Timothy strode away swiftly, back down the hill.

Lois gazed after them. "What did Lycon come for? Why would he interrupt an afternoon's weaving to walk up this hill and then go right back down again?"

Eunice checked the impulse to retort, Perhaps to give you another opportunity to let him know he is unwelcome. She picked up the spindle. Lois reentered the cottage.

Here in this fieldstone farmhouse with its three comfortable rooms and its paved court, its shallow cistern beside the stone stairway that rose to the roof, Lois had lived for more than fifty years. Here three sons had been born to her to die in infancy. Here she had borne a daughter who survived. From this house Lois had gone to bury her husband Gedaliah not long before Eunice, just turned fourteen, fell wildly in love with the Greek weaver Epaphras. In this house Epaphras also had come to dwell, though the house of his family in the Street of Weavers just outside the city wall was larger and the looms where he worked each day were there. Still, he had dwelt here in the hope of appeasing his strong-minded mother-in-law, who would have been left to dwell alone if he had taken Eunice to the house of his people.

Now Lycon came often, climbing the hill road. He was patient and he was kind, and he loved the young widow and the son of his dead brother, all the more so because his own marriage had not been fruitful.

The question of Timothy's circumcision had been for Epaphras an ultimate test of his own manhood. He had yielded to Lois in many things. By the time his son was born it had become clear to him that in no way could he make peace with the embittered older woman short of himself becoming a Jew. This he refused to do. When, without consulting either parent of the infant Timothy, Lois had brought Rabbi Zebulon to the house on the eighth day for the circumcision, Epaphras had taken the child in his arms.

"There will be no Jewish butchery here today," he had declared. "If I hear any more on the subject I will take my wife and son and return to the house which is my inheritance."

Eunice had wept in secret as days went by and her son remained uncircumcised. Yet she was proud that Epaphras had asserted himself and that Lois had been obliged to yield. When Epaphras suggested that the question be laid aside until the boy's thirteenth birthday, when as a man he could decide for himself whether to observe this Jewish rite, Eunice accepted the compromise, relieved that the argument need not be resumed for thirteen years. But during those years Lois had spoken often and bitterly of her uncircumcised grandson, harping on the matter, until Timothy had come to regard circumcision as an act disloyal to his dead father. He had firmly announced on his twelfth birthday, more than a year ago, that he would never submit to circumcision and so deny his Greek heritage.

But Lois would not let the matter drop. "I want only what is right for the two people I love. Upon me the burden is laid! You refuse to realize what it is you cast aside when you spit in the face of the Lord God and turn away from all that God gave through Moses to the Chosen People. For this I am called quarrelsome. For this I am unloved, though I do only what a responsible and loving Jewish mother must do."

Her pleas for understanding were too often mingled with self-pity. Under the oaks Eunice was remembering

also. I am twenty-eight years old, she thought rebel-
liously. I am a woman, though she thinks of me as a child.
Soon Timothy must give up synagogue school and begin
employment at the loom. He is to learn the weaver's
trade, and he is lucky to have the chance to learn in the
house of his father, taught by the brother of his father.
He has had his years of study at the synagogue, and it
is enough.

Perhaps the most recent outbursts from Lois stemmed
from awareness that Eunice and Lycon had discussed this
with Timothy but not with her. The worst of their
quarrels had begun, not with Lycon's marriage proposal
but earlier, when Rabbi Zebulon called to urge that Timothy continue his studies till he was old enough to go to
Jerusalem and study in the School of Hillel, while the
great Rabbi Gamaliel still lived and taught there.

"This boy has a deeply spiritual nature. He loves the
literature, the wisdom writings, the poetry, the histories.
A way must be found to turn him upon the path his feet
ought to follow. Above all, he must not postpone longer
the essential rite of circumcision."

Zebulon was a thin, spare little man with jutting ears
and jawbones which his curling forelocks did not serve
to soften. He had large, intelligent eyes and a way of
speaking so warmly reasonable and sincere that one forgot the odd angles of his ears and jaws.

The rabbi had clasped Timothy's shoulders in his bony
hands. "Let him study with me till he is sixteen. Then let
him go down to Tarsus, and thence by boat to Jerusalem to study. Never mind the cost. This community has
wealth which would be well spent on such a project, for
this is no ordinary boy. This is a gifted and sensitive lad,
and our people know that money cannot be spent to
better purpose than for training such a boy to serve the
Chosen People."

Timothy had shrugged away from the rabbi's embracing arm. "I will never be circumcised. I will never be a rabbi. I will be a weaver, like my father."

The recent storms in this cottage on the hill above the ancient city of Lystra had stemmed from that day. Lois had surely learned by now that there was no point in opening the subject of Timothy's future, for neither the boy nor Eunice would engage with her in such discussion. His future had been discussed, but not with her, and Lois was a bitter and deeply disappointed woman.

The spindle whirled, as Eunice paid her mother the silent tribute of understanding her even while she remained determined, rightly or wrongly, to side with her son about his own future.

The spindle whirled, and the finished yarn became a thick hank. From her stone bench beneath the oaks Eunice had a fine view of the broad valley, its stubbled fields, its vineyards heavy with grapes ready for harvest, its olive orchards in silver shimmer. Through the valley ran a stream, a trickle in its sandy bed now that summer was ended. But in spring, when snows melted on the mountains, the broad channel would be filled with pulsing current. The stream flowed east, under the city walls and out again on the eastern side, to lose itself beyond the next range of mountains, perhaps by passing underground.

It flows from nowhere to nowhere, thought Eunice, restive in the dull monotony of her life. I wonder what the next valley is like? And the one beyond that? Her life seemed narrow and barren, moving like the stream from nowhere to nowhere.

On the Iconium road two strangers appeared, dusty enough to have made the entire journey from Iconium, eighteen miles, since sunup. If Timothy were here he would perhaps run out to invite the strangers to pause and bathe their feet and drink a little cool water, for they looked to have traveled through the heat of the day without pause. There was something Jewish in the style of their beards and the drape of their Roman coats. They swung along in a practiced, tireless stride, brisk, confident, joyful. Joyful? They had no more possessions than could be carried on their backs, yet there was indeed an air of joy about them that made you marvel. What journeys have they made? she wondered. What cities have they seen?

In the vast store of Greek legends, two had Lystra as a setting. In both, Zeus and Hermes came walking into this valley. Those two yonder could easily pass for the gods of those legends, returning to pay a third visit to the ancient village which had become, in the period of the Seleucids, a walled city. Their bearing had authority. The larger man, with his beard in two fat curls, was handsome and dignified enough to serve for a model of Zeus-before-the-Gate, whose statue stood in the portal of the marble temple at the foot of this very hill. The smaller man (no bigger actually than Zebulon) moved with a lively grace, swinging a light cane as dusty from the road as his worn sandals. The grace and swiftness of his movements were such as the Greeks ascribed to the messenger Hermes. A sculptor could take him as he walked, his strides matching those of the taller man, his movements expressive of swift purpose, and, adding only wings to his sandals and his staff, make a very credible Hermes.

Lois emerged, vigorously shaking a skin of milk to make cheese. She liked to walk about while churning. "Those are two Jews in togas," she said, making no effort to lower her voice. "I hate to see Jews deck themselves in Romish garments."

"Oh, Mother!" Eunice voiced the protest softly.

The men paused on the road. The larger man raised a hand in greeting. "You Lystrans have a reputation for inhospitality, good mother. We would not want your neighbors to loose their dogs upon us."

The smaller man scratched his chin, clawing through

the dark, heavy beard. "Have you a rabbi in Lystra, Mother?"

Eunice spoke quickly, lest Lois make opportunity for further rudeness. "You will find our rabbi, who is called Zebulon, at the synagogue. When you enter the city, go to the agora and take the street called the Street of Bakers. It leaves the agora at the southeast corner and angles down toward the river. A Jew called Philip sells food-stuffs in the corner booth. He will direct you."

She watched the two move briskly down the Roman road, and was still spinning under the trees when the sun had progressed halfway down the sky. Lois had finished her churning, put away the cheese, and scrubbed out the churn, and had come out to sit and rest with Eunice when Timothy came racing up the hill, his face crimson with excitement or exertion or both.

"Mother! Grandmother! Jonas is walking. Two strangers came and—"

Lois said sternly, "Where is the oil?"

The blue eyes widened in contrition. "I'm sorry! Two men came to the gate where Jonas begs and—"

"We saw the men. Jews wearing togas. As for Jonas, I always said he would walk when he grew tired of sitting. A man with clubbed feet—"

Eunice laid down her wool and rose and slipped an arm about the boy's sagging shoulders. "What was said? Did you hear? Did you see it happen?"

"I was in the agora. I was talking to Philip. Jonas came stumping along over the cobbles toward Philip's booth and the strangers were being mobbed! People were shouting that they were gods, and some brought garlands, and some were buying little presents in the booths and, oh, Mother, come and see! The city is in turmoil! You come and see, Grandmother."

Lois snorted. "Go and buy oil! If you return without oil there will be no cakes today at sunset."

Eunice gathered up wool and spindle, took them quickly into the house, and got her favorite mantle, snowy white with touches of color in the fringes, a gift from Lycon. "We'll get oil," she said, and took the boy's hand. They went rushing down the paved road, which had been built by Roman soldiers after their conquest of this high Asian hinterland.

Lois watched them go, feeling lonely. There they went, like two children, swinging hands and chattering, without a care in the world.

They don't need me, she thought. They don't even like me.

She resisted the impulse to get her mantle and go pelting after them. She lifted her eyes to the distant mountains. Who knows what is happening beyond those ranges? Wonderful things could occur, and we would never know, she thought, until strangers came walking into Lystra, bringing the news. I will live and die and never lift my eyes to the glittering towers of Holy Jerusalem. And here is Timothy, with all his gifts and graces—here is Timothy who could go to Jerusalem the Golden and become a scholar. Who could, but never, never would.

Eunice and Lycon will turn that boy into a bent and hollow-chested weaver, uncircumcised, to live his life out caring equally as much for Greek myths as for the Holy Writings.

Lois pushed back the heavy hair from her neck. So Jonas was on his feet! She had told him more than once, when he held up his beggar's bowl in the gate, that all he lacked was gumption. Yet there he had sat all these years, his skirts carefully arranged to display the ugly feet. One of those two Jews had had the wit and the spunk to rebuke Jonas in terms that finally stirred him to stand and walk.

Well, it wouldn't last. The men had come from God

knows where on God knows what errand, for they led no donkeys and, therefore, weren't merchants with goods to peddle. Soon they would take the road to Derbe or somewhere else—probably to Derbe and soon, if they hoped to get through the Cicilian Gates to Tarsus before winter snow closed the gates to travel.

This road crossed Asia from Ephesus on the Aegean Sea all the way to Tarsus. It was a road along which conquerors had marched, Hittites, Assyrians, Egyptians, Persians, Greeks, and finally Romans. But whoever came and whoever went, the people tilled the soil and sheared the goats and pressed the olives and the grapes, paid their taxes and were quiet.

Lois cast a final, lonely glance after the two lively figures who were approaching the foot of the hill and the temple of Zeus-before-the-Gate. Then she rose and entered the cottage. There would be cheese for the sunset meal, and she would grind the barley and if Timothy and Eunice managed to remember the oil they would have cakes with the cheese. That was food enough. Praise God there was always food enough in this house, even without the miraculous pitcher Zeus had given to Baucis.

2

TIMOTHY RUSHED EUNICE down the hill, surefooted on the blocks of stone with which Roman soldiers a century earlier had paved the ancient road of armies. "Mother!" he cried, "you ought to come away oftener. You look young—young as me!"

She gasped, "I feel young! Sometimes, at home, I feel older than Methuselah." Then, "Timothy! Slow down!"

The boy's eager feet slowed, but not much. "It *was* a mighty work! Getting old Jonas up on his feet was a mighty work."

"Indeed!" Then, curiously, "I wonder which of them did it."

They had come up behind the modest temple that blocked off their view of Lystra's west gate. From the rear one could see the cracks in the marble, especially a large one that angled across the rear pediment with its antique, weathered relief in which Amazons offered garlands to a central figure Lycon called the Moon Maiden. The throng overflowed the pavement that fronted the temple. A tumult of voices eddied and pulsed ever louder as Eunice and Timothy drew nearer. Now they were in the midst of the tumult. Timothy wriggled through the crowd toward the flight of worn marble steps that ascended to the portal, dragging Eunice with him. Half-way up Timothy finally halted.

"I can't get through!" He bent and shouted in her ear.

Eunice clung to his arm to keep from being separated from him. The broad porch above the flight was backed by a row of pillars with simple Ionic capitals. At the right end, the end nearer the city wall, a tall podium rose between the pillars, from which priests were accustomed to harangue the people. Within the shrine, beyond the open doors, stood an antique statue of Zeus done in gleaming white marble. The beard on the benign face hung in fat curls not unlike those of the larger of the two strangers who now stood, engulfed by yellow-clad priests of Zeus, there in the porch above the crowding people.

One of the priests leaped into the podium and raised his voice in a chant in praise of the immortal Olympians. He lifted his arms, beckoning to all to join in the lovely lines of iambic hexameter. Timothy pushed his face close to Eunice and murmured, "Old Miletus must be feeling great to have so many people here today."

Indeed, Eunice had heard more than enough of Miletus' complaints about Greek neglect of the old gods. He was a kinsman of Epaphras and Lycon, which of course made him some sort of distant relation to Timothy. Miletus had resented Epaphras' alliance with Jews as fiercely as ever Lois resented her daughter's mixed marriage.

"I don't ask you to accept every knavish adventure of the Olympians," Miletus would say to the brothers while they bent to their looms. "Homer wrote both to enter-tain and to inspire. But men must honor the gods. They are the Olympians! They are Greek!"

Epaphras had been willing to argue with Miletus, but Lycon never would.

Eunice heard the piping voice of the boy join in the chant, a voice that shifted into the deep voice of a man between one line and the next. She tugged at him and shook her head, but he continued chanting, grinning at her, proud to have stored away in his memory so much that was beautiful, whether of Hebrew or of Greek.

On the platform the struggle intensified, the effort to force upon the strangers the homage of the garlands. Timothy leaned close to murmur, "That little one looks more Jew than Greek."

"They are Jews. They inquired the way to the synagogue as they passed."

The boy's grin broadened. "Zebulon will have plenty to say to them! I hope I'm on hand to hear him!" His slim body jerked with the rhythm of the chant. He watched the lively scene with interest and delight. Suddenly Eunice was caught by the aspect of the larger of the two strangers. He was crowned with three garlands, and others lay across his shoulders. He gazed out over the crowd, his eyes gleaming with friendship and good-will. The great pillars glowed with age, forming a background of simple dignity for the turmoil. And Eunice no longer found it shocking that Jews were here in this place of worship amongst the Greeks. Epaphras had taught her to appreciate the architecture of fine Greek buildings. She found this temple, marred though it had been by occasional earthquakes, far more satisfying to the spirit than the squat and squalid synagogue where she went with Lois on the Sabbath to ascend to the dim gallery reserved for the women of the congregation.

Miletus appeared on the porch, clad in yellow. Draped over his shoulders was a young ram, which he gripped by the legs. His strident voice rose in the chant, praising the deathless gods, omnipotent Zeus, swift-footed Hermes.

The chant ended. Miletus called out, "We have been taught by what cunning devices you have formerly tricked men of Lystra into betraying the baseness of their natures. Greeks, you will say, have forgotten the gods the ancients praised. You will find this is not true in Lystra. We love the gods and honor them."

His tufted, yellow beard jutted. His hands gripped the ram's legs. As a crescendo of shouts greeted his speech, the animal gave a sudden lunge and a jet of urine sprayed over the yellow robe and onto the coat of a nearby priest.

Then the smaller of the two strangers leaped into the podium. He lifted his hand, demanding silence, but the shouting continued. The throng stretched all the way down the steps, across the pavement, across the highway, and on into the grassy park beyond. From all this throng came shouts of praise to the gods, immortal and Olympian, who apparently were honoring this city by a third visit. Jubilant priests led the shouts, nor did the scuffle and racket abate, nor the shrill cries, "Hear us, O mighty Zeus! Give ear, swift Hermes."

Then the man in the podium caught a garland flung at his head and tossed it back into the crowd. He took his toga between his hands and rent it from neck to hem.

At the sight of this typically Jewish gesture the shouts dwindled. A voice rang out, an orator's voice, speaking from the podium with a pure diction the Greek of these Asian lands, the Greek of a man who had spent his youth in the pursuit of knowledge.

"Keep your gifts and your garlands. Stand upon your feet. Do not offer us obeisance. We are mortals, like yourselves. You blaspheme in calling us gods, as if our own power had raised your fellow townsman and set him on his feet. We are men, come from beyond the mountains and over the Great Sea to bring Good News to Lystra."

Confused, the priests looked toward Miletus, awaiting their cue. The chanting had died. Miletus' hands tightened on the ram's legs. "We know you well, O glib and witty Hermes," he shouted. "You were ever a trickster.

We applaud your wit, but we are not deceived. Now do us the grace to come down to the altar, where we will sacrifice this flawless ram to honor you."

As Miletus spoke, the ram freed one leg that became entangled with the flowing, yellow hair of the priest.

If ever a throng was confused by mixed emotions this one was. One and another began hiding their offerings in the folds of their coats. Still, they could blame the priests for misleading them, and the priests, of course, could always blame their leader, the volatile and arrogant Miletus, who was by now too busy dealing with the ram to keep abreast of the altered mood of the people.

The man in the podium shouted, "I am called Paul, a man of Tarsus, a Jew and a Pharisee of the Jews. My companion is Barnabas by name, a coppersmith of Cyprus, while I am a tentmaker by trade. We have crossed seas and mountains to bring you this message: Lord Messiah, even the Christos, has come!"

The drama of the announcement was lost in confusion and chagrin. Miletus had somehow got rid of the ram, which was being lowered to an apprentice priest from the end of the porch. The people were murmuring in confusion, and some were trying to escape through the throng, mortified that they had been made fools of. Most, however, were still curious enough to remain.

The voice of the man of Tarsus rang across pavement and park. "The Christos was born a Jew as our prophecies foretold. But his message is for all men. He laid this command on his followers, 'Carry the Good News to all nations.' For this reason we have come to Lystra, to declare that all men are children of God, who made men, having first created the earth and the firmament of heaven and all living creatures. By whatever name He is called, He is the mighty God. Messiah brought salvation and a new and glorious life to every man who accepts him as Lord and Savior, whether he be Jew or Greek, slave or citizen. God is the Father of all men, and the Christos is the very Son of God, sent to redeem humankind from sin and evil, that they may dwell in peace and love together."

A shrill voice rose. A thin, ragged figure limped upward from the pavement toward the porch, as people parted to let the beggar pass. As he jerked his way upward he shrieked, "Blessed are you, O glorious messengers, for surely God sent you to deliver me from my infirmity, who never walked until today."

The hubbub faded, as Eunice lost contact with her surroundings in the mighty meaning conveyed by the man from Tarsus. The Christos has come! For how many hundreds of years had Jews awaited the fulfilment of the promise. Lois should be listening to this message! Messiah has come, but not to Jews alone. Messiah has come for all men! All, all are the children of God.

Timothy's hand was squeezing her shoulder. "Old Miletus has got himself into a mess."

A sort of pity for Miletus touched her briefly. He could not turn against these men he had hailed as gods, not while Jonas was hobbling upward to the porch. Whatever Miletus did next, it would be wrong. She murmured, "Sh, Timothy. Listen to that man. Hear what he is saying!"

The coppermaker from Cyprus was in the podium now.

Miletus cried desperately, "Tell us by what power you made this lame man walk."

"By the power of Jesus of Nazareth, who came to bring the water of life to all men."

Timothy had vanished from beside her. When Eunice saw him next he had wormed his way up toward Miletus and the strangers. The man from Cyprus was speaking, but she could not force her mind to absorb more, having heard the astounding statements of his companion. She was filled with the radiance of Paul's message. I want to go home. I want to tell Mother. Oh, Mother, believe! Please believe! She reached the roadway, turned for a last look at the strangers, and saw that Timothy was standing close to the podium. The last thing she heard as she walked away from the milling throng was the voice of Miletus. "Don't be misled, men of Lystra. These are gods. Don't be tricked into misbehaving as in times long past. The quicksilver Hermes was sent with mighty Zeus to deceive you and tempt you into churlish behavior toward the gods. His duty is to uncover the worst as well as the best in men—"

Eunice closed her ears. Timothy would be all right, either with the strangers or with Miletus. No harm would come to the boy today. This confidence was part of the ineffable peace that filled all her being. I did not sin when I married a Greek husband and brought into the world this blue-eyed boy. Whatever Mother may say hereafter, I will hold my peace, knowing that I did not sin. All men are the Children of God.

She was halfway home when she remembered that no oil had been bought, nor was Timothy likely to remember it. Well then, there was bread in the house, and a goat tethered on the rocky slope, waiting for the evening milking.

As she neared the house Eunice saw the familiar figure, sturdy, invincible, a strong pillar upon which a family had leaned for almost twoscore years. Eunice felt a surge of love for the old woman. We are a family! We need one another and we rely on one another. How long had it been since she had felt the impulse to kiss her mother?

Lois grunted, "You've been gone long enough."

"I saw Jonas. He is indeed walking."

"He could have walked long ago, when he was a child, if he'd had more gumption. I told his mother. I told Philip. I've told him, times enough."

"Of course you did. And Philip told him, every time he sent oil or barley to Matilda from duty, not from affection or concern. Still Jonas did not walk. Now he walks. Two strangers came to Lystra and now Jonas walks. It was a mighty work, Mother. And these men say —Mother, they came to tell us that Messiah has come."

Hope sprang into the brown eyes in the dark face, hope and a terrible longing. "I suppose—oh, I suppose you believed them. You are gullible enough."

"What I believe makes no difference, Mother, except to me. They believe. They made a heartbreaking journey, over the mountains, from city to city, not for themselves, but for only one reason—to spread the Good News. They will accept no gifts. People were pressing gifts upon them but they accepted nothing. Give them a hearing, Mother. They will be here in Lystra, telling their story to all who will listen. Give them a hearing."

Lois grunted and went to the mill, where grain for the evening meal was half ground. She knelt and began laboriously turning the upper stone upon the lower one. Eunice folded her mantle and laid it on a shelf and knelt to help turn the heavy weight.

"Mother, do you still believe the old prophecies?"

"Of course!"

"Do you believe Messiah will come?"

"Certainly."

"Do you think he might come in our lifetime?"

"Don't be a fool. Messiah will come when God wills. Many have claimed to be Messiah, only to die as rabble rousers and disturbers of the peace, while their followers scattered to the four winds. Zebulon has told how they come to Jerusalem with the return of every Passover, creating disturbances and vaunting themselves. Myself, I will want some evidence. I hope I am not such a fool as to believe a pair of wandering Jews who come down the road wearing togas."

"The little one tore his toga from neck to hem when the people would not listen to him." Eunice went to the granary for more grain. "Timothy was with those men, standing between the tall one and Miletus up in the podium when—"

"The podium? What podium?"

"Miletus and the people dragged the two men up to the temple of Zeus—before—"

"The temple? That Zeus temple down there?"

"Now, Mother, don't jump to conclusions—"

"They preached the coming of Messiah in the temple of Zeus?"

"Mother, I've never seen the city in such an uproar."

"Blasphemy!" Lois sat back on her heels, her dark face mottled with rage. "Blasphemy! You came away and left Timothy with those—those blasphemers and that pagan priest he is related to! What kind of mother are you?"

"Like you, Mother. I want the best for my child. If Messiah has come, and as they said, has come for all men, whether Jew or Greek—since God is the creator and the father of all men—then these men have things to say that I want my son to hear. I also want my mother to give them a hearing."

Lois was walking about the court now, wringing her hands. "You have found two blaspheming strangers who offer a doctrine that exonerates your folly and guilt in mingling Jewish blood with Greek. Now you will call me bigot, and marry Lycon. You will turn from your own people once again on the testimony of two charlatans who preach Messiah from the porch of a pagan temple. Wherein have I sinned that God has given me so wicked a daughter?"

Eunice rose. She tugged the mill off the spread linen, and Lois held the pan while Eunice poured the ground meal into it.

She said, "I am a woman. I no longer require chastening from you." She turned blindly and left the house, feeling desolate. How could she have supposed there was a way to reach that pigheaded woman?

The shadows of the oaks were long on the slope. Figures were climbing the hill. Timothy bounded excitedly ahead of the others. The strangers were in the group, and others also, men and women. She felt the presence of her mother beside her.

"Oh," she cried, "how can I bear to hear what you will say to those good men, guests my son is bringing to his house?"

3

Lois GLARED at the approaching group. "Charlatans! They take advantage of a growing boy to come uninvited to the house of a widow."

"This is the house of two widows. Mother, don't humiliate Timothy."

"He's got no oil! He brings guests but no oil. What am I supposed to offer them, with sunset at hand?"

"We can offer the fare Baucis and Philemon set before Zeus and Hermes. We have bread and milk." She tucked her hand in her mother's arm. "Don't let them see that we are quarreling. Smile!"

"I taught you all the manners you know. Be quiet." Then, very softly, "All those people! Half a score, coming at the hour of the sunset meal."

The company moved in close formation, excited, happy voices mingling. Jonas stumped along in their midst. Timothy, with the two outlanders, was in the lead.

Eunice murmured, "Philip is with them. He has a cruse of oil on his shoulder. They bring fruit and bread. Mother, they are bringing their supper."

"What is Philip doing in that mixed company? Five of them are Greeks. God help us! Those two men have their beds on their backs. They must intend to spend the night here."

"Give them a hearing. They are well able to speak for themselves. The mountains rim our valley, not the world."

Timothy broke away from the group and arrived in a rush of excitement. "Mother! Grandmother! We have guests! Oh, Grandmother, wait till you hear the news the strangers bring."

Lois said, "Go fetch the rabbi."

Eunice gripped the boy's arm. "Fetch Lycon. He is your next of kin."

Timothy glanced from one to the other, then made his decision. "I will bring Lycon. Tomorrow I will take Paul and Barnabas to the synagogue for morning prayer." He appealed to Lois. "They are good men. You will love them." He raced away down the hill to fetch his uncle.

Lois approached the visitors, hands outstretched. "Welcome to our dwelling, such as it is, for we are two widows and that lad is all we have."

Barnabas said warmly, "He is a fine lad."

Paul straightened his thin shoulders as if casting off all the weariness of a long and troubling day. "Good mother, we came here by a child's invitation. But we bring something in return for hospitality. You shall not lift a hand on our behalf until you hear our message. Then we will remain or depart, according to your wish, for this is your dwelling, and we are strangers."

Lois replied pleasantly, "That seems fair enough."

Eunice said, "I heard you speak at the Zeus temple, sir. I am Eunice, a spinner by trade, and this is my mother Lois. The lad has gone to bring his father's brother, who is our next of kin."

Lois said, "The evening breeze is pleasant under the trees. Rest here. You will meet our rabbi tomorrow. He is a man of learning, who studied in Jerusalem for two years with the great teacher, Gamaliel." She bent a sharp glance on the weary little man which seemed to say, You see, we are not all ignorant and gullible people in the back country of Asia.

Barnabas said, "Praise God for a scholarly rabbi. Paul also studied with Gamaliel. Sit down, Paul. Rest. It has been a harassing day. Think of it, Paul. You will have a scholar in Lystra with whom to engage in disputation."

He glanced around at the company, who were making themselves comfortable on the grass before the cottage. "We have so far found no rabbi of comparable training in Asia. I am a man of business, not a scholar, and Paul often finds me a disappointing companion."

Philip set down the cruse of oil beside the portal. He looked somberly at the strangers. "You will find Zebulon more than ready to dispute the propriety of preaching Messiah from the porch of Zeus-before-the-Gate."

Paul was pacing restlessly amongst the relaxed people, unable to rest until he had cleared up a few matters. "It is our custom in every city and town to go first to the synagogue, or wherever Jews are to be found, and preach to them. Afterward we preach wherever we are given a hearing—in the gates, in the agora, in the portals of public buildings. We did not choose the setting today. The crush of people drove us out through the gate, and suddenly there we were, two men in the midst of hundreds. However"—and he paused to look down squarely at Lois, who was sitting beside Eunice on the bench—"I see no impropriety in preaching the coming of the Son of God amongst men in any place where men and women will listen. We have never before preached our first sermon in a city to so large a company. Yet it sticks in my mind that this is an unfortunate beginning for us in Lystra, and it would not have happened had I remembered that my mission is preaching, not healing."

He stood brooding over Jonas, who sat as he had sat in the gate, with the ill-formed feet extended and exposed. They were tender feet, and walking on stones today had bruised them. Paul addressed Jonas firmly. "My friend, we will now speak of your healing. It came about through your faith in God's power, and God's power is infinite. Give God the glory. The Lord Jesus during his ministry healed countless sick. When he commissioned his apostles he commissioned them to heal the sick, cleanse lepers, open the eyes of the blind, cast out demons, and make the lame walk. I was not one of that company, nor was I so commissioned. I myself suffer from an infirmity, a fever that returns to sap my strength until I feel that I trudge these Roman roads bearing a body of death upon my back. I pray for healing, but God, who reads the heart, finds in me a need for the discipline of suffering. You, Jonas, will walk with pain until the tender flesh has toughened. Your infirmity remains, and your spirit must be strong. Remember, every day you live, to give God the glory. Remember that God's chastening is designed to make us strong."

Paul looked searchingly into the thin face of the man who had begged in the West Gate for so many years. "Because this grace has been given to you, we begin our ministry in Lystra cumbered with the enmity of the priests of Zeus and also of many right-thinking Jews. The priests made fools of themselves today before all the city, and well they know it. God help them, for we could not prevent their stubbornness and their folly. The throng swept us along, up to the portal of that pagan shrine, where, to avoid the blasphemy and the sacrilege of having a ram sacrificed to us as if we were gods, we were compelled to speak out in the name of the Lord Jesus.

"I ask myself, Jonas, why did I speak the word to you today? I can only reply that the Breath of God moved me to speak that word. The hand of God is upon you, Jonas. Be worthy of this grace. When we are driven from Lystra by offended and affronted men, bear in mind that you are the walking symbol of the power of the Lord Jesus. You carry on those feet not only the burden of your body but also the heavy weight of our ministry."

Eunice dared not meet her mother's eyes. Had she provided this preacher with a list of her mother's objections and arguments, she could not have elicited more apt comments than these. She rose and entered the house, bringing back a basin, a pitcher of water, and a towel. She knelt to bathe the tender feet of Jonas, but his wife Matilda, Philip's kinswoman, took the utensil and the towel. Eunice poured the water, and Matilda bathed the bruised feet and dried them.

Barnabas said, "You must get sandals made to fit these feet, my friend."

"I've never needed sandals till now," Jonas said humbly.

A Greek called Porphyro said, "I will make sandals as my gift to you, friend." And Eunice knew that the sandals would be well made, for Porphyro had been making sandals for Lois and Timothy and herself as far back as she could remember.

Philip was an elder in the synagogue, a man of substance, respected throughout the city of Lystra. There had been a scandal, years ago, when first Jonas began begging in the gate, since Matilda was Philip's kinswoman. But the talk had died down, for Philip was widely known for honesty and rectitude, as well as for practicality and piety.

Barnabas leaned back comfortably against the bole of an oak. "A remarkably fine view," he observed. "We have had a long day. We fled Iconium at the beginning of the night's third watch."

Lois straightened. "What happened in Iconium that you fled?"

Paul said darkly, "Certain fanatic Jews in Antioch of

Pisidia made themselves our enemies. When we first preached in Antioch we were given a hearing in the synagogue as well as in the street. But more and more people turned to us, and in the streets you could hardly pass because of the throngs who lingered to hear us. The Jews grew jealous and quarrelsome, and the rulers of the synagogue ordered us to go hence and preach in Antioch no more."

"It was time for us to go on," Barnabas said quietly. "Yet in every city our joy in the converts and our desire to remain until they are fully grounded in the new faith must struggle with the urge to preach and found ecclesiae in more and yet more cities. In Iconium, when we had preached for a month, the approach of autumn warned us we must move on if we are to reach Tarsus before winter closes the mountain pass. We yearn to return to the churches in Antioch and Cyprus and Jerusalem which launched us on this journey, and report how God has blessed our ministry. Yet we linger, loath to leave, until God gives us enemies who send us forward on our mission.

"In Iconium, when we had preached for a month, enemies from Antioch followed us and roused up certain factions in Iconium against us. There was threat of stoning, but we left the city and spent the night with a shepherd—last night that was, though it seems a long time ago—and this morning we were on our way to Lystra before dawn brightened the sky. And I do firmly believe that it was the hand of God which brought us here, and that God will bless our mission in Lystra as He did in Iconium and in Pisidian Antioch, and in certain cities of Cyprus also, where we ministered before we crossed to this Asian land."

"It has been a very long day," Paul remarked. He had not yet ceased from prowling about.

Lois said, "I am sure many of these people were eager

to offer you hospitality. Yet you accepted the invitation of a child."

Barnabas smiled, completely relaxed against the bole of the tree. "Timothy was the first to invite us."

Paul stood above Lois, looking down upon her. "The lad is of mixed blood. His home is peculiarly appropriate, since we preach to men and women of every race and calling."

A flush tinged Lois's cheeks. "You speak of our shame."

Barnabas said quickly, "He is not a boy to be ashamed of."

As he spoke, Timothy and Lycon appeared on the road, climbing the hill with great, eager strides. Timothy waved and shouted, but the evening breeze whirled away the sound of his words.

Lois said, "You know of course we have no way of testing the truth of anything you choose to tell us."

"You have the evidence of your heart, good mother. It is easy to believe when you see wonders and miracles. But to recognize truth because the message rings true— no, I ask too much. First you must hear our witness. I myself was a scoffer and an unbeliever until I was struck by blinding light on Damascus Road. I have great sympathy with those to whom faith in this message comes only with difficulty. I fell from my horse that day, stunned and blinded. But I was led to the house of a good man in Damascus who believed on the Lord Jesus. His ministry washed away both the blindness of my eyes and the blindness of my heart. The grace of faith comes easily to some. To me it came very hard."

Lois grunted, and Timothy and Lycon joined them. "My father's brother, good sirs," Timothy said proudly. And after concluding introductions, "Please tell Lycon and my grandmother all about Messiah. What was he like? Had he a seraph's wings? Had he powers of levitation? Did he walk on water?"

Paul looked kindly on the spindly, excited boy. "He knew God. Through the Lord Jesus all men can come to know God."

He still stood, gazing down upon Lois. "Through faith we sow the seed and cultivate the soil. Through faith men marry and bring children into the world. For Jonas today it took a singular act of faith to rise and walk. Faith is the substance of all we hope for, the evidence of what we do not see but know certainly exists. Faith is proof that the prophets spoke as God moved them, and that God's promises have been fulfilled in the Lord Jesus. You are a Mother in Israel, Lois. I need not explain faith to you."

Lois said heavily, "Faith in God is not the same as faith in a story told by two strangers, dusty from the road, having been driven hence from both Antioch and Iconium, strangers who preach Messiah's coming from the porch of a Zeus temple."

Barnabas smiled upon her with great sweetness. "Your grandson is half Greek. Do you really believe God sent Messiah to the earth for Jews alone?"

"You use my greatest misfortune as a reproach."

Paul said, "Lois, this lad is no reproach to you. Think carefully. Would you say that all men have sinned and fallen short of the glory God offered in the act of creation?"

Lois pushed back her dark hair in an extremity of frustration. If there was one thing Lois knew for certain, thought Eunice with wry pleasure, it was that all men share in the world's wickedness. Here were two men who surely read the heart! She saw that Lycon was watching her instead of the strangers, and motioned him to a place beside her on the bench.

Paul persisted, "All men, Lois? Jews and Greeks, Romans, Egyptians, Syrians, and the Lycaonian tribesmen of these hills? Have all men sinned?"

Lois said somberly, "All have sinned and fallen short. But Messiah—"

Paul said, "God has provided through Messiah forgiveness of sins and a way to turn again and live at peace with God. Would you then say that God would provide this priceless boon to all men? Or would God offer forgiveness and reconciliation and peace of heart to Jews alone?"

Lois made a final plea. "Forgiveness? Is that what your Messiah can bring? Only forgiveness?"

The tentmaker from Tarsus sank down at last, exhausted yet triumphant, since this tough-minded old Mother in Israel was on the point of yielding. Oh, he coveted this strong, stubborn woman, for the sake of the lad, for the sake of the handsome young woman, the lad's mother, but most of all for the strength she would bring to the company of believers he would leave in Lystra when he moved on to other cities. He had recognized from the beginning of his ministry that converts easily persuaded were too often easily lost. The core of every ecclesia must include such as Lois to hold it firm. The miracle was not in winning converts in each city, but in shaping them to survive and grow, to bear leaves, flowers, fruits, and finally seed to spread, luxuriate, and go forward forever until the earth was filled with the knowledge of the Lord Jesus.

Paul said, "Forgiveness, repentance, righteousness through knowledge of God and the indwelling Breath of God. Ah, Lois, did you think the Kingdom of Heaven on earth is only an empire with Jesus on the throne instead of Caesar? What strangely human creatures we are, so to warp the divine meaning of our special destiny! God's kingdom is in the hearts of men. Righteousness is God's supreme gift to men. Knowledge of God through our blessed Lord Jesus, who dwelt among men for a season—this is the open door by which all men may enter the Kingdom. This is the Good News we have trudged down many a dusty highway to bring to Lystra and to this household."

Lois tore her gaze from the magnetic eyes of the outlander, stared wildly about at the company, until suddenly she was caught by Timothy's look of kindness and longing and love. The boy threw himself down beside her and embraced her. "Tell the truth, Grandmother. Tell these people how you love the Greek part of me the same as the part that comes from the Chosen People."

Lois wilted. "Philip, do you accept this strange doctrine?"

"Jonas is walking. His feet are the same, but he is walking. This is a mystery of the spirit. I accept the teaching of these good men."

Lois slowly rose. "I must hear more, but there will be time for all that. Timothy invited you here. Eunice welcomed you. I—went through the motions in the name of courtesy. Now I welcome you, each of you, all of you. You have come to hear these men and to know them and their message better. Let us spread the sunset meal that you have brought, and break bread together. Timothy, bring water to bathe the feet of our friends who walked today from Iconium to Lystra, and who have endured much since reaching our city."

Suddenly everyone was bustling. Women spread the meal upon a cloth Eunice brought from the house. Lycon carried the two beds to the roof and Timothy got his own bed and carried it up there.

Amid the bustle a moment came when Eunice found Lycon standing beside the cistern in the court. He drew her close, looking deeply into her eyes. "What does it all mean, my beloved?"

"I am not sure yet. It means more than we can learn in an hour or an afternoon. But as a beginning, it means that I now have the courage, dearest Lycon, to marry you."

4

Timothy was off for school, rushing breakneck downhill.

He had been rushing to school, arriving late, half the time since the preachers took up residence in the cottage. Talking—there had never been such talk, surely, in the city of Lystra or in all this great, high valley.

The Good News—the Power of Salvation—how to become a Christian; how to live like a Christian. Both were the gift of the Lord Jesus, the one by his death, the other by his resurrection.

Sometimes Timothy fell asleep only to wonder next day whether he had dreamed all the things he seemed to remember. Paul and Barnabas, laboring to strengthen the new ecclesia, preparing it to prosper and grow after they continued their journey south and east, to Derbe, on through the pass and down to Tarsus, then home to Antioch of Syria and Jerusalem—home to report where they had been and what had been wrought.

Eunice and Lycon had married two weeks ago and gone to live in the loom house beside the city wall. Sometimes Jonas and Matilda came to spend a day and a night on the hill. Jonas found the barley field comforting to his feet after the cobbles of Lystra, and talked of learning to plow the field after the early rains.

As he neared the foot of the hill, Timothy overtook a trio of strange-looking travelers. Two men strode briskly along, men whose gaudy coats and scarlet turbans proclaimed that they were traveling entertainers of some sort. Of what sort was apparent as Timothy jolted to a halt near the weird little creature they led.

Attached to her owners by a cord which hooked into the leathern collar of her slavery, a child half walked, half trotted. Without missing a step she stared round at Timothy with strange, wild eyes. She wore a single garment, a threadbare shift of some sort. It did not reach her knobby knees, which, like the skinny arms and bloated belly, suggested that she was more than half starved. The child was filthy, with wild, matted hair of no particular color except the color of dirt. Her bare feet had been bloodied on the stones and blood was on her legs in caked rivulets. Yet she seemed unaware of her misery as she stared round at Timothy.

Suddenly she shrilled, "You too will walk down many a dusty road. But the master you serve will bind you with cords of love."

Weird language from this weird and revolting child! But of course! Timothy had heard of such things. The child was demoniac, possessed! The men led her from city to city to tell fortunes.

She had told Timothy what his future was to be! Could it be true? But I am bound to stay with Grandmother now, he thought. I promised when Mother married Lycon and went to live in the loom house. Still, a demon had spoken through this child. The fortune must be true. I know the meaning. I am to travel with Paul and Barnabas. I am to become a servant of the Lord Jesus, a companion to evangelists. It is my destiny!

Filled with joy and gratitude he asked, "What is your name?"

One of the men, the one who held the leading cord,

turned. His bristling gray brows shadowed tired eyes in deep sockets. His face above the gray beard was deeply lined and very dark. "Don't meddle with Merza, boy. You've heard your fortune. Now let's see the color of your penny."

Timothy gasped. "I have no penny." Then, "I did not ask for my fortune." I did not ask, but oh, I am glad to have heard it.

The younger man gave the cord a cruel jerk. The jerk would have toppled a child less nimble and experienced. This was a thick, burly fellow, cruel, self-indulgent, not a man one would choose as companion.

"How many times—" He jerked again, a savage jerk, to which the child accommodated herself by her incredible footwork. "How many times must you be told? Wait! Tell fortunes only when ordered! First we bargain. After we see the money, then you speak."

He approached the child with cocked fist. She dodged past him and ran whimpering to fling herself behind the older man.

Timothy cried, "I can pay you. Not with money, but come to the cottage up there on the hill, with the oak trees in front. There is milk from our goat, and cakes fresh-baked this morning. A warm coat I have outgrown which Merza can wear. Sandals—I have outgrown a good pair of sandals this year. They would last Merza all winter." He liked to say the name. It had a sound of mystery and power.

The big man scowled. "Don't waste pity on Merza. She feels neither cold nor heat. She is demon-possessed, and such folk feel nothing."

The older man said quietly, "She is flesh and blood, Bias. She can die of abuse like anyone else." To Timothy he said, "Your father. Where is he?"

The message was clear. They would go to the house of

a widow. They wanted no truck with a house where a vigorous man was in charge.

"My father and my grandfather are dead. I live with my grandmother." No need to mention that Barnabas was there, and Jonas and Matilda. Paul had gone down into the city quite early.

The older man said thoughtfully, "Tell me, does your grandmother make cakes with sesame oil?"

"With olive oil, sir, and the barley well ground and sifted."

The reply had caught Bias' attention. Still he said impatiently, "We are losing the best of the morning. We'll eat in Lystra. There's no profit in dawdling on the road."

"Be wise, Bias. The girl needs cleansing, and a woman to teach her how to keep herself decent. Her times of uncleanness have begun, and she has no notion how to look out for herself. A grandmother—a firm Jewish grandmother by choice—could teach her. Moreover, I would like a breakfast of cakes made with barley flour and olive oil, new-baked. Sandals and a warm coat for Merza—you'll find she is worth more to us clean than foul."

From behind him came a thin, childish voice, unlike the shrill voice which had predicted Timothy's fortune. "I want my grandmother. I'll be still as a serpent in the hole."

Bias said, "Boy, are you a Jew? You look Greek to me."

"My father was Greek. My mother and grandmother are Jews."

Bias said contemptuously, "They are a mixed lot. Well, come on then. No use dawdling here." He set off swiftly up the hill.

Timothy ran ahead to warn Lois about the unsavory

guests he was bringing. Yet he was not anxious. Lois would be as bedazzled as himself by the future the girl had predicted. It was better than being a rabbi, which had always been Grandmother's dream for him.

The girl must be older than she looked. The times of her uncleanness had begun. It was a mystery belonging to women, and Timothy did not bother his head about such.

Slaves were often a pretty miserable lot, though Timothy had never seen one look as miserable as Merza. He hoped Bias knew what he was talking about when he said she felt nothing.

The Lord Jesus had cast out demons! Oh, if Paul—but no. Paul did not choose to do mighty works, but only to preach. Besides, what would happen to Merza if she lost her powers? Her owners would treat her even more cruelly, perhaps leave her to starve and perish. Nothing could be done for her.

Fast as he ran, Timothy reached the cottage only a step ahead of Bias. "Sit here." He waved toward the bench. "I will fetch my grandmother."

As he entered, he heard the rasp of the grinding mill. In the court, Lois and Matilda were kneeling on opposite sides of the heavy affair, turning the upper stone over the nether. Matilda faced him, but Lois did not see him till he touched her shoulder.

"What are you doing here at this hour?" She sat back upon her heels, looking up at him in astonished displeasure.

"I met a soothsayer. She told my fortune—oh, Grandmother, such a marvelous fortune! But I had no penny to pay, and her owners—well, I had to give them something, so they are here to get some breakfast. Barley cakes, I told them, and—"

Lois was on her feet. "Her owners! Timothy, what got into you?"

"Grandmother!" cried a thin, childish voice. The girl had entered and was crowding round in front of Timothy. "Oh, Grandmother, you did not need to sell me. I would have made no trouble, ever again. These are bad men. Bias hurts me. I am cold, and in winter the stones bruise my feet. Give back the silver to Zenon. Buy me, Grandmother. I will earn money for you. I will tell fortunes."

Lois stared in horror and pity at the creature who clutched her skirts. Tears rolled down her cheeks. She put her arms about the thin girl in the threadbare shift. "Oh, my child, I would help you if I could. Tell me your name."

The girl pulled away. "You have forgotten me. Never for a moment did I forget you! Now you look at me as if I were a stranger."

Timothy said softly, "It is not true, what Bias said, that Merza feels nothing."

Lois said, "Matilda, give over the grinding. Take up the meal and make cakes for the men, the owners of this poor girl. I will bathe her and find some clothing. A decent coat, and some tunics—Timothy has been growing so fast. Timothy, pour out the warm water in a basin and put more to heat. Stir up the fire. Bring in fuel. Come, child. Come, Merza, dear child. Let's have a look at you."

She led the girl toward her sleeping room, which opened off the court to the left of the portal. At the stairway she called, "Jonas, never mind the beds. Go get water. The cistern is quite dry, and we shall be fetching water from the spring till the rains come. We will need plenty of water to cleanse this—to cleanse Merza."

At the bedroom door Merza lagged, reaching toward Matilda. "I am hungry. I am very hungry. What is that that smells so good?"

From the top of the stairway Jonas protested, "Brother

Barnabas has gone for water. Wife, give me a pitcher. I will go and milk the goat."

"Husband, the goat was milked long ago, at dawn. Get more water, for one pitcher will not suffice. Then you can sit and talk to the child's owners. How fortunate that we have a man in the house at such a time."

Lois exclaimed, "Timothy, you brought those men. Your duty is to sit with them while Matilda makes their breakfast. Matilda, give this child the cakes left from our meal. Bring milk in a cup. Then make the cakes for those men. You will find we have already ground enough meal for that purpose."

"I will get water," said Jonas, and took a pitcher from Matilda and went limping out through the portal. "We're sure to need lots of water today."

Timothy looked longingly after Lois as she vanished with Merza, who was greedily stuffing cakes into her mouth. He had not shared with Lois one word of his wonderful fortune!

Barnabas was sitting with Bias and Zenon under the trees, a large pitcher of water propped between his knees. This was clearly not his first encounter with these entertainers who, like himself and Paul, traveled the Roman roads that linked the cities of the empire. Timothy took the pitcher into the house, emptied it into the sooty pot that sat among the stones of the fireplace.

"Barnabas is talking with the men. Tell Grandmother he is here. He has encountered these men before. Tell her, oh, Matilda, do tell her Merza told a truly wonderful fortune for me. She said—"

He saw that Matilda, unable to listen and work at the same time, had given over patting out the barley cakes and was sitting on her heels, waiting with avid eyes and open mouth to hear his marvelous fortune.

"I'll tell you later, Matilda. The men are impatient for their breakfast." He returned to his unsavory guests.

Bias was grinning at Barnabas. "So this is where you

holed up when they chased you from Antioch. Refugeed with a widow and her grandson, eh? Clever. Where is your fiery little friend who turns the world upside down?" Then, impatiently, "Boy, how much longer must we wait for food?"

"The cakes are on the fire. It won't be long. Grandmother is bathing Merza. Matilda is baking the cakes."

Barnabas and Zenon fell into conversation about certain violent incidents which had occurred in Antioch of Pisidia when the rulers of the Jews grew envious because of the crowds attracted by Paul's preaching. Timothy listened avidly. One day he would be a participant in such scenes.

Zenon said, "We heard they meant to stone the little fellow in Iconium. How did you get away?"

"We spent the night with a friend in the hills and set out for Lystra before the sun rose next morning."

Bias laughed. "You won't be so lucky this time. We saw those Antioch Jews on the road yesterday. They were headed for Lystra. They'll smell out somebody in Lystra to help them. They'll stone that little fellow yet."

Barnabas rose and wrapped his coat about him. "Thank you for the warning. Paul is in Lystra, and has been since quite early. I must go and find him. Take care of that little sybil of yours or she won't last out the winter."

Timothy cried, "I'll come with you, sir." He was suddenly terribly frightened for Paul.

"Your place is here, Timothy." Barnabas strode away swiftly down the road.

Bias shouted, "What's keeping the girl? If there's to be a stoning down there in the city it will be great for business. I'm not going to waste the morning here!"

Zenon said, "Sit down, Bias. We will wait till she has been cleansed and fed. Merza has value, and we will indeed lose her unless we learn to take better care of her. She is twelve years old, and no bigger than when we got her from her grandmother at the age of nine."

Matilda emerged, soft, plump, clean, anxious. She set a dish of smoking barley cakes on the bench between the two men. "I'm afraid the milk is gone," she apologized.

"Milk!" exploded Bias. "Wine is what I drink, not milk."

Matilda looked harried. "We never serve wine for breakfast."

Zenon interposed, "Eat your cakes. You'll get wine when the girl earns money to buy it."

Bias grinned, his mouth stuffed with cakes. "Your fire-eater friend is probably dead of stoning by now."

"What's that?" cried Lois from the portal.

Zenon said, "I apologize for my companion. He enjoys frightening people."

Timothy felt as if he were suffocating with fear for Paul, but he managed to say calmly, "It's all right, Grandmother. They saw some Jews on the road who have come from Antioch, enemies of Paul. Barnabas has gone to warn him. I'm sure the rabbi will not allow anything to go wrong in Lystra."

Bias growled, "Where is the girl? We're going." He scooped up the last of the cakes and rose.

"She is drinking her milk. She will be with you in a moment. Is it true her grandmother sold her to you?"

Zenon said, "The family was destitute. She would have starved. But she has the gift of clairvoyance so I bought her, and hired Bias to come with us as our protector."

Lois looked hard at Bias. "She bears the marks of many beatings. Poor child." A tear ran down beside the prominent nose which gave so much character to the dark, strong face. "Is she Greek? Her name is Greek."

"I gave her the name," said Zenon. "It is a good name for this business we are in."

Bias belched. "She's mixed breed, like your boy." He wiped his mouth on his coat sleeve. "I'm going, Zenon." He strode away down the hill road.

Lois said, "The girl ought to remain in women's quarters for the days of her flux. Find a place where she can rest and be warm at such times. Also she needs food and plenty of petticoats at these times. If you don't take better care of her she will go into the wasting sickness. You live off her affliction, yet you abuse her. Do you want to lose your living?"

Zenon said softly, "Actually, I don't want to lose Merza. She is an appealing little thing, when the demon lets her rest."

A plaintive voice cried, "Grandmother! Where are you?"

A strange little figure appeared in the door to crowd against Lois. The girl's wide, hazel eyes seemed enormous. The tangled hair had been cropped very short and lay in rich, chestnut-colored ringlets all over her head. The pale, thin face had a translucent look. She wore the blue coat Timothy had saved for Sabbath-best till he outgrew it. Apparently she was wearing several garments under it. On her feet were sandals formerly Timothy's, the broken cords replaced by twined lengths of bright yarn. The strange eyes, peeking around Lois's skirts, sought out the figure of Bias striding off down the road. "He is a beast. I hate him. Grandmother, give Zenon silver. Don't let him take me away again, Grandmother."

Zenon rose, holding the leash loosely. "You are not for sale, Merza." Then, to Lois, "You have done wonders, good mother. I will try to follow your suggestions. But I am an old man, and tired, and the life of those who follow the roads is not easy."

Lois embraced the trembling girl. "Keep her shod, and warm, and feed her, and for the sake of mercy, leave off beating her."

Merza shrilled, "Grandmother! Don't send me away again!"

She was squealing and hiccupping against the tug of

Zenon's hand on her arm, against his attempt to attach
the cord once more to her collar. Then suddenly her attention was caught by a group ascending the hill, and
the others also turned to look. Matilda it was who first
recognized the bloodied, stumbling figure in the midst
of the group, though Timothy had already identified
Barnabas, Zebulon, Lycon, and one of the Christian Jews
employed in Philip's booth. Matilda screamed, "Paul,"
and began to run.

Merza screeched, "They stoned that little preacher!
They stoned him in the city and dragged him into the
field to die." She ran after Matilda, and now all of them
were running, all but Zenon, who followed slowly, wind-
ing Merza's leash about his arm.

5

TIMOTHY CAUGHT a last glimpse of Merza, trotting erratically downhill, clumsy in the unaccustomed sandals. But he had eyes only for Paul, who limped painfully upward. Someone grasped an arm to help him along. Paul exclaimed sharply, "Don't touch me!" The rich, curling beard was matted with blood. His face was so bloodied that, of all his features, only one eye could be distinguished. Even the great, impressive nose seemed lost in the smear.

The rabbi walked beside Paul. Timothy thought achingly, Rabbi, Rabbi, could you not have prevented this? Stoning is a ritual, prescribed by Law, with every step charted. You are his friend! Stoning was the penalty for a man convicted of blasphemy or a woman convicted of adultery. The field of stoning was outside the walls, within view of the loom house of Lycon. Twice it had been used within Timothy's memory, both times for adulterous women. Pious Jews kept it neat, with stones in piles and the earth free of weeds. How could this thing have happened to Paul, when the rabbi was his friend?

How could Paul possibly have survived?

Timothy rushed into the house and up to the roof to bring down Paul's bed and spread it near the fire. He poured water into the blackened vessel which stood always among the coals. Oil was at hand for anointing the wounds. Bindings, towels, what else?

Clothing for Paul. His toga had been destroyed when he rent it in the porch of Zeus-before-the-Gate, for it had been too threadbare to stand patching. He was today wearing his only coat, and it apparently was torn to shreds and quite wrecked. Someone will provide a coat, he thought. Lycon had been weaving a new coat for Paul, but it was unfinished. Timothy rushed back to the roof to rummage among Paul's meager possessions, and the tunic he found was the last one in the bundle.

The company was at the portal as he descended again to the court. Paul said again, sharply, "Don't touch me!" Then Barnabas, "Zebulon and I will cleanse the wounds. Lycon, keep the company outside." Then Paul was beside the fire, and the rabbi was stripping off the torn coat before he and Barnabas helped the bloodied figure down onto the bed.

Lois entered to bend over the fire, test the temperature of the water, poke at the fuel Timothy had laid over the coals. She brought a clean sheet to wrap the patient. And Timothy watched, murmuring brokenly, "Paul, you live. You were stoned, yet you live. God be thanked, you live."

Lois brought out a small jar of precious ointment Timothy had not even known she possessed. Then Barnabas said, "We are Levites, Zebulon and I. We have been given medical training, and will attend to these wounds. Mother Lois, go out to the company and lend them your strength. Paul is a modest man and will not tolerate a woman's hands or a woman's gaze. Timothy will remain and be useful."

Despite his awe of Paul's tenacious courage, Timothy was desperately fearful. O God, don't let him sicken and die as my father did of putrefaction, for he is a man of mighty courage, with a great work still to do. O Lord Jesus, let him live, and let me grow fit to become his companion and servant.

Barnabas and Zebulon knelt on either side. As they cut away the tunic Timothy saw that in addition to innumerable bruises, there were deep and jagged wounds high on the chest, above the eye, and on the front of the thigh. Other wounds on the back were later revealed, but the face wound seemed to be causing the most trouble because of the copious bleeding. Now Timothy tore himself away from horrified contemplation to gather the moist and sticky rags. He poured water into a basin and thrust them in to soak. Washed and dried, they could be torn into strips for bandages for some future occasion.

Barnabas said, "Bring more water, Timothy."

The cistern had chosen a bad day to go dry. Timothy took the pitcher. With a last, anguished look at the slight but apparently indestructible figure, he left the court and went out into bright sunshine. Strangely, it was no longer morning. The sun was overhead and shadows were short. Under the trees the Christians were gathering. More were on the hill road. Their questions peppered Timothy as he emerged.

"Please," he said, "they need water. He lives. His wounds are being cleansed, anointed, and bound. Pray God he will survive this dreadful thing."

"What is the rabbi doing in there?"

Timothy did not reply but went rushing up over the hilltop and down to the spring. Few of the Christians were aware of how many hours the rabbi and Paul had sat disputing together the books of prophecy and their fulfillment in the life and death of the Lord Jesus.

Deliver us from evil, he prayed as he ran, stumbling over stones, recovering his balance, and running on. Deliver Paul from evil, from suffering, from death, from the hatred of misguided and wicked men. Let none follow him to this house to drag him back to death in the field of stoning. O God, Lord Jesus, God, deliver Paul.

When he returned, the group before the cottage was still larger. Eunice sat among them, spindle whirling. Philip was telling how he had heard, in his booth in the agora, commotion and loud voices at the far end, near the West Gate, but was readying his wares for business and did not realize who was involved until certain Jews rushed past his booth to go and fetch the rabbi.

"They're stoning your preacher," they had shouted to him in passing.

"I don't understand," mourned Philip. "Our Lystra Jews revere the Law. A man must first stand trial, then he is taken to the field of stoning. Who would stone a man in the agora and afterward carry him to the field outside the wall? It was most irregular. It was contrary to the Law."

Lois said, "Enemies of Paul came from Antioch and Iconium. He had eluded them in Iconium. Perhaps they feared to delay action lest he escape again."

Lycon said, "Greeks were involved. I saw Miletus among those who laid him in the field of stoning."

Timothy entered the cottage. In his haste he had slopped out more than a little water from the pitcher.

Barnabas said, "Thrice have I nursed Paul through the fever. We were friends from our youth, and made many a journey to Jerusalem together to celebrate the Passover. I have dressed his wounds after other attacks by zealots."

Zebulon was probing the chest wound, seeking the exact shape and depth, which continuing issues of blood seemed to conceal. "God help you, friend, you have a clavicle of iron," he said. "Had this blow struck nearer the throat, or lower in the chest—but as it is, your clavicle saved your life."

"That was the first stone," said Paul. "Rabbi, I have

never known a stoning so disorganized from beginning
to end. The wrong people were hurling the stones—
Greeks, and Jews from other cities. They gave me no
hearing at all. There was a noisy, undignified argument,
then suddenly a Greek priest—that fellow Miletus—
threw a stone that struck my clavicle, and one of the
Antioch Jews caught me above this eye here, and I went
down on all fours and heard and saw no more for the
thud of stones upon my back and shoulders and thighs.
Somebody came up shouting that it was illegal to do this
in the agora, and I lost consciousness for a time. I suppose the men who carried me to the field of stoning
thought me already dead. Whoever that man was who
interrupted the affair, I suppose he saved my life."

Paul opened one eye and touched the hand that was
binding his chest wound. "I suppose he was one of your
good Jews, rabbi."

"It was myself," said the rabbi. "And when they picked
you up I, too, thought you were dead. I think our Lystra
Jews had little to do with this."

Barnabas said, "Lie still, Paul. Your lips are oozing.
Timothy, bring wine. See if you can just drip the drops
into the mouth without touching his lips. You've lost a
tooth, Paul, and may lose another. You need fluids so
hold still and don't talk."

The sound of voices raised in one of the hymns Christians sang came from beyond the portal as Timothy
began to drip wine from a spoon into the opening between the mashed lips.

Barnabas said, "Again God has sent enemies to drive
us forward on our mission. We have lingered longer
than planned in Lystra. I have seen snow on the mountains. We will go on to Derbe. If our preaching prospers
there we will give up hope of reaching home this winter,
preach in Derbe for a while as the spirit moves us, then
perhaps return as we came. Timothy, when you're

through with the wine, go and bring Lycon and Philip. We must make our plans."

Paul pushed away the spoon. "Enough, lad. Rabbi, you and I are of a size, and I am naked. My last coat is gone. Lycon is weaving one for me but it is unfinished. I came on this journey determined not to be a burden but—"

Zebulon interposed, "I have tunics to spare, and a coat that will do you through the winter. But this notion of moving on at once is folly. That thigh wound will keep you bedfast—"

Barnabas and Lycon and Philip were arranging a sunset meeting for today when Barnabas would speak the farewells for both Paul and himself.

Zebulon said, "You are a stubborn man, Paul of Tarsus. I do not know how Gamaliel tolerated a zealot such as you."

Paul's eyes closed. "He is tolerant even of zealots. I will return to Lystra, Rabbi. I am not through with you yet."

Suddenly the court was empty. Outside, the Christians were departing, to return for the sunset meal when all would break bread together in memory of the Last Supper of the Lord Jesus. Timothy sat beside the bed where Paul lay as if sleeping, his breathing deepening and slowing, his body jerking at times as if he dreamt.

Timothy was lost in a sea of confusion and pain. Paul and Barnabas were leaving. Wounded, with blood still seeping from thigh and facial wounds, Paul fully expected to set out on foot for Derbe, twenty miles to the southeast. They hoped and intended to go on down to Tarsus, then Antioch of Syria, and so to Caesarea and Jerusalem, visiting everywhere with the apostles who had followed the Lord Jesus in his lifetime, had witnessed the Crucifixion and seen the Lord after the Resurrection. Paul and Barnabas would report on their journey and the converts and the ecclesiae. Who will guide us? Who will

answer the questions which arise? We are new to The
Way. We are ignorant, dependent on Paul and Barnabas
in scores of ways.

The day is passing, he thought, and I have told nobody
at all the marvelous fortune Merza predicted for me.
If I cannot tell Paul I should at least tell Barnabas. And
Grandmother.

I will never be stoned, he thought, feeling reassured. I
have not been circumcised. I am not under the Law. The
thought echoed and reechoed. He caught his breath, for
without intending to, he had spoken aloud. "I have not
not been circumcised."

The unbandaged eye was open. Timothy said to it,
"I am neither Greek nor Jew. I have nothing to do with
those who stoned you."

"I was stoned by both Greeks and Jews. Do you not
accept the view that all men are brothers?"

Timothy's head ducked in embarrassment. "I want to
go with you when you set out for Derbe. I guess I was
trying to think of an argument to persuade you. Oh,
Paul, today a soothsayer told my fortune. She said, 'You
will walk down many a dusty road.'" His voice choked
with emotion. It was the first time he had repeated the
wonderful phrases to anybody, and here he was telling
them to Paul! "She said, 'But the master you serve will
bind you with cords of love.' All day I have known that
this is my future, that I am to go with you, to be your
servant—your companion. All day I have known it, and
I have told nobody until now. Oh, dear Paul, do say I
may go with you, to share your mission and your dangers and to walk beside you on the roads."

Paul's hand grasped the boy's hand. "What of your
responsibility to Lois?"

"You had responsibilities. You left them. You did not
marry. Neither will I. You told us Jesus said, 'A man
must forsake his family to follow me or he is not fit—'"

"Your grandmother would rejoice to see you embark on such a career. But Timothy, there are some decisions you cannot make at your age. I suppose there was never a man who enjoyed the company of women more than I do. You cannot measure the cost of celibacy until you are a man, with a man's needs and emotions. Vows are not to be taken lightly, my son. There are many things to consider, sacrifices to be made by yourself and by those who love you. I could have been killed today. I seem to be a man with a great talent for making enemies. I endanger myself and my companions also."

Timothy's voice was low. "They will not stone me. I am half Greek."

"True. You have not been circumcised."

Timothy said shyly, "The rabbi says I am an exceptional scholar and a good scribe. I have longed to copy the book you carry, the Sayings of the Lord Jesus, so that I might stand and read from it when our ecclesia meets and there is no preacher to address us."

"An excellent thought. When I return—"

"Oh, Paul, I want to go with you!"

"Spoken like a child. Lad, two things are essential if you would be my companion on the roads. First, to be a man and a Christian. Second, to be master of a trade."

Timothy said, "And I am not yet a man, nor have I learned my trade." He sighed. "Tomorrow I will begin my apprenticeship as a weaver. When you return—"

Paul's eye had closed. "Tomorrow you must also begin learning to win souls to The Way. You must start with Zebulon. And Miletus."

Timothy cried, "But I don't even *like* Miletus!"

"He is your cousin, and Zebulon is your teacher. I leave their souls in your charge. Now you must let me rest. I say only one thing more. I will not embarrass myself by asking the good Jewish women who invite my companions and myself into the hospitality of their homes to take in an evangel who cannot decide whether he is Greek or Jew."

Timothy leaped to his feet. "*You* want me to be circumcised? *You?*"

"Lad, you would be an embarrassment to us. I have trouble enough without going in search of it. Moreover, it would greatly comfort Lois, who will miss you more than you can imagine."

Paul had accepted him! This was the meaning of the entire conversation. I will do everything he says! Oh, I will work as nobody ever worked before! I will ask Zebulon to help me find every prophecy in all our books which foretell the coming of Messiah, and he will help me discover how each applies to the Lord Jesus. Miletus —oh, I know not how to approach him—I am afraid of him, really. But today he cast stones with the Jews. He must be in a dreadful state of mind. I will talk to Miletus. I will learn to know him as a cousin and a Christian ought. Circumcision? Oh, I have been so foolish about that! But I will wait for that until Paul returns. It will comfort Grandmother when I go away with Paul. It will be my gift of love to Grandmother in parting.

Then suddenly, as he saw that Paul was apparently sleeping again: I must find Merza. I must thank her for the wonderful thing she has done for me. None of this would have come about if Merza had not come today, to make that strange and beautiful prediction of my future. Where is she? I must find her, and see how she fares, and say thank you, Merza, for the splendid fortune!

The boy was gone, and Lois had come to sit beside him. Still Paul kept his eyes closed. His lips had begun to bleed again. There would be much that needed saying before the two of them set out tomorrow morning, and he must not talk when it was not necessary. He kept very still, breathing steadily, deeply. Best if they think him asleep, for now. This good Mother in Israel was one in whom, more than anyone else in Lystra, Paul put his trust. She would steer the ecclesia through the shoals and the deeps ahead. Silently he took inventory of his condition. The legs were sound, so Barnabas said. They had sore spots, bruises, but nothing to keep him from using them. The thigh wound was still seeping a little, but a fresh bandage before they set out at dawn would do for a time. A day's journey from Lystra to Derbe. Well, perhaps in his case it would take longer. They could take shelter for the night tomorrow in some shepherd's hut, and find another soul to whom to preach the Good News. Today I walked away from the field of stoning, he thought. Tomorrow I will walk away from Lystra. I bear the wounds of the Lord Jesus. Forgive my pride, O Lord. Forgive my incurable vanity, which makes me stand firm, inviting trouble, when wisdom would dictate a milder course. You chose me for my zeal, Lord Jesus. I must not complain when it proves inconvenient.

The boy Timothy will shape up very well. He would like to go with us, at least as far as Derbe, but no, he must lose no time learning his trade. That is the first lesson. Once a plan is made, lose no time. Heretofore my companions have set out on the spur of the moment with me, blessed by the elders. Mark turned back when we left Cyprus and came to this high, Asian land. As if God could not see beyond the Taurus Mountains! As if these people had not souls equally as precious as Cypriot souls! The lad Timothy will become for me what John Mark could never become, for Mark loves Peter first and most, then Barnabas, and I come in a very poor third with that lad. One needs always to be training up the young to take on our burdens and bear them with us. The hand of the Lord must surely be on Timothy, and he will be a comfort to me in years to come.

Upon me the burden is laid. Upon me, fever ridden,

incautious, brash, misreading all too often the hearts of men. Offending where I would persuade. Those good men in Jerusalem have never grasped the terrible and urgent mandate: Go into the world. Preach to every nation. O God, I thank Thee that I was born both Jew and Hellenist, a man of a great city who knows there are cities on every shore of this Great Sea, and that God is father of all. Of all. No man loves Jerusalem and the Temple more than I, Paul, called to be an apostle. But Paul grows tired of the pain and the conflict, homesick for Heaven and the Presence of the Lord Jesus. But not yet. Not until I can bear the glory, knowing that the labors that were laid upon me have been discharged as ordered.

The wound was seeping again, and he reached to press the linen firmly against the flesh, feeling the damp of warm blood. Lois rose and brought a fresh bandage, and he took it and held it in place till the seepage stopped. O God, You chose me for this towering task. Why did You not choose a vessel more fit? When I am not prostrate with fever I am making enemies who abuse me when they can, and but for Thy mercy destroy me.

Yet I live. I walked here from the field of stoning, and tomorrow I will walk as far as I can on the road to Derbe. Yet how can a man make Christians of all the world, especially a man who understands so well how the arrogance of a little knowledge can blind the mind to truth? What will become of each little ecclesia when I am driven hence? Year after year our friends in Jerusalem and Antioch preach the same message to the same people, guiding each step, shoring up the broken walls, bringing in new converts to enrich and refresh the old. While I preach for a brief season in a city, then go my way, leaving the shorn lambs to protect one another from the storm. Without ministers, without books, with no firsthand knowledge of The Way as Jesus taught it.

Ah, but I leave with them the great gift, the Breath of God. Where wisdom fails, inspiration must come to their rescue.

My time is not yet, Lord Jesus. When I come to You, I will leave behind me such a chain of ecclesiae, such a cloud of believers, praising Your name, that they will become for me a cloud of glory to usher me into Your presence. Forgive the weakness, the longing to lay down the burden, O Lord Jesus. For until Your apostles have carried the Good News to all nations, Your time to return to us has not come. For when You come again, it must not be to a manger in Bethlehem, but riding upon clouds of glory, to be welcomed in every nation as Lord and King.

6

Through a city seething in the aftermath of violence, Timothy made his way. Booths sagged where stones to shore them up had been seized and cast at the vulnerable body of the missionary. Cobbles were missing, where pried loose by one of the maddened attackers. Here and there blood could be seen on the cobbles of the agora, Paul's blood, on cobbles scuffed and muddied by rushing feet.

People milled about, full of gossip. The Antioch visitors had departed. Law-abiding Lystra Jews must have given them no welcome at all, after the deed was done.

As he crossed toward the booth of the Jew who had gone to fetch Zebulon to the scene that morning, Timothy heard a shrill, penetrating, familiar voice. "Your hands drip blood, and it is the blood of a righteous man."

Merza! And the tall fellow in yellow at whom she was screaming was his cousin Miletus. Merza sat on the pediment of a statue of some long-dead Seleucid general, but this was not the girl who had come all clean and pretty from Lois's ministrations this morning. Pure evil darted from her hazel eyes. The chestnut curls were tousled. The features were twisted in malevolence. The face was suffused, a deep red that was almost purple. The mouth was stretched wide and twisted downward. The hands curved into talons as she rushed madly at the priest. She drove her head into his midriff, at the same time scratching her clawed fingers down his arms. Miletus caught and held her away from him, while her eyes rolled, her mouth twisted, and bits of foam dribbled, foam mixed with blood, for by now she was gnashing her teeth upon the lolling tongue.

Then Zenon had her, one arm holding her tightly while the other hand slipped a bit of whittled stick between her teeth to protect the tongue. He apologized to Miletus. "The demon seizes her. The demon drives her to excesses. Please forgive—"

The girl was struggling, and it took his entire strength to keep her from further injury to herself. Her body had grown rigid, the tension in her legs and arms so terrible her hands and feet shuddered. Her sandals had been twisted off her feet.

There was, near the agora, a pen where animals could be watered and left to browse while their owners were occupied with business. Now as the day grew late it had emptied. Zenon picked up Merza and carried her toward this place. Timothy ran to the statue, where he had spied the missing sandals, and would have followed Zenon, but Miletus had his arm in a tight grip.

"Tell me the truth, boy," he demanded. "Did that preacher rise from the field of stoning and walk to your cottage today?"

Timothy said softly, "Cousin, how dared you stone a citizen of Rome?"

Miletus grew pale. One long arm bent across his forehead. "Great Zeus save us! A citizen. He wore a toga once, to deceive us, and never again."

"Miletus, you were never a stupid man, till now. The toga was worn threadbare. When he rent it, it was fit only to be torn into bindings, some of which are now wrapped about the wounds you inflicted. Hear me, Cousin!" Suddenly his dislike of Miletus vanished in a yearning to open his eyes to recognize and accept wisdom. "Suppose the mighty god you call Zeus were a thousand times more powerful than he seems in the tales the poets told of him? Suppose he were in the whole earth supreme, creator and father of all men, the same Ineffable One the Jews call by the Name they fear to pronounce? Suppose Zeus is indeed the Mighty God, one and the same in every land in all the earth. Suppose He had sent out messengers—these same preachers who came to Lystra and got Jonas up onto his feet before ever they entered the city . . .

"Suppose they were sent here by God to test and try our hearts and our understanding, and they came walking into Lystra—men, to be sure, just as they seemed to be— but messengers of God nonetheless. Suppose they wrought a mighty work at the city gate, not by their own magic but by God's will. Suppose you were misled because you had been too well indoctrinated in the ancient and beautiful and inspired literature of our people?

"Suppose they wrought a mighty work to test and try the hearts of men. And you, Miletus, chief of all the priests of Zeus, were yourself misled in your longing to believe the gods had come again to Lystra.

"Ah, Miletus, you were not wrong. You did not make a fool of yourself that day, except in one thing—your excess of zeal. You tried to make deities of two men sent as messengers of the mighty God. And they, being righteous men, conscious of their humanity, could not permit you to offer to them the homage which belongs only to God, since that is sacrilege.

"They had no wish to embarrass you or humiliate you. They were driven to extreme measures to avoid sacrilege, and you were not easily persuaded. You, Miletus, and Paul of Tarsus were two devout and stubborn men in collision. Cousin, should not a priest care for truth above all, and not let pride separate him from deeper knowledge of the God you have sought all your life to serve?"

"Boy, are you trying to make a Jew of me?"

Timothy was suddenly conscious of the sandals in his hand, and itching to get back to Merza, even while he felt uplifted and astonished because such a flow of wisdom had come pouring through him—from somewhere—and this cousin of his had listened as a man listens to a man. It had been a heady, a most wonderful experience, and strange. Yet he rose, for it was time to find Merza. He said, "Talk to Lycon. He is a Christian and also a Greek. You know that many Greeks have joined our company."

"I'll talk to that troublemaker. I'll face him and demand an explanation."

"Miletus, Paul was stoned today! You cannot see him. He has been treated for wounds and lacerations. He is resting and nobody will be allowed to disturb him. Perhaps you can find Barnabas and get him to talk to you, though I doubt it. You'd do better to go to the loom house and talk to Lycon and Mother."

Timothy walked away. I did not do badly, he thought. Where did all that sudden insight come from? Most of those arguments never entered my head, till today.

Called to be an apostle, he thought, as he walked away from the agora. Will it happen to me also? Then, Merza, but for you I would be the same today as yesterday, a child with no great plans for what I would become. But today I have been accepted by Paul—with reservations —to become in time his companion in his travels. Tomorrow I will begin, oh so willingly, to learn my trade as a weaver. Today, today I began seriously to study how to lead men to become Christians. That is the great work —to open men's hearts and minds to the Good News.

Merza, Merza, you were a messenger of good news to me today. I wish I could do something good for you in return. You are the most pitiable creature under the whole sun, and I can do nothing, nothing for you.

Timothy found Zenon sitting on a bench against the wall of the corral. His coat was spread on the grass where Merza lay, pale as death but quiet and apparently sleeping. What long lashes she had, darker than her hair —very dark against the pale, hollow cheeks. Timothy handed the sandals over to Zenon.

Zenon said, "She is resting now. When she wakens she will be as if it had never happened. I will try to get a little wine into her before she sleeps tonight. She is always weak, exhausted after one of these seizures."

Timothy said softly, "Already the fortune she told me this morning is beginning to work. I talked with Paul. I will be his companion on his preaching missions, after I master my trade as a weaver. Perhaps one day I will meet Merza again in some distant city. Merza and you also, sir." And he smiled up at the tall, thin figure dressed in those outlandish garments of red and yellow. "I would love to see Merza again, somewhere. Will she live to grow to womanhood?"

"I'm sure I hope so, boy. She is our bread-and-butter, our living. Bias and I would be in a sorry plight without that little girl. I have been told that if we starve her we also starve the demon and it will trouble her less. But I can see that in starving the demon we also starve the girl. She shall be better fed from now on. I am resolved upon that. I will try also to give her a few days' rest at special times, as your grandmother suggested. She should have rested today, but in this business you have to grasp opportunities when they come, and when there is a stoning our business always picks up. She has done splendidly today."

Timothy swallowed. For a moment his mind had room

only for the picture of the wounded and bleeding apostle
climbing the hill. Zenon also had seen it. But then, Zenon
had been seeing strange and terrible sights in many places
for many years.

Timothy asked, "Where does Merza come from?"

"The north country. Bithynia, near the Propontis. A
village, not a city. Her grandmother sold her to me four
years ago. After the demon had entered into her she began having screaming spells and the neighbors complained. Also the parents and the grandfather were dead
and the grandmother and child were starving." He
shrugged. "Poor people will always sell children as slaves
rather than watch them starve. You cannot blame that
grandmother."

"Has Merza had the demon all her life?"

"Her grandmother said not. She told me they had had
a neighbor, a woman of violent and evil temper. One day
the neighbor threw a small kitten against the wall of the
house with such force it crushed the little creature,
breaking its bones. Yet this same woman was entrusted
with the care of her own grandchildren, while their parents worked at their trade in the Street of Bakers.

"One day the son-in-law came at sunset to get his
children. He found the woman strangling his son, an infant, while nearby lay the remains of his other child.
He killed the woman, took his wife, and fled from
Bithynia, lest he be executed for the murder of his
mother-in-law.

"Merza began having these attacks within a few days
of the event, falling-down spells and also a spirit of clairvoyance, of divination. She began telling the fortunes
of whoever entered the house, until all the village was
afraid of her. It was concluded in the village that the
soul of that evil old woman had entered into the child.
She was given to screaming and destruction though she
had been mild enough before all this happened. For a

time the grandmother kept her bound, and when Merza grew noisy she threw water on her."

Horrified as he was at the story Zenon was telling, Timothy still registered his sudden recognition of what the strange thing was about Zenon. He was a showman, an entertainer, yet he used no tricks. Except for his flamboyant costume he was as simple and straightforward as one's neighbor on the next farm. This was a story such as men invent, yet Timothy believed every word of it. Zenon looked him in the eye. He spoke simply and sadly, as if sharing the fascination and the grief Timothy felt for the unfortunate girl who slept so quietly nearby.

"I heard of the case. I found the village and the house, and made an offer of silver pieces for the girl. The grandmother sniffled a little as she took the money, but one sensed that she was glad enough to get the girl off her hands. Merza grows increasingly valuable as she learns her trade and comes to understand what is expected of her. Taking care of Merza is good business. It is my business. I took Bias into a sort of partnership to protect us from thieves—there are those who would like to take the purse, but worse still, there are those who would steal Merza if we did not keep her on a leash day and night."

Timothy asked, "Where will you go from Lystra?"

"Maybe north. Maybe east. The cities of the royal road have been very good. We won't go back that way just yet, though I want to try Ephesus again. We have been there twice, but Merza gets better as she matures. Often she decides which direction we shall take, and we never lose by that. She never has read her own future, or mine for that matter. But when she chooses a direction to take at a turning of the road it usually works out."

Merza was stirring. Her cheeks took on a healthier tinge. The hazel eyes opened. She sat up, looked curiously at Timothy, saw the sandals, and put them on her feet with an air of curiosity and pride. She said, "I saw you before. You were at the grandmother's house. I will see you again, someday. Somewhere."

Timothy said, "In Ephesus? Will I see you someday in Ephesus?"

"Somewhere. When we are older. When we are older and taller."

Bias came lumbering and stumbling toward them, his scarlet headcloth askew, his beard dribbled with wine. He roared, "Stay away from Merza, boy. She is nothing to you and you are nothing to her. You've heard your fortune. Skedaddle. Go away!"

Timothy rose. "I really must be going," he said politely to Zenon. "Thank you for talking to me." He took Merza's hands in both of his. "I will never forget you, Merza," he said. "I will pray for you every day, and ask Grandmother to do the same. When I go on the roads with the preachers I will look for you in every city."

"Somewhere," she murmured, staring at him from her seat on the grass. "When we are older and taller."

7

ON THE FIRST LORD'S DAY after the evangels went away south, the Christians came together at sunset in the court of the house on the hill. While Paul and Barnabas remained they had been meeting under the trees, but within days after their departure the winds had shifted, more snow had appeared on the distant mountain range, and they now met inside, where cooking fires took the chill off the sheltered air in the courtyard.

Hymns were sung. Barnabas had taught them hymns, some with words of prophecy from Isaiah or the psalms about Messiah's coming. Some were passages taken from the book Paul carried with him, the Sayings of the Lord Jesus. The melodies were familiar Jewish hymns, which the Greeks picked up readily so that they sang as lustily as the Jews.

Timothy loved the singing, even though his own clear soprano voice had deserted him and he was struggling with the necessity of learning to harmonize. Lois and Eunice sang well; Lycon and Philip also, as did others in their company. But the finest voice was that of Matilda. She set the pitch and charmed them all with the beauty of her singing.

The favorite hymn was the triumphant story of the

Resurrection, as composed by a Jerusalem Christian called
Silas. It was longer than most hymns, a sermon, a Scrip-
ture reading, and a hymn all in one, or so it seemed to
Timothy.

On the first day of the week, as dawn was breaking,
The women went to the tomb, taking spices and perfumes.
The stone had been rolled away, rolled away from the tomb.
They went inside, but the body was gone.
          The body was gone . . . gone!
Then two men in dazzling garments were with them, saying,
"Why seek ye the living among the dead?"

There were stanzas recounting various appearances of
the living Lord Jesus to different apostles and followers.
Matilda had memorized all the stanzas and could sing
them without flaw or hesitation. Timothy was confident
that he also would soon have them all letter-perfect. The
final stanza of this lovely hymn told of the appearance
of the Lord Jesus to a company upon the mountain called
Olivet, outside Jerusalem, when he promised that soon all
of them would be infused with the Breath of God.
     The hymn closed:

As they looked on him thick cloud enveloped him
And he was seen no more in their company . . . no more.
But two men stood with them, saying,
"This Jesus who was taken from you will come again.
He will surely come again."

As the song ended, Timothy felt the assurance: Paul
and Barnabas have left us. They have gone to continue
their work in another place. But they will come again.
They will surely come again!
     Philip and Lycon had been elected elders. On this first
Lord's Day following the departure of the two preachers, Philip was to open the meeting while Lycon would
close it. Now Philip said, "We have discussed what
should become our order of worship now that we have

neither Scriptures to be read nor preachers to bring a sermon. Barnabas told us how in Jerusalem the apostles met together after the Lord Jesus was taken from them. They sang hymns, and afterward each in turn witnessed, relating what they remembered best of the years when the Lord Jesus was among them. Sometimes they recounted sayings of the Lord Jesus, or spoke of their experiences as Christians, and of problems encountered in faith and living. Let us do likewise, each in turn to witness as the Spirit moves.

"Now today I want to witness to certain changes which have come into my way of doing business. True, a man of business has his ethics. Yet one does not call attention to inferior wares by spreading them for a customer to examine. Yet how can I compare a few coins with the gifts our brothers Paul and Barnabas have brought to us?"

He paused, and Timothy saw with a deep stir of understanding something of the struggle against habit which had occurred in Philip, that solid and not-too-imaginative man of business.

Philip continued, "Formerly I would have covered rotting grapes in the basket with fresh grapes, hoping for a top price for the lot. Now I remember our brother's preaching. I separate the fresh grapes, exposing the overripe fruit. When buyers poke at it in surprise that it is exposed, I mention that overripe grapes are cheaper. I suggest uses to which they can be put, for they can be mashed to make a wine that is sour but nourishing, or at worst they can be fed to fowls women fatten in a corner of the court."

The smile that lighted the heavy face held both astonishment and sweetness. "Now this I did as a sacrifice, an offering to the Lord Jesus. But I find that business improves. Women who formerly bought from Demetrios come now to me. They do not sniff at my oil but ask only, 'Is it rancid?' and if I say it is fresh they believe me. So now I ask, what have I done wrong? A man should pay a price for the joy he has in serving the Lord Jesus. But I have known only profit in my business and joy in my soul."

Lycon asked, smiling, "And what of Demetrios? You are hurting his business with what seems to him unfair practices."

"I have explained to Demetrios what I am doing, and why. I have invited him to hear the preaching of Paul and Barnabas. If there is more I can do, I will gladly do it. Perhaps you can reach him, Lycon, where I have failed. We are not really competitors, for Greeks go to him and Jews to me. Yet lately I have been selling food-stuff to Greeks also."

Others spoke. Timothy listened, longing to rise and tell of the fortune Merza had predicted for him, and of the subsequent conversation he had had with Paul. He had not shared the exciting secret with anyone else, and dared not, until he found courage to tell it to Lois. In fact, he was keeping his secret, fearing ridicule, until he had accomplished some part of Paul's assignments, for example, if he were able to bring Miletus to join their fellowship.

Jonas hobbled to the fire to begin again a long narration of how Paul had healed him. He had told the story several times. It was beginning to grow in the telling. And Timothy thought, If we don't find a more inspiring order of worship we will begin to bore one another, for we know each other too well. We must find something fresh to say. Else when we bring in new converts they may decide that The Way has little to offer them. And he thought of the snow on the mountains and pinned his hopes on the likelihood that Paul and Barnabas would have to take the long route home, and would come back this way before winter was too far advanced.

Jonas spoke with much circumstance of how the day had been, how few coins had come into his bowl, his mounting despair. He spoke of the goodness of Matilda, who sent him out each morning full of hope and courage which dissipated as the sun rose hotter and higher and the bowl did not gather many coins. Noonday passed, and the wall no longer shaded him, and the full heat of the sun beat down.

"I wonder if you know what it means to beg from the poor. We have few rich in our city—just poor folk who scratch for a living—yet they are the ones who pity and who give. Even when it is known that the beggar's wife comes from a family in comfortable circumstances, the poor share their pittance. Well, I have spent many years asking poor people, and strangers, to share with me. A beggar's life is a humbling life. Yet there I sat, my encumbrance exposed, extending my bowl to traders who had concluded the day's business and were leading their donkeys onto the highway to return to their farms.

"Then they appeared, two strangers with something about them to lift the heart, something all have seen these past weeks, something that opened the doors of the soul. And Paul fixed his eyes upon me. I was swept out of myself by that compelling glance. The soles of my feet began to tingle and my ankles to cry out the longing to perform their function.

"Paul took my hand. Power ran through me as he touched my hands. People do not often touch beggars, my friends. They toss a coin, and one learns to watch where it spins and to catch it in the bowl. They toss a coin—but they do not touch.

"Then he said, 'God can raise you up, my brother. God can set you upon your feet to walk like other men. Do you believe in the Power of God?'"

"'I believe!' I cried, for I was swept out of myself by this stranger, by his message, his voice, his touch.

And as I spoke those two words, power filled my body and I was upon my feet, scarce knowing how I got there, and I was walking and praising God."

Jonas wiped his cheeks with the sleeve of his coat. Matilda also wept, and her face was radiant. And Timothy remembered how Lois had said, when Matilda married Jonas and all the Hebrew congregation marveled that a handsome and gifted young woman of good family had chosen to marry a beggar, "She has been mothering one thing and another from childhood. Now she will mother Jonas."

When Jonas had concluded his story, repeating much that was no longer new to anyone present, Matilda said, "Jonas has such pains in the muscles of his legs. I rub them each night, or he would lie awake with the pain. Yet he keeps saying that the pain will pass as the legs grow stronger." She sent a dark, troubled glance at Philip. "I am glad my cousin has found only prosperity in serving the Lord Jesus. It has not been quite that easy for my husband. Yet Jonas is brave. He makes light of pain and difficulty, for the work in the booth, walking on those dreadful cobbles all day, is very hard."

Lois spoke out strongly. "It takes courage for any man to stand upon his own feet. It takes more courage in the case of one who never did it until now, but spent coins others had earned by their toil. Jonas, we love you for your courage, as we see it exhibited day after day. We pray that God will continue to heal you more perfectly as the days and weeks pass. I for one firmly believe that time and courage will bring this to pass.

"Jonas, you have faced the fact that you can either stand on your own feet, or you can bring ridicule and reproach upon our company, and most of all upon Brother Paul, who suffered stoning, yet rose and walked to this house, and the next day walked on to Derbe.

Messengers have brought the news that Paul and Barnabas reached Derbe safely. Since snows are now falling on the mountains we can feel quite certain that Paul and Barnabas will not attempt the Cicilian Gates. We can be confident that when their ministry in Derbe ends and the autumn rains have ceased, they will return to visit the three cities of Galatia where they organized ecclesiae, and go down to the coast by the route which brought them here, to return to Syrian Antioch by ship. This prospect will surely hearten us all in the Christian Way, that we may give them a good report when they come."

Matilda said, "Paul certainly gave us the impression that Jonas was truly and completely healed. I never imagined he would suffer such pain."

Timothy wanted to cry out, Oh, Matilda, your sympathy weakens Jonas more than the pain.

Lois was speaking again. "You have been a patient and loving wife, Matilda. I myself am a stiff-necked woman and stubborn. Now that I am alone in this house from dawn till dark, while Timothy is at the loom learning his trade, I find my mind dwelling too often on the burdens I bear, on the neglect I receive from those I love."

How will I tell her I am to go with Paul? Timothy wondered. I dare not leave her alone in this house. Suddenly he was remembering his one visit to the cave in the Street of Beggars where Matilda dwelt with Jonas. In every city, he was told, there are caves dug into the base of the city walls where beggars are permitted to eke out their miserable existence. It was to such a cave that Matilda had gone when she married Jonas, leaving the comfortable dwelling of her cousin Philip. And Philip, angered that she had chosen such a husband, refused to lift upon his own back the burden of supporting Jonas.

He sent them an occasional gift of oil or vegetables or grain, but he did not bring them up out of that noisome cave.

Jonas had risen to answer the plaint of Lois about her loneliness. "Sister Lois, suddenly I have the courage to ask a great boon of you. It is not right that you dwell alone on this hill while we— Oh, Sister Lois, I have longed to return to the clean air of this farm, to the comfort of soft earth beneath my feet instead of cobbles. May we bring our beds once more to spread in that small room you use for winter storage? May we spend tomorrow among the earthy beauties of your vineyard, tying up the tendrils loosened during grape harvest? May we rest at evening under the brilliant oaks at your portal? Oh, I long to lead your goat to pasture, to sink my bruised feet in the rich earth which nourishes your household." Then, with a rush, "Ah, Lois, I cannot express how deeply I have longed to get my dear wife out of that stinking cave beneath the city wall!"

There was a general stir among the people. And Timothy thought with longing, If she will only consent! It will set me free for my work and my destiny. It will solve many problems.

When he looked up, Lois was looking directly at him, a smile of great tenderness lighting her dark face. She knows about my mission; Paul must have told her. She has known all this week, while I kept silent. She has deliberately opened the door for Jonas to make this request.

Lycon rose as moderator for the close of the meeting. "What do you say, Mother Lois?"

"I say yes. With all my heart, dear friends, bring your beds and your belongings and we will make a home for one another."

Then Lycon said, "I talked with Brother Barnabas

the evening before they went away. I asked how we were to survive as a Christian community without preachers or any written word to guide us, and he replied, 'Bear ye one another's burdens and so fulfill the law of Christ.' This is the keystone of our Lord's life and gospel. It is better to give than to receive. Our Lord Jesus suffered death upon the Cross to give us life, abundant life. Can we do less in return than to love one another and to bear one another's burdens? You see here today a perfect example. Jonas and Matilda have a need, a pressing and most appealing need. Lois also has a need since I took her daughter to my house when she became my wife, and since Timothy is learning his trade at the loom, even while he also continues to improve his skills as a scribe by going daily to the synagogue school. Yet Lois is in a position to meet the needs of Jonas and Matilda, and they are in a position to give to her the love and companionship she no longer receives from daughter or grandson. They bear one another's burdens and so fulfill the Law of Christ."

Lois was looking fixedly, and most lovingly, at Timothy, who stared at her in return with astonishment and delight. The boy had chosen to keep his secret from his grandmother, though it surely concerned her more deeply than anyone else, other than himself. He had not trusted her to rejoice in his splendid prospects.

See, my beloved Timothy, how I give you this great gift—your liberty. You need not trouble about what will become of your old grandmother when you become a companion to Paul, an evangel, carrying the Good News!

The message was communicated between them, without words. And Lois thought, If I were a man, how gladly would I set out on such a mission to the world! How broad the horizon of this valley will become for me the day Timothy sets out to cross those mountains which hem us in. Our lad Timothy, who will be circumcised at last, and will become a Messenger of Glad Tidings in cities of which I have never even heard. Ah, lad, I would make any sacrifice, bear any burden, to open such doors to you!

She reached to touch his hand, which enclosed hers in a tight, warm, loving clasp.

BOOK II
Philippi

8

Paul had dreamed again.

Twenty days of hard travel had brought the three of them over the uplands of Asia and down to the Aegean Sea at Troas. There, for the third time, Paul dreamed, and in consequence of the dream the party again changed direction.

There had been no preaching since they had left Galatia behind. "The Spirit forbids me to preach in Asia," Paul said after the second dream. The morning after that dream the three had stood beside the purling, glittering waters of the Macestus River, on high land from which there was a splendid view north, down the valley where the river cut its way toward the Propontis. This was Asia. They had left Galatia and Bithynia behind, and if Paul was forbidden to preach in Asia, where would he preach? For beyond Asia was the sea, and Macedonia beyond the sea.

For a day they rested beside the purling mountain stream. Timothy washed their tunics and stretched them on bushes where they dried quickly. Silas mended their sandals, and Paul communed with himself, wrapped in silence, staring down into the lush valley. Autumn was upon them, The mountain roads were chill except when

the sun was high. The Macestus valley and the shores
of the Propontis would have provided a splendid setting
for a winter's preaching. But the Spirit had forbidden.
On the following morning they took the road west to
Troas and the sea. And at Troas Paul dreamed for the
third time, and the travelers, numbering four now instead
of three, took ship for the land whence had come Timothy's Greek ancestors, whoever they might have been,
and however long ago.

Three years had passed since the first visit of Paul
and Barnabas to Lystra, three years while Timothy and
the other converts awaited Paul's promised return. Timothy considered himself an adequate weaver at the end
of his first year's apprenticeship. Lycon pronounced him
ready when the second spring came, bringing news that
the Cicilian Gates were again open to travelers. But Paul
did not come.

Timothy had been dreaming of the little sybil, Merza,
all through the second winter and spring and had con-
soled himself that summer would bring Paul and Barnabas
to Lystra and launch Timothy on his travels. In his
dreams he always found Merza in Ephesus, with the
fabled temple of Diana of the Ephesians rising behind her
as she told fortunes in the square. He knew what the
temple looked like because he had seen it imprinted on
Ephesian coins once or twice, and had been told of its
massive size, and that it was counted as one of the great
wonders of the world, the largest temple known to man.

The second summer passed, and Paul did not come. A
peddler from Derbe, Gaius by name, visited the Christians in Lystra and Iconium and Antioch now and then.
Gaius had been one of Paul's converts in Derbe. Paul
and Barnabas had dwelt with him in that city. Converts
in Derbe had been fewer than in the other cities of
Galatia. Derbe was a city created for and populated by
retired Roman soldiers and the wives they found in this

high country. Gaius made it his business to carry reports
between the Galatian churches, binding them into a fellowship. And when Timothy learned that Paul did not
come that spring, he settled himself for another year's
work at the loom. He would save what he earned this
year to be used on the journey when Paul did come.

The third spring brought Paul, and with him a solid,
muscular man called Silas. Barnabas did not come with
Paul this year, having gone instead with his nephew
Mark on a missionary journey in Cyprus. Silas was a
Christian from Jerusalem, a sweet-faced man with the
strong, gnarled hands of a vineyard and orchard keeper,
a splendid singing voice and a store of hymns sung in
the ecclesiae of Jerusalem and Bethany.

So Timothy was circumcised. Paul and Silas remained
for three weeks to strengthen the church in Lystra and
to baptize about a score of converts who had joined since
Paul's departure. One of these was the Greek priest
Miletus. Zebulon was still a friend to the Christians but
could not bring himself as yet to join their company.

Then Paul and Silas and Timothy set out for Iconium.
The third month of summer ended before their visits in
Iconium and Antioch of Pisidia were concluded. They
had followed the royal road thus far, and had planned to
continue on it until it brought them down to the sea at
Ephesus. But Paul had dreamed the first of the three
dreams that changed their course. They left the royal
road, turning north. And now they began to move with
speed. When they reached the most northern of the four
roads that cut west across Asia till they reach the Aegean
Sea, they took this road. And again Paul dreamed, and
they continued on this mountain highway, after crossing
the inviting Macestus valley, until they came to Troas
and the sea.

Twenty days at the swift pace Paul set wrought a
change in Timothy. Heretofore he had spent his days

bent to the loom and to the scrivener's desk. Now he felt the swelling of his lungs as he walked, breathing deeply the clean mountain air. His mind also was swelling to hold and ponder thoughts discussed by Paul and Silas as they traveled. For if Paul had a feeling for the peoples of the world, Silas had a feeling for the places. Behind him were years of encounters with pilgrim Jews from many lands who came up to Jerusalem to celebrate the great feasts.

"We have traveled more than twice the distance from Dan to Beersheba," said Silas, as they rested beside the Macestus River. "Yet our journey has only begun. How can a man's mind grasp the vastness of the world which borders the Great Sea? Brother Paul, I feel that I am only beginning to comprehend the challenge of your vision to carry the Good News to all the world. Twenty lifetimes would not suffice to fulfill such a mandate."

"God will give us scores of lifetimes, scores of evangels," said Paul. "Timothy is an example. This Asian hinterland through which we have passed will be reached and taught by men from ecclesiae we launch."

Paul was often taciturn while traveling. He drove himself hard, and Timothy's legs stretched into longer strides, his skirts well girt, to maintain the pace of the two evangels.

Silas had two subjects of endless interest on which to discourse as he and Timothy strode along in Paul's wake. One was reminiscences of the days when the Lord Jesus had visited Bethany, of Simon the Leper whom Jesus had healed, of Lazarus the Farmer whom Jesus had brought from the tomb. The other topic was the lands through which they passed, for what he did not already know he learned from conversations with travelers on the road, or innkeepers when they were fortunate enough to find a hostelry wherein to spend the night. And when he was not discoursing on one or another of these topics, he

sang the Christian hymns, his great, lusty voice ringing
through the hills. Timothy had learned all the hymns
Silas knew before they reached Troas.

When Timothy realized that the city of Troas was
believed to be located on the site where Troy had stood,
he began relating the tales Lycon had told him much as
blind Homer must have sung them when he sat at kings'
tables. He passed the miles telling of Odysseus and Ajax,
of Hector and Priam, of Achilles and Menelaus, and of
the battles fought on the plain before Troy. But when he
spoke of the beauty of Helen, prime cause of the seven
years' siege, Paul said sternly, "Enough. Say no more of
the evil and death wrought by the concupiscence of men
and the enticement of a loose woman. We do not make
this journey to celebrate Greek myths. There are souls
in Troas to be won to The Way, if the Spirit permits
me to preach in that great outpost of Asia."

Abashed, Timothy told no more Greek tales. He followed the obstinate, swift figure. He had been about
Paul's height three years ago. Now he was a head taller,
a weedy figure, hollow chested until they set out on this
journey. Paul's beard still flourished, but when he removed his headcloth one saw that he was becoming bald.

Silas said presently, "Greeks brought their language to
all this vast land. The conquest of Troy undoubtedly
opened Asia to Greek settlement. Had it not, your ancestors, Timothy, might never have reached Lystra."

Paul said, "Timothy is a Jew now. He has been
circumcised."

Autumn came early in the mountains. The oaks were
vivid, reminding Timothy of the oaks which stood before
the cottage at home. He felt no homesickness, only the
wish that he could share all these sights, sounds, emotions, conversations with Lois and Eunice and Lycon.

As they reached the last pass, from which the first
distant glimmer of the sea was visible, Paul announced,

"We will winter in Troas. I pray God we may preach to good effect in this harbor city, for whenever we establish an ecclesia among seafaring men we can hope that our converts will in turn carry the Good News to other harbors on other shores."

"The plan is good," said Silas cheerfully. "Our funds are low. Timothy and I must find employment while you preach in Troas. We must replenish our purse. We made this journey in twenty days, not counting the Sabbaths and the Lord's Days, when we have rested. But without hospitality from converts along the way, we have made sad inroads upon our resources."

And Timothy reflected, gratified, When spring comes we will turn south along the coast, and pass through Smyrna and come at last to Ephesus.

When we are older and taller we will meet in another city. This Merza had said. In all his dreams of finding Merza, the setting was Ephesus.

They crossed the last height, and there below was the city, and in the distance the blue Aegean Sea, dotted with lush, green islands. How God must love the Greeks, thought Timothy, to give them so fair a sea for their ships.

"No wonder my ancestors were seafaring people," he said softly.

Troas was unlike any other city Timothy had seen. Its walls were high and thick, the gates of oaken beams studded with iron and decorated with bronze. The road ran alongside the city till it came to the western tower, then circled in such a way that they entered in late afternoon with the sun at their backs. They were jostled by dark-skinned sailors smelling of strange cargoes, speaking outlandish tongues.

Timothy was awed by a sense of the vastness of the world. He had passed beyond the mountains at last, and here were men who had never seen the high plains of

Galatia. When his eyes met the blue, delighted eyes of
Silas, the two smiled at one another, two travelers awed
by encounter with strangers from strange places in a vast,
strange world. Paul did not seem to share their excitement. He had long understood the vastness of the Roman
world. Moreover, Paul had grown pallid under the leath-
ery sunburn of their summer's travels. When Silas ques-
tioned him he said, "The fever is the curse of coastal
cities. I have felt it coming since this morning."

They made their way to the agora, and thence to the
stall of a Jew who sold meats and poultry. Timothy had
supposed Paul would ask for the synagogue, for in most
cities, as in Lystra, the synagogues maintained an adjoining shed supplied with clean straw where Jews might bed
down safely without charge. Instead, Paul said, "Can you
direct us to an inn, my brother?" He spoke in Hebrew,
as was his custom with Jews. A tremor was visible in his
hands.

The merchant was deftly binding the legs of a white
hen. Feathers clung to his heavy beard. He handed the
hen to a scrawny child who wore the leather collar of
a slave. "The boy Eutychus will lead you to a decent inn,
friend." The merchant reached into a coop made of
wickerwork and dragged out another fowl.

When the boy was staggering under the burden of
six hens with beating wings and raucous squawks, he
lifted his chin above a wing, blew feathers from his lips.
"This way, sirs." A wing was beating his dirty cheek.
Feathers drifted about his dark, anxious eyes.

Timothy reached to take two of the fowls, but the
child twisted quickly aside. "Please sir, no sir. She will
beat me—my mistress."

Paul said, "Peace, Eutychus. We will not molest you
or your property."

They turned into a narrow street between houses built
to a height of two or even three stories, with laundry

flapping overhead from one housetop to its opposite, making a rustling canopy. Dirty water from recent rain sloshed between the uneven paving stones. The child grew so distraught with his six lively fowls that he stumbled in and out of puddles, though the paving was spaced to allow one to step easily from stone to stone. Fruit peelings and offal, the stinking discard of butchered animals, chicken feathers, and other truck muddied the narrow gutters. There was no flow to the water to carry off the garbage.

In the dialect of the hill people Timothy said, "I would willingly help you, Eutychus. We are men of goodwill, sent here to bring good news. Even to slaves are we sent. We would not injure anyone." He spoke with pride. This was the first Christian message uttered in this city. He reached to grasp the legs of two or three fowls.

The boy shuddered away from his reaching hands. In his fright, Eutychus lost his grip on two hens. They flopped about, splashing filth over themselves and the travelers and the slave child. When Eutychus tried to recover them, two more hens escaped.

Then Silas took two of the wet creatures by the feet, holding them with heads hanging. Timothy also took two, and once the heads were down the creatures quit flapping. Silas said, "Now hold your two hens by the legs, Eutychus. See how quiet they become? It is much easier if we each carry two."

The boy glanced about fearfully. "My mistress will beat me if she sees the guests helping me. Give them back before we reach the tavern." He added to Timothy with pride, "You need not speak hill dialect to me, sir. I learned Greek long ago." The show of pride in the dirty face was touching.

Timothy asked, "Do you get many soothsayers in Troas?"

"How would I know of such things? Where would I get a penny for a fortune-teller?" The boy had grown bolder now that his problem of transporting the hens was solved. His narrow shoulders took on a bit of swagger.

"But if they stopped at the inn of your mistress? Two men called Bias and Zenon, and a girl called Merza, who is a sybil?"

"People come and go. I do not notice them. I work. I eat my crust. I sleep as near the kitchen fire as I am permitted. My mistress would beat me if I spoke to guests or noticed them."

Paul said kindly, "I will speak to your mistress, that she cease to beat you. As for yourself, Eutychus, be obedient, and zealous, that you tempt her not to anger. Virtue is pleasing to God, in slave and mistress equally."

The dark eyes were fixed doubtfully on Paul. "Yes, sir." He stumbled, muddying himself. Silas helped him regain his balance.

"How far, Eutychus?"

"Just ahead, sir. Two houses down. The big one with no laundry. Quick, give me the hens." He gathered them all, three pairs of legs clutched in each grubby fist, and darted around to an alley entrance of the tavern.

Silas led the way into the tavern, bending his head in the low doorway, and taking a coin from the scrip attached to his girdle. A greasy landlord with dank, gray locks and a habit of licking his lips greeted them civilly, while his eyes darted toward the street, taking note that nobody followed them with their luggage, that all they had was the beds on their backs.

"Dinner for three also? Our wine is the best."

They had stopped before leaving the hills to eat their usual loaf and bit of cheese. Silas said, "A little space for our beds for tonight, friend. Tomorrow we will see what further needs we have." He proffered a copper coin.

The man led the way to a dark balcony. Torches gave

a flickering light to the room below. The dimness of the balcony was alleviated by an opening just under the roof. Paul had been shuddering spasmodically throughout the afternoon. As they climbed the dank and dirty stone stairway Timothy was aware that now Paul's teeth were chattering.

The landlord said sharply, "The mistress does not like fever in the place. It stinks up the house, and a death never brings luck to an inn."

Silas said sharply, "The sufferer does not like fever either, nor do his friends. But this is not a man who will die of fever, for God is with him."

Timothy had already unrolled Paul's bed and he was down upon it, and Timothy had removed Paul's sandals and was rubbing his feet. Silas brought an extra coat from his own roll to wrap about Paul. It was Timothy's first experience with the fever, for it was not an ailment common in the high plains of Galatia.

Now Silas said, "Barnabas was very good with illness. He has instructed me, however, and we will do the best we can. The object is to keep the patient warm until the fever breaks. Sweating is then profuse, and the problem becomes one of bathing away the sweat and making the patient as comfortable as possible."

A dark-eyed, trim young man in a clean coat of blue wool crossed to them, bringing with him a small copper lamp with one wick lighted. "I know something of medicine. Will you permit me to be of assistance?" Then, as Silas looked at him doubtfully, "There will be no charge. You are Jews and I am Greek, but I recognize this man. He is Paul of Tarsus. I have heard him preach in that city and am confident he will welcome the services of a Greek, even from a freedman like myself. I was educated in art and medicine at the University of Tarsus."

Paul had sunk into a writhing, muttering stupor, so

rapidly had his fever risen. It was as if he had held it
at bay by force of will till he lay down, then opened the
gates and let it flood in. As for the young freedman, it
was obvious that Silas trusted him on sight. Nor did he
seem at all astonished to meet an acquaintance of Paul in
this distant city, a physician, indeed, and at a moment
when Paul sorely needed one. There was dignity in the
young man's bearing. He moved with competence, as if
his very touch could ease the patient.

"My master sent me to school," Luke said. "On his
death he gave me my freedom. I lived in Philippi as a
child, and am now returning to my native Macedonia,
where I hope to use my skill as a physician to help my
people. Ever since I heard this man preach of how all
men are equally dear to God, I have made it the aim of
my life to pass on to others the kindness I have received."

The Greek crossed to his sleeping place and brought
another coat, which he laid over Paul. Timothy saw the
deep flush of fever which had replaced the earlier pallor,
and was thankful that Silas had someone so competent to
help ease Paul's sufferings. Nor did anything about the
appearance of such a man at such a time astonish him.
The Christian faith was built on far more astonishing
events than this one.

The Greek said, "You are Timothy? Will you kindly
ask the landlord for hot stones to hasten the breaking of
the fever?"

Timothy found the landlord engaged in drinking beer
with a group of merchants he had seen upon the road
earlier that same day. All affability and good fellowship
now, the landlord waved Timothy toward a low doorway. "Ask in the kitchen. They attend to such things."

From the kitchen came the sound of an open palm
smacking flesh. "Clumsy fool!" shrilled a voice. The
kitchen was littered with feathers, especially in the
corner nearest the fire. Feathers floated in a pot of soup

which stood amid smoke and flames. Eutychus was himself covered with feathers also, but struggled to remove more of them from the headless hen he held between his knees.

Timothy approached the angry hostess. "I must have heated stones for a sick man upstairs. Your husband said—"

"My husband is a fool. If you want stones go to the alley. Heat them in the atrium. Guests are not permitted to enter the kitchen. Go! Go!"

She bent to skim feathers from the soup, all the while shrieking at Eutychus. The boy muttered to Timothy, "You will find stones beside the door, sir."

While the stones were heating in the central room the boy came softly up beside him. Most of the feathers had been brushed away, though two or three still stuck in his tangled hair. "He promised to speak to my mistress, that little man with you. Is he ill? Is he dying?"

"He will be well in a day or two. He will not forget his promise."

After delivering the hot stones to Luke, Timothy went out into the darkening street and asked directions to the Street of Weavers. Tomorrow he must seek employment. He did not care to lose any time about it.

But that night, after the fever broke, Paul dreamed for the third time on this journey. At dawn he told the three of them about his dream. "A young man clothed in white sat beside me as I slept, saying, 'Come to Macedonia. Come and help us, for we are ready and yearning to learn of the Christos.' "

What of Ephesus? Timothy did not voice the question, but his disappointment was deep. Macedonia was north and west, beyond the blue Aegean Sea. Ephesus was counted a five-day journey on foot, due south from here. He looked at the neatly groomed, handsome Macedonian freedman in his white sleeping robe, the young physician who had sat beside Paul's bed all that night. Who could say what had brought such a dream to Paul?

Paul said, "Silas, go to the harbor and inquire about ships for Macedonia. The season is late, and we dare not waste time or we will be winterbound in Asia, where the Spirit has forbidden me to preach."

Silas drew from his scrip the last of his coins. "We must winter here, Paul, till we have earned the price of our passage to Macedonia."

Luke said, "Put away your money, friend. My master left me money in his will, and I have enough and to spare. I myself have passage on a boat that sails tomorrow —the last one this season. Rest here today, Brother Paul. I will go down to the ship this morning and secure passage for the three of you."

9

MERZA FELT HOT AND ITCHY inside the heavy folds of the woolen coat. Julia had given her the coat before Zenon and Bias took her aboard the boat at Ephesus. That was early in the spring. Now that midsummer had come the coat was too heavy, too hot, except for sleeping when nights were cold. But where can you safely leave your coat if you don't feel like wearing it?

The sun glared on marble. Her eyes hurt. The paving stones were hot. Summer was a bad time to be on the roads, though not as bad as winter. Faces crowded her, closing her in. They seemed to surge in and away, in and away, till she was dizzy from all the faces. All, all were staring at her, waiting to hear her tell them something marvelous about themselves. I wish, she thought in her wretchedness, that just once somebody would say something marvelous about me.

"You will find a new friend three days hence. This friend will speak only truth to you."

The oily, harried little Greek glared at her. That was not what he had asked about. Still, he handed over a grudging drachma to Zenon and went mumbling away.

His anger gratified Merza. Oh, it was easy enough,

except for the heat—and in winter, the rains. People came and went endlessly. When you were finished in one city you moved on to another, following Zenon and Bias along the endless Roman roads. Really, it was fun sometimes, with everyone looking expectant, delighted with what you said even when, as today, the demon was quiet and you just invented what you told them.

Now here was a woman who looked to be about ready to deliver a child. Nobody who had a richly embroidered mantle like hers to wear should look so worried. Merza took the gold bracelet, touched it against her cheek, breathed deeply, and returned it. "Your son will be born to trouble but live to triumph."

That was a good fortune, and she had never used it before. It had just popped into her head while she held the bracelet against her face. A fortune like that ought to be good for three drachmas. Zenon was pleased with her today. He looked dignified, and this was important to their act—a master showman presenting Merza, the Pythian, the Sybil, the Soothsayer. The deep, leather purse was hidden inside his clothes. Bias ought to be somewhere in the crowd, in case of trouble an old man like Zenon could not handle. But he wasn't here. Most likely he was off somewhere guzzling or whoring or bragging or fighting. Zenon sometimes plotted ways to be rid of Bias—not that he ever admitted it, but this was one of the things she knew without being told. Bias was of little use on the road, yet it was Bias who grabbed most of the money Merza earned, to pay for his whoring and his guzzling and the enormous meals he ate. Still, Zenon was an old man. You needed a strong man with you when you traveled the roads. But Bias—if I had a knife I would get rid of him, she thought. Zenon could find another partner. In fact Merza could pick out a better partner for Zenon in any city.

"Be of good courage, my lady. You will need courage for three years. After that your stars will shine brilliantly and all will be well."

Anybody who could be of good courage for three years of trouble could survive whatever followed that. Even I, she thought. The demon did not produce a vision for every occasion. There were even days when visions came that seemed to have nothing at all to do with the demon, visions that came when she felt as clear and untroubled and lucid as today. But for days like today, when the demon rested and her spirit was quiet and no visions came, she had garnered a store of pretty phrases. Good days brought a good meal at sunset, sometimes even a good bed, free of vermin, and certainly no beating or other trouble with Bias.

She lifted the heavy hair off her neck, running her arm under it to let the air dry the sweated flesh under the tangles. I will demand a bath tonight, she resolved. I know my trade. We have prospered ever since Ephesus. When we leave Philippi we will follow the highway to Corinth. That is said to be a very rich city, and if I do well there, Zenon has promised to take ship for Italy. One day I shall tell fortunes in Rome! Corinth, they say, is the place to make a fortune! Enough, surely, to buy tickets for three to travel to the greatest city in the world.

A face in the crowd leaped at her. The eyes were blue as the seas of Greece, but the face was dark—darker than the yellow hair and the faint, young, yellow beard. The boy was too tall! That face belonged to a little boy who took her to the grandmother! This boy's face looked across at her above the faces of the crowd. The eyes stared with astonishment—joy! Nobody ever looked at her that way! Those odd blue eyes asked nothing from her, offered only concern, compassion, delight! People never looked as if they cared about her—only about themselves, hoping she would tell them something wonderful.

Merza's eyes swerved from the strange blue eyes of the tall boy. But it did no good, for the faces of everyone else had become the faces of the two grandmothers. Merza's mind was blank with despair. She stood in the broiling heat with the pavement burning her feet through the thin soles of the worn sandals. People were jostling one another to get closer to her, holding out their baubles for her to touch while telling their fortunes, poking coins at Zenon, shouting, "Me next! I've waited all morning!" and Merza could not think of one thing but the grief she had felt when the two grandmothers, first one, then the other, had turned her out on the roads to go with Zenon.

This was real trouble. Here were all these people, clamoring to hear their fortunes, clamoring to give coins to Zenon. Her demon had deserted her. None of the convenient phrases she kept ready for such times would come to mind.

The cord jerked. The tight collar gagged her. She must speak to that oily face under the yellow headcloth. The man looked to be from some Asian province, Lydia perhaps, where the costly purple dyes were made.

Merza shrieked, "The child will be born safely. A girl child. Later it will sicken and die."

Had Merza's child sickened by now, and died, the child she had given to the lady Julia? Merza felt as if the collar would choke her. It had been too tight for a long time—ever since Ephesus and the birth of the child. This was an old man, this merchant. He had not come to ask about childbirth. What had he asked?

Zenon moved in close and spoke softly in the Phrygian tongue. "A business venture in Thessalonica. Speak up. You have done well today. Now behave yourself.

We will quit in another hour, and I will buy you wine if you like. Speak up, girl." His voice sounded friendly to the people, no doubt, but his glance burned its warning. Do well and I protect you. Do badly and Bias can have you. Zenon squeezed her fingers over the onyx beads she held. "This is his chaplet. Speak to him. Speak up, girl."

Merza shrieked, "Avoid it! You will not prosper in it."

She threw the beads at the oily face and clutched her coat with both hands, opening the heavy woolen folds to let whatever air there was blow through the thin tunic to cool her sweating flesh. "Disaster!" she shrieked. "Earthquake, pestilence, shipwreck, disaster!" She wanted to shriek, but dared not, "O God, deliver me from this life."

In his astonishment, Zenon dropped her cord. She doubled it within the folds of her coat and began to run. Zenon was too old to overtake her. Also, he was confident she would return. Where else could she go? She was his slave. She ran madly, desperately, and now the tall, yellow-haired boy was running beside her.

"Merza, this way! Turn here." So he knew her name. Well, why not? You had only to stand among the idlers in the agora to hear it.

They turned into a street, broader than most, with buildings of stone—many of marble—lining it. A voice came, a voice whose tones and diction brought flashing memory of the second grandmother, who had cleansed her and cut her hair, then returned her to Zenon. At the portal of a Roman thermae stood a small man with a splendid beard, piercing eyes, a beaked nose. The penetrating voice echoed along the street.

"Hear the words of the Lord Jesus, 'Come to me, all who labor and bear heavy burdens. Come to me for rest.' "

Her lips opened but only her heart cried, "I come. I

come for rest, for the burden is too much and I can endure this life no longer."

The man was a Jew. Anyone could see that. Maybe that blue-eyed boy was a Jew also. He was clean enough. The grandmother was a Jew. Who else ever looked at you with so much compassion? Maybe I am a Jew. Oh no. Jews do not, however impoverished, sell their children to such as Zenon.

Now she was seeing the little preacher in a shifting panorama of settings. He was writhing and shivering, ill with fever. He was swimming in the sea, swimming for his life, his hands gripping a floating timber while beyond him a ship rose on end for the plunge into the deep. A sword appeared over the sea, and the timber had become a wooden block, and he laid his head upon the block and the sword slashed down, severing the head, while an incredible gout of blood gushed up between the two bony shoulders.

Merza screamed, and heads turned and the little preacher stopped speaking to look at her with annoyance, resenting her intrusion on his message.

Merza cried, "This man serves the Lord God Jahweh. Do not molest or harm him! He speaks the living words of truth!"

She whirled to run again, miserable because she had annoyed such a good man, miserable because she had not meant to cry out but only to listen, miserable because so often visions came to torment her when they did no good but only harm. It was not I, but the demon, who cried out! She ran with more than human speed, lest the demon disturb him again. And from the depths of her own being, depths to which not even the demon could reach, came a prayer, "Lord Jesus, I come to you for rest, for the burden is too heavy. Deliver me from the life I lead."

She ran straight into the arms of Zenon, who had heard

her scream and had tracked her down this street. He will never deliver me, this Jesus of the little preacher, she thought numbly, and herself handed to Zenon the trailing cord of her slavery. Zenon led her slowly back to the square and across it to the tavern, all the while cursing softly in the Phrygian tongue.

Zenon was angry, and the demon was angry, and Merza shuddered and her teeth chattered. Kill me then, demon, if you will not leave me! But the demon would never leave her or kill her. It would drive her only so far as Merza could endure and survive, lest it be left with no shelter in the lonely dark of a houseless world.

Zenon shortened the cord so that she was obliged to walk close beside him. "You are lucky, girl. Bias is off skylarking. You know I cannot protect you from him except through hope of gain. You must earn money to pay for his pleasures or he will take you for himself again, and I cannot prevent him. Behave yourself! Your folly today has cost as much as you might earn in an ordinary week in some of the cities we have visited. Behave yourself, and hope that Bias does not hear of this day's irresponsible actions."

Even the demon grew quiet at the threat. The demon could not rest when Bias took her. Since Merza had given birth to that squalling thing in Ephesus, Zenon had made her spread her mat beside his. He kept her cord wound about his body at night. Yet Zenon was an old man, and could not protect her when Bias came in the dark and cut her cord and dragged her away to use and abuse her. When the demon drove her to fight Bias with a strength greater than her own, the aftermath of the struggle left her unfit to appear in the streets and gates and squares of whatever city they were in. Zenon did the best he could. But her one real protection was in her earnings. Loss of earnings was the worst of all possible misfortunes.

During the months when the child was within her the demon had been quiet, as if it feared the life which stirred in her womb. The last months before they came to Ephesus had been poor pickings for the travelers. In Ephesus she was fainting in the street when the lady Julia took her home, and after the child was born she had done badly for several months.

Perhaps Bias had learned something. The child had clearly interrupted her earnings. Moreover there might not be a lady Julia to befriend her if Merza was got with child again.

Tears were soaking her mantle, and Merza could not contain her sobs. "Dear, good Zenon, you are an old man. Bias will have me when you can no longer follow the roads. Please, when you grow helpless with age, kill me, for I cannot kill myself. The demon prevents it. Do not leave me to follow the roads with Bias alone."

But for the demon, Merza would long ago have strangled herself on the tight collar. If they did not provide a larger one soon, she might indeed strangle despite the demon.

Zenon said, "Peace, girl. You made a spectacle of us both today. I ask little of you but to tell people what they pay to hear. After they have paid for their fortunes, ask for favors. That Lydian merchant had a silver denarius for me, had you given him something other than witless babble."

Then, because she had humiliated him with the reminder that his years on the road could not last forever, "I will be leading you down the roads for many more years. You will be a hag with no teeth before I am gone. But you will be a hag with a demon, and still profitable to Bias."

Clearly through the turmoil of her misery came the conviction. The little preacher could deliver me from this life. He does not want to, for the law forbids him

to interfere between a slave and her owner. He has
troubles enough with Jews who stone him from their
cities. He will never choose to risk trouble with Romans
by breaking their laws governing slavery. He will never
willingly help me. Yet I must keep asking, for unless he
delivers me from this life I will never be delivered
from it.

10

THE DAYS THAT FOLLOWED held moments of triumph in the confident mastery of her art that were quickly followed with overwhelming disgust at the prospect of a lifetime spent in this fashion for the gratification of Bias. Then hope would return. The little preacher could change her life if only he would. He followed the roads. He might depart for Thessalonica, or Athens, or Corinth any day, and take all her hopes with him. Never in all the years had any promise of what was in store for herself come to her. Yet on most days the demon served her well, remaining quiet and unobtrusive yet sending visions to fit most fortunes demanded of her, and she was doing so very well that business was better than at any other time or in any other city she could remember. The deep leather purse grew heavy. Bias had plenty of money, and she seldom saw him. Zenon grew careless and complacent.

Twice or thrice she saw the tall boy in the crowd, and managed to escape and follow him to where the little preacher was speaking. "He can help you," the boy assured her. "Ask him."

But whenever she came near she could not ask. The demon prevented, putting his own words into her mouth. She could only scream, "Hear this man, for he is the servant of the Most High God."

The little preacher was annoyed by her interruptions.

With her deepest insight she understood him very well. He wanted to help her; he pitied her. But he did not want to run afoul of the laws of the Romans, or let anything whatever interrupt his preaching, for that was preeminent with him. He scowled when she screamed out in the voice of the demon. He tipped his beard toward the tall boy, motioning him to lead her away. Still, she thought, I have spoken in his behalf. I have brought him business. People follow me! They believe what I say. They stand in awe of him when I announce important truths about him. I have witnessed for him. In the end, if I persist, he must consent to use his powers to set me free of my demon. Then I will become useless to Zenon and Bias and who knows? Perhaps I will become the slave of the little preacher.

A night came when she slept, exhausted after days of inner turmoil. In her dream, women touched her with ministering, gentle hands. They bathed and anointed her so that she knew the joy of being clean. The grandmother was one of the women. She cut short Merza's tangled hair and washed it and brushed it into curls and gave her a clean tunic that was large enough, and a blue woolen coat and sturdy sandals that were only a trifle large on her bruised and toughened feet. Then the grandmother who had been so kind returned her to Zenon, and Zenon rushed her away, back to the roads.

But as she ran, stumbling in the unaccustomed sandals, she encountered this same little preacher. He was bleeding from the wounds of a recent stoning. Other men were about him, but he refused their help. And now at last Merza knew that it was the sight of the bloodied and suffering little preacher, toiling up the hill, that had caused the grandmother long ago to let her go without a word of farewell or regret or blessing.

Merza wakened, feeling strong but still. The demon slept. Her mind was easy within her. The little preacher must help me, she thought. He owes me a debt.

Zenon led Merza to the West Gate, where the highway entered the city. This road crossed the mountains of Greece, passing through cities and villages to a far harbor from which one took ship for Italy, for a passage of only a few days. Is that my fate? What do I want with Italy or Rome?

My life is changing, beginning today. I will not stand in agoras and gates, playing the Pythian, after today. What will become of me? What does it matter? I will still be a slave. Ah, but if I escape from Bias, never to see him or be touched by him again! O God, let it be so. Let it be so. And she remembered the grandmother of a single day's encounter, so long ago, so very long ago, when the yellow-haired boy was smaller. If I could find her again, to be her slave—or perhaps—her granddaughter—I would be loved. How does it seem, to be loved?

She told casual fortunes in the West Gate, her ears alert for the sound of the little preacher's voice, her eyes glancing for a sight of the tall boy with compassionate blue eyes and tufts of yellow beard. The West Gate was a busy, noisy, confused place, with traffic moving, tangling, crowding the few who waited for fortunes, pushing them back and back against the dark and hidden angle of the city wall. This was dreadful. The first principle of the business was to be seen, to be out in the center of things. Now there came from beyond the gate the exhorting voice of the little preacher.

Then Bias arrived, in strident voice berating Zenon for bringing Merza to so poor a stand. While they were preoccupied with their quarrel, she doubled up her leash within her coat and, bending, vanished behind a donkey whose master was taking in the quarrel with open mouth. Crawling, she reached the gate and beyond, where, on a platform erected for the use of public entertainers or city officials, stood the little preacher.

She had escaped Zenon and Bias, but not the demon. She opened her mouth to cry out to be healed, but instead came the scream the little preacher hated and dreaded to hear. "This man serves the Most High God!"

Now at last the little preacher turned his full attention upon her. He knelt to bend from the platform and laid his hands upon her head. What he said she did not hear for the roaring in her ears and the writhing of her body under the onslaught of the tormented demon. When the struggle reached her throat, bound in the tight leather collar, she was lost in swift blackness. For moments only she twisted and writhed on the filthy cobbles of the roadway, unconscious, unknowing, while watchers drew back, frightened, awed.

Her mouth stretched wide, wider, she convulsed one final time, then was still except for a frothy spittle that dribbled down into the dirt under her cheek.

Someone screamed, "She's dead!"

Someone else cried, "The demon strangled her."

One of her owners, the big man, stood over her, pushed her with his foot, then bent and unlocked the collar and departed, shoving it into his clothing. And the watchers followed, for the two owners were shoving the preacher along toward a pair of soldiers who were policing the area around the gate.

Merza wakened on a clean bed, with folds of thick linen between her aching body and the cold stone floor. The clean-washed smell of the bed was her first waking awareness, then pain, raw pain in her throat and on her cracked lips. She felt weak, exhausted, empty. Then she noticed the silence. When you sleep in taverns you have no experience of waking to silence.

Her neck felt strange. Her fingers touched the ridges made in the flesh by the collar, but the collar was gone. Then she found a raw bruise above her ear, and a cut on the lobe where blood had clotted.

"Merza. Are you all right, Merza?" It was the voice of the tall boy.

She opened her eyes. The room was dim and cool, with slitted windows high under the roof's overhang. Between her bed and a curtained doorway stood the figure of the boy. He knelt and took her hand in long, strong hands. He blinked, and she thought, He's weeping. Why is he weeping?

His fingers were callused. "You are a weaver," she said. "I think you are also a scholar." It was automatic, the habit of years, to say something personal to anyone you touched, or whose baubles you handled.

He blinked and smiled. His hands tightened. "Merza, Paul has cast out your demon. You are no longer a sybil. You were convulsing on the cobbles in the West Gate. Then you were still, and did not seem to breathe. I thought you were dead. Others thought so, too. Bias must have thought so, for he came and—and pushed at you with his foot, and he cursed, and leaned down and took off your collar. Then he and Zenon took Paul and Silas over to the Roman soldiers. I don't know what happened to them next. I saw you move, and you were alive after all, so I picked you up and brought you to this house. It is the house of a dyer, a woman called Lydia."

He must not tell her yet of the terrible trouble Paul and Silas were in, now that the Romans had taken them into custody. Let her rest easy while she could, for it had been a dreadful experience she had had there in the gate.

Seeing how puzzled she looked he said, "You will find good friends in this house, for these people are Christians."

Death is the penalty for slaves who attempt to escape. The boy must be a fool. But she was too exhausted to argue with him. Her body ached and her throat was raw. She turned away her face lest the boy see that she wept. She was ashamed to think Bias had abandoned her for dead, leaving her to be carted out and dumped like an

ass fallen under its load. How many times had she filled
the leather purse for Bias to empty on his whoring and
his guzzling and his gluttony! Yet he and Zenon had
gone away, leaving her in the street, thinking her dead,
not caring, except to abuse the little preacher because
he had cast out her demon.

She said, "The demon—it has been with me ever since
I can remember, and before that. I wanted the little
preacher to change me, and he changed me. Now I
know not what will become of me, or of the demon.
Where will it find a home now? It must find a home,
or wander houseless and alone in the world, having no
hope, finding no rest."

The boy looked down at the dirty, bruised, discolored
face, the dark hair in which was tangled the filth of the
pavement, and remembered how pretty she had looked
that day after Lois had washed her and cut her hair.
Now she stank from the filth she had rolled in. Oh, it
was a pity there were no women in the house to bathe
her. They had rushed away when they heard the news he
brought, that Paul and Silas had been arrested and taken
before the magistrates for trial. He plucked a clump of
dried dung from her hair. Pity drove back, for the
moment, even the awful fear he felt concerning the fate
of Paul and Silas.

How many times had Paul rebuked him for bringing
the girl to him, saying, "My mission is to preach. I am not
called to heal the sick, nor have any been able to heal
me of my own affliction."

Everything about Merza had seemed to him a miracle.
How disappointed and anxious he had been last autumn,
more than half a year ago; when Paul's third dream, that
night in Troas, had set their feet on the last ship of
autumn to cross from Asia to Macedonia. Yet the ministry
here in Philippi had been marvelously rewarding from
the first, and the gentle and scholarly physician, Luke,

had proved to be a God-sent addition to their company. Timothy had found employment with a weaver named Clement, who was also one of the Christians. And when summer was half gone Merza herself had—wonder of wonders—appeared in the agora. Silas had told Timothy of the event, and he had excused himself on certain afternoons each week to follow the girl and listen to her. Most of all, he had redoubled his prayers for her.

Now here she lay, a pitiful sight, apparently dozing. But when Lydia returned she would be bathed and cleansed, and would look as pretty as she had looked when Grandmother finished with her that autumn day four years ago.

He said softly, "Perhaps someday I can take you to Lystra. My grandmother has prayed for you all these years. So have I. Ever since you visited us in Lystra we have prayed that you might live in health and somehow, through God's mercy, be delivered from the life upon the roads."

Merza turned the words over and over in her mind. Why should they pray for her? Why should they even think about her? Why should anybody care what happened to her, once she had told their fortunes and gone on her way?

Her averted eyes stared up at the patch of blue sky beyond the high window. She said softly, "She never was my grandmother. I had a grandmother, long ago, who sold me to Zenon because I was noisy and the neighbors complained. She was my grandmother. The other grandmother was yours. She was never mine. Her name is Lois, and she was not my grandmother at all."

I I

MERZA WAKENED, feeling strangely quiet. The door curtain had been tied back. Beyond spread the atrium. By
the slant of sun through the roof opening she knew it
was past noon. Still, the house was utterly still, empty
apparently of everyone except herself.

She lay remembering Julia, who had brought her last
winter to a house as fine as this one. Past the age for
bearing children, Julia had come to the square fronting
on the great temple of Diana-of-the-Ephesians on a day
when Merza, exhausted and great with child, was telling
fortunes. Merza looked upon the sad and solitary woman
in her rich coat and embroidered mantle and saw her
with three little ones clustered about her knees.

When she heard the fine fortune, the lady Julia gave
Zenon a gold piece, asking in return that Merza, who was
near to fainting with exhaustion, come to her home to
remain till after she had given birth. And Zenon, fearing
that Merza might perish on the roads if she did not have
rest and care, let the girl go.

The delicious luxury of warmth and cleanliness, of
privacy in a quiet house, had been marred only by the
discomforts of the last days of swollen pregnancy, end-

ing in a quick and all but painless delivery. The demon
had not troubled her during those days. But once the
child was born, she could not bear to look upon it or
even hear its lusty wails. She could not bear to have the
squalling, clutching creature in the same room with her.

"Only look at her and you will love her," the lady
had urged.

"She looks like Bias. I hate her. She is a slave, like me.
So let her be your slave." The lady Julia was wife to
Philologus, who was an Asiarch, having recently served
his one-year term as archon of the province of Asia.
Perhaps the lady would not want a child begotten by
such as Bias. "If you don't want her, let someone leave
her on the midden for the dogs and the birds." And
then, at last, lest the lady hate her for her indifference to
the child, "What would I do on the road with a squalling
nursling in my arms?"

Julia said softly, "She shall be my own child. She shall
be elder sister to the children you have promised that I
shall bear. Dear Merza, you have given me hope, and a
child—gifts beyond price. I will not forget you."

Merza had had little luck in Ephesus after she went
back to Zenon, and so they had crossed to Athens. They
had had little success there either. They moved north
through coastal and mountain villages and cities, following the highroads. When they reached Macedonia the
purse began to fill again. They did well in Dion and
Pydna, in Beroea and Thessalonica. But nowhere had
they done better than here in Philippi. Oh, Bias and
Zenon could make plenty of trouble for the little
preacher, who had driven out her demon and robbed
them of their sybil.

Her hand went to her neck. It's really true! The
collar is gone. They had abandoned her for dead and
would not come looking for her. How many times, she

thought bitterly, have I filled that deep, deep purse! And they would not spare a drachma to bury me, but left me to be swept out like a dead dog!

Merza touched her hair. Her fingers came away smeared and stinking of dung. Were there no servants in this fine house to bathe away the filth? She felt deeply humiliated. When she talked to Timothy before, he was seeing her in this nasty, stinking condition. When the people whose house this was finally got around to speaking to her, this was how they also would see her! Oh, it was monstrous to leave her in such a condition!

If Zenon and Bias have lost their living, what then has happened to me? How will I survive? I have no skill or art save the one I have practiced. If I am to stay in this house, what service will I be asked to render in return for bread and a roof for shelter? Surely there is some slave in this house who could have washed my face and brushed the filth out of my hair! Surely someone could have found a clean garment to replace this stinking coat I am wearing!

Merza got stiffly to her feet, feeling the pain of bruised flesh with every movement. So she had convulsed in the street. They had all had quite an eyeful at her expense—that boy, and every drover and carter and burden-bearer who passed through the West Gate of Philippi during the noonday watch today! Yet the demon was gone. Some strange stillness within her testified to that fact, as did the raw pain within her throat left by its passing. What does it mean that the demon is gone? Perhaps it means that I shall never convulse again. Never roll in filth, with my clothes in a tangle and my limbs exposed, gnawing my tongue and gurgling raw shrieks. And in exchange? I am an ownerless slave, abandoned to whatever chance brings, and if Zenon and Bias lost their living today, why so did I!

The atrium was paved in stone of a soft gray color.

Beside the pool two stone benches stood, slabs of reddish granite set on wedges of dressed stone. Beyond the atrium was the peristyle. A gallery ran around two sides of the atrium, and someone, a slave and a Greek, no doubt, had painted murals on the third wall, showing dye pots steaming with a fire beneath and a slave in leather apron stirring with a pole the stuff in the vat. Various scatterings of vegetation depicted artistically about the central figure were, thought Merza, giving only half a mind to the subject, vegetables useful in producing various colors. Still she had little mind for observing the house, for the boy had brought her here, and the boy lived on the roads as she did, as the little preacher did. They, like herself and Zenon and Bias, were traveling entertainers who moved from city to city. If they had managed to secure housing in the home of a dyer in this city, well, she had managed to secure housing in the home of one of the Asiarchs in Ephesus. But they were transient, and she was transient, and who knew where they, or she, might go from here?

There was a broad archway between the atrium and the peristyle. The garden was neglected and weedy. A flowering almond tree stood just beyond the archway, and near it the empty shrine such as people of wealth erected to shelter their household gods. But no gods were sheltered in this shrine.

The woman called Lydia who owned this house must not care much for it. Perhaps she was not really rich enough to afford its upkeep. Or perhaps she was rich but ruled with a slack hand. The thought was momentarily reassuring. A mistress who rules with a slack hand might be useful to a slave with no identity she can prove.

This woman of Lydia had given shelter to the little preacher and his companions. The boy had felt free to bring Merza here without first asking permission. So she was a mistress with a slack hand. The kind who would go out and leave a strange girl alone and untended, not even knowing whether the girl might be insane, or a thief, or a companion of thieves.

But not only the mistress was gone. The entire household was gone. Where were they? What had taken them all hence at the same time?

The stone paving was cool under her bare feet. She crossed to the pool, dipped her hands into the water, which had been warmed by the sun of midday. Something moved and she turned, hands dripping. A door opened at the far side of the garden. The boy came quickly across the diagonal walk.

"Merza, you ought not to be out of your bed. How do you feel?"

"Very strange. And very dirty. Where are the people who live in this fine house?"

"Merza, you ought to stay in bed. You are bruised and beyond what is evident to the eye—the demon was cast out of you today, and surely you were wounded as the demon struggled within you."

"I am filthy from rolling in the street. Can I have water in a basin and a towel and something clean to replace this torn, filthy thing I am wearing? Isn't there one woman in the place to help me get clean? Oh, if only your grandmother were here, she would not leave me as I am!" Merza sank onto the cool stone of the nearby bench, staring down at her bare feet.

"I'll try to find the things you need." Timothy sat beside her. "Dear Merza, I did not want to tell you this. Paul and Silas have been arrested and taken for trial before the city magistrates. All their friends have gone— all the others, all but me—have gone to the court. I do not know why they are gone so long. But Zenon— Bias—" He put an arm about her, filled with compassion for what she must feel to know that Paul and Silas were

in desperate trouble because of the thing Paul had done
for her.

Merza shuddered away from his arm. "Don't touch
me!" The boy was too humble, and humility confused
her. She was a slave, and if the boy desired her, filthy
and half-fainting as she was, she was too sick to put up
much of a struggle. What ailed him anyway? He should
know that there is no other person in the world as
defenseless as a slave whose owners have abandoned her.

She said fretfully, "Look at that shrine. No lares in it.
No penates. In this house they neglect the service due
to the gods."

"In this house they worship only God."

"Like the little preacher. Are they Jews?"

"The lady Lydia is a Jew by adoption. When Paul
and Luke and Silas and I came to Philippi she heard the
preaching, and believed and was baptized, with her household. Then she brought us here to be her guests so long
as we remain in Philippi."

"Lydia is a province, not a person. I have been there."

"I, too," said Timothy. "The lady's name is Euodia, a
woman of Lydia. She calls herself Lydia for business
reasons. She is a widow and she is a dyer. Her dye shed
is beyond the peristyle, through that door." He gave her
an anxious glance. "Are you all right? You belong in
your bed."

"After I bathe."

Timothy rose and went somewhere, returning with
basin and towels. He dipped water from the pool. "If I
knew where to look for clothing I would bring you
something. Well, at least I can get a tunic you can wear
till the lady returns."

Merza stood beside the bench and washed her face,
her neck, her arms. The water felt so refreshing she
stripped off the torn coat and, setting a foot on the end

of the bench, began scrubbing her legs. Timothy was coming down from a room off the balcony, and at sight of her with her tunic up around her hips he turned scarlet and averted his face.

"You'd better go to your room to finish your bath. Let me get clean water for you."

Merza sank onto the bench, dizzy from her exertions. Timothy had dropped a clean tunic at the end of the bench and was pouring out the water around the base of the almond tree. Merza said, "The demon—and the collar—are gone. I feel naked, hollow, almost—lonely. What will become of me? Where will I go? What will I do? That empty shrine! Why don't they at least put flowers in it? In the house of Julia the shrine was honored. Every day the entire household prayed in the peristyle."

Timothy picked up the tunic and sat beside her. It was a tunic Zebulon had given to Paul. Timothy had thought Paul's tunic would come nearer fitting the girl than one of his own. He said, "I have thought of you often, these four years. I used to dream of finding you. In the dream I always found you in Ephesus. I always dreamed that I took you away to live with my grandmother. Would you like to go there? Do not worry about your future, or what will become of you. You are among Christians. Christians love one another and they will love you. As I do."

Merza said sharply, "I know what you mean by love. I learned all about that, from Bias! I gave birth to a child in Ephesus last winter!" Then, as Timothy touched her with horror and pity, "Don't touch me! I cannot bear to be touched!"

He ducked his head. "I would never hurt you. Never."

"Then you are a fool. What are you crying about? Men don't cry."

Timothy wiped his cheek with the tunic he held

crumpled in his arms. "I am weeping for you, for what has happened to you, for slaves who are abused and cannot defend themselves. And I am weeping for Paul and Silas. They are in the Roman tribunal, on trial for preaching the worship of the Most High God. Romans are forbidden to worship any but Caesar, but until today Paul has never had trouble with Romans! I am afraid for him."

She laid her hand on his arm. "Do not fret about the little preacher. He is destined to survive many things. I saw him, during the days when I ran after him in the street. I could have told his fortune if he had cared to hear it. He will not die in Philippi. He will die in Rome, and when he dies his hair will be all gone and his beard white and his face full of lines and wrinkles. It will happen after many years, and in Rome, not in Philippi."

She covered her face with her hands. "Don't ask me how he will die. I cannot bear to remember what I saw." Then, her voice shrill, "Why did you follow me in the street? Why did you take me to the little preacher? I did not want to make trouble for him. He will have plenty of trouble down all the years, and I did not want to add to his trouble by getting him hurt in Philippi."

"Merza, four years ago, when you and I were both children, you told my fortune. You said, 'You will walk down many a high road, but the master you serve will bind you with cords of love.'"

She stared at him, astonished. "Did I say that to you?"

"You said it. As a result, I prepared myself in the ways Paul directed, to become his companion on the roads. I owe you a great debt. I thought if Paul cast out your demon that would be a kindness to compare with what you have done for me."

"Poppycock," cried Merza. "I told fortunes for money, not kindness. If you want to show me kindness, let me finish my bath and be clean." The boy was a fool.

Still, the day he appeared she had begun praying to be loosed from the life she led. And that was a new thing. One possessed by a demon did not often pray. Hate was the weapon of such folk.

She crossed to the room where her bed was spread on the floor. "You were a fool to believe that fortune. I invented half the fortunes I told. Do you think I had visions for every face in the crowds? I learned long ago what people will pay to hear."

"Mine was a true fortune."

"I suppose so. Some of them were bound to be true, or I would have been abandoned and left to starve long ago."

Timothy emptied the basin over the plants in the garden and dipped clean water from the pool. He took it to the bedroom and set it on a bench made of stone. She stood holding the tunic in her arms, her face in her hands. "The lictors are scourging the little preacher, beating him with rods. I can't bear it!" She threw the clean tunic to the floor. "Take it away. Bring me something to wear that does not belong to the little preacher."

Timothy picked up the tunic. "Merza, your demon is gone. You need not pretend you still have visions, for I know you don't." He shook out the tunic and folded it over his arm. "I'll try to find something else for you to wear."

"Bring me some bread. I'm starving."

Timothy left Paul's tunic on a bench and went to the kitchen. Ah, Paul, Silas, dear friends, are they indeed beating you? Surely the girl invented all that. Both Paul and Silas were Roman citizens, immune to rough handling by Roman officials. The girl had invented all that. How could she know what was happening? He found clean towels, and a loaf, and some fruit, and returned to the atrium, and across it, praying as he went for the evangelist whose coming to Lystra years ago had changed the direction of his whole life.

Still absorbed in anxiety for his companions in travel, Timothy pulled back the curtain to deliver the food and towels to the girl. Merza laughed at sight of his scarlet face. Her tunic lay in a crumpled heap. "Come here, stupid. Scrub my back." She offered a dripping cloth. "Oh, you should see yourself." What a fool, to let the sight of an abandoned and ownerless slave embarrass him! What a fool, and yet he was the only person on earth who still felt some sort of responsibility or concern for her welfare or even for her safety. Whether she lived or died meant nothing to any other soul on earth!

Timothy hurled the towels toward her and dropped the curtain between them. He leaned against the wall, his hot face buried in his hands. He could not exorcise the haunting image of that bare, bruised, emaciated body, the jutting ribs, the small, pointed breasts. He had felt their pressure against himself when he carried her over his shoulder through the streets today. Her calves and thighs were bunched with muscle, as if all the nourishment she received had gone to strengthen her legs for journeying on the roads of Galatea and Asia and Hellas and Macedonia.

She called, "Timothy, I am covered with bruises and abrasions caused by convulsing on the cobbles. Do find ointment, or at least bring some oil."

He found oil in the kitchen. He reached round the edge of the door curtain, his eyes averted, his face hidden, extending the cruse. She cried, "Oh, fool! Bring it!"

Still averting his eyes he entered and set the cruse on the bench. He found a towel and wrapped it around her naked body. "I like to hear you laugh," he said. "Even when you laugh at me. Whatever happens, Merza, I will love you and pray for you always."

She turned in his arms and twitched aside the towel. If she had safety anywhere in the earth it was with this ridiculous, fumbling boy. "What a fool you are," she said softly. She put her arms about his neck, pressed against him, rising on tiptoe till her mouth found the generous, full-lipped mouth framed within the sprouting beginnings of yellow beard.

He kissed her, fumbling and uncertain at first, then fiercely, swept out of his senses by an emotion with which he had had no previous experience. She moved her body knowingly against him. "If I am truly loved, perhaps I can forget all the past. Love me, Timothy, love me! There is so much I must be taught to forget. Love me and heal me."

Timothy's arms tightened convulsively. "You will be my wife. I swear I will find a way to make you my wife." Yet even as he said it he remembered with horror all his assurances to Paul. "You did not marry, Paul, and neither will I. I am yours to command."

Merza broke from him and slapped his face furiously. "Your wife! Who wants to be your wife? Buy me, or Zenon will find me and sell me as a whore in some tavern. Bias always said that would happen, if ever I quit telling fortunes. I am a slave, so make me your slave! There is no other safety for me."

The reminder of what her life had been struck Timothy like the dash of cold water with which Lois used sometimes to waken him. He took the oil, poured a little into his hand, anointed the bruised face and shoulders, the wounded flesh of the abused, starved, debased body. Then he wrapped his own coat about her, and picked up Paul's tunic and carried it from the room. Halfway up the stairs he paused, leaning his head against the cool stone wall.

"O God," he prayed, "You know I would not hurt or abuse her. Give her a true friend in Lydia, to teach her to be modest and womanly and compassionate, to heal her of all the sorrows she has known. Heal her mind, and heart, and body." And then, desperately, he prayed, "Deliver her from evil. And deliver me from lust."

12

WE ARE THREE WIDOWS, thought Lydia, and a child, and
Rufus. My household. My family. A small household
with a too-large house. And now a girl I know nothing
about, a street girl accustomed to displaying herself in
every public place, has been brought here. I know nothing about her character. I have no faith or trust in her.
She has brought all these terrible things to pass, inter-
rupting the ministry of Paul and Silas. They have been
beaten by lictors, confined in the stocks in the torture
chamber of the inner prison, and she brought it all upon
them. Yet I must somehow make a place for her in my
house, among my dependents.

Lydia squeezed her eyes tight shut and shook her head.
She dared not give way to the anguish she felt.

Lydia was a tall, Junoesque woman, twoscore years of
age, with dark, beautiful, compassionate eyes, and a look
of incisive intelligence. One knew she would rule her
group wherever she was, yet rule it for good. Her upper
jaw was overshot, but not unattractive. Rather, it seemed
to add strength and character to her face. Her brows were
cleanly arched above the intelligent eyes. Her movements
were definite, sure, adept.

She said kindly, "Erethrea, you will have us all weeping before long. Please be comforted. Where is your faith, dear?"

"Where is your handkerchief, dear?" said Syntyche sharply. "You are creating a spectacle in the public street. You make all this harder for the rest of us because you have no self-control. Do you think only you saw the blows, the blood, or heard the thud of rods on those bare backs?"

Niko gave a little shriek, and Lydia touched the child's shoulder comfortingly. She said, "Syntyche, do be silent."

Erethrea sobbed, "I keep thinking of them—Brother Silas so pale. Brother Paul so thin, his ribs showing—and the blows—and they so brave, so good and kind always. Oh, I cannot bear it."

Lydia said, "I should have left you at home. The girl needed care and a woman to sit with her. I was wrong to take you with us."

Niko said, "Timothy is with the girl."

Erethrea mopped her mottled cheeks and blew her nose. "She needed a woman to sit with her, or to bathe her while she slept. She was fearfully dirty, and I should have thought of her. I know I am too cowardly to be taken along to these public punishments. But I would have died of the anxiety of not knowing whether they lived or died, had you left me at home."

"So you are weeping in the streets instead of at home," said Syntyche.

Lydia said, "Rufus, here is the alley. If you want to hurry on home by the back way—the wool has been too long in the scarlet. It needs stirring."

"Timothy promised to stir it, my lady."

"Nevertheless, you are the dyer, not Timothy. We will manage the rest of the journey without a man's support. You may leave us here."

"Yes, mistress," said Rufus. He touched his hand to his

flaming red hair. The hands and arms of the dyer were colored with every shade of dye the House of Lydia offered its clientele. Under the clean white coat, his chest also was stained with many colors. He strode swiftly away down the alley.

"Such manners in a slave," said Syntyche. "How do you endure him?"

Niko cried, "We all love him. So do you, Syntyche, though you pretend otherwise."

Erethrea said, "He is a slave, but the Breath of God has entered into him, and he has been given the gift of tongues. Indeed it is true—we all love him. Forgive my weakness, dear Lydia. I have behaved as if I suffer more grief than others for our dear preachers. Of course I know better. But, oh, those dear men." She sniffled piteously.

Lydia said, "Come, my dears, we must not dawdle. You know I have sent word to the Christians. They will come at sunset to pray for Paul and Silas. We must get along home and prepare food for the company. You must bake more bread, Erethrea. Syntyche, perhaps your mistress can spare cheese."

"I will ask, if you wish. However, fasting with prayer is more appropriate to this occasion."

"Our hearts are heavy. This occasion does not call for fasting." Lydia added, "We must think what to do for the little sybil also. She has had a terrible and painful experience today, terrible, yet wonderful. I suspect she will be very hungry. You must certainly bake plenty of bread, Erethrea."

"I am ashamed to have gone off and left her with only Timothy," said Erethrea. "She desperately needed a bath, and the anointing of her wounds."

"She may have slept the whole time we have been away," said Lydia.

Niko said, "I wish Luke were here. I miss him when he goes away. He would know better than we what to do for Merza."

They turned into the street of weavers and dyers, at whose far end stood the House of Lydia, with its dye works in the shed behind the peristyle. Syntyche turned with them, though Lydia had assumed she would go on to the Street of Cheesemakers and turn there. Perhaps Syntyche wanted first to satisfy her curiosity about the soothsayer, thought Lydia.

Lydia's business of importing the costly purple from the city of Lydia in Asia brought to her door the richest and most ostentatious residents of Philippi and its environs, as well as merchants from other cities. The house was far too large for her needs, yet because her customers came to the house to do business she had not disposed of it when her husband died, though she had, with the passage of time, cut in half the staff required to keep up such a place. These past months, with Paul and Silas, Luke and Timothy all dwelling under her roof, had made her feel for the first time in many years that the house was not, after all, too large. The atrium and peristyle provided quarters where the ecclesia could meet. Thus the great, expensive house had at last justified its existence.

The portal bore beside the door a painted reproduction of the madder plant and a bunch of grapes. Over both, greatly enlarged, was a splendidly tinted reproduction of a single murex shell, open and empty of the occupant whose life processes had created it.

Away to the south and west rose the great mountain for the sake of which King Philip of Macedon, more than three centuries earlier, had fortified this city and given it his name. Throughout his turbulent reign he had taken a thousand talents of gold each year from the mines of Mount Pangaeus. His son Alexander had created a Greek world that stretched across Asia and Syria and on to

India. He had created this mighty empire out of his own genius, his warrior's training in his father's camps, and the wealth of gold which continued to flow from Mount Pangaeus at Philippi.

The Romans revered Philippi for another reason. On the plains of Philippi was fought the battle, following the murder of Julius Caesar in the Roman Senate, which ended the Republic and set young Octavian, adoptive heir to Julius, on the throne as first of the Roman Emperors. The crowning of Octavian, who changed his name to Caesar Augustus, ended a long period of internecine wars and marked the beginning of the Pax Romana, which had endured now for well over half a century and looked to last indefinitely.

Augustus was followed by Tiberius Caesar, who was succeeded briefly by Caligula (Gaius Caesar, nicknamed Caligula, Little Boots, by the soldiers of his father, Germanicus). Caligula was followed by Claudius, the fourth Caesar to reign as princeps in Rome.

Last year (or was it the year before?) the emperor had expelled the Jews from Rome. Whatever his reasons, provincial governors had become nervous of men charged with preaching in the name of the Most High God, meaning the God of the Jews. And this was the charge brought against Paul and Silas today. Any official inclined to be lenient with such prisoners put himself in the position of Pontius Pilate two decades before when he was told, "If you set him free, you are not Caesar's friend." To Lydia it seemed a miracle that Paul and Silas still lived.

At the portal of her house Lydia said resolutely, "Our dear friends still live. Be comforted, my dears, for I feel every confidence that they will return to us. They live, and God is with them." She realized, but did not say, that even though they lived, even if by some miracle they were released quickly, today's event marked the end of their ministry in Philippi. Paul was sure to regard this event as God's signal that he had stayed long enough in one city and should move on to another.

Niko squeezed Lydia's hand. "I do hope she is feeling better—that girl, Merza. I am going to give her my ribbons. Oh, I hope she is awake."

Syntyche said spitefully, "She caused all this trouble. Niko, I wish I had your forgiving nature, but she is to blame. Paul let her know more than once he wanted to be left alone, that healing is not his ministry. She is to blame, and I for one do not propose to forget it. Luke would have been caught with the others, had he not gone to Mount Pangaeus."

Two days earlier there had been an earthquake at the mine, and Luke had gone to minister to the injured.

And Lydia listened and thought, I am no sweeter natured, no more forgiving than Syntyche, and I will not pretend that I am. I do wish Timothy had not brought that girl to my house!

The girl was in the atrium, sitting near the pool. She had washed herself after a fashion and was wearing Timothy's coat, pulled together because he had not given her a tunic to go under it. Her hair had apparently been washed, after a fashion. It hung in damp tendrils over her shoulders. Her feet were bare, but clean. Lydia crossed to her, touched by her look of exhaustion and neglect.

"You have surprised us, my dear. We expected to find you napping. I am Lydia. I hope to be—your friend, Merza. Timothy, is that coat the best you could find for Merza to wear?"

Timothy was pale with strain. "Where are Paul and Silas? Tell me what happened."

"They are in prison. We must be thankful they did not get a sentence of death."

Erethrea fled sobbing to the kitchen. Timothy said, "Merza says they will come back to us safely. But I couldn't help fearing the worst."

Niko cried, "But, Merza, you aren't a soothsayer any longer."

Timothy put an affectionate hand on the little girl's shoulder. "This was a vision of the streets, of days past, before the demon was cast out."

Merza was not listening to the talk. She was looking intently at Lydia. She hates me, thought the girl. She blames me for what is happening to the little preacher and that other man, the one who sings.

The lady said, "Timothy, you have lost much of this day's weaving. Clement is expecting you to come and make the best of what daylight is left. He will tell you what was said and done at the magistrates' court. We will all be together at sunset to pray for our beloved friends."

Syntyche said, "I'll get along home now. I will try to bring cheese at sunset—whatever the shop can spare from the regular customers."

The two of them, Timothy and Syntyche, were gone, and now Lydia turned to Merza. "My dear, we will try to make you comfortable and pretty. Niko, bring scissors. You don't mind if I cut off some of this mass of wet hair, do you, Merza?"

"I will cut my own hair. It grows fast and I have cut it whenever I can get scissors. But I have had no scissors since we were in Ephesus." She took the scissors Niko brought and began whacking off her hair above her shoulders.

"Have your wounds been anointed, my dear? Did Timothy find oil for you?"

"Yes, thank you. And I am feeling much better, my lady." This was not a woman to whom one confided every ache and pain. Indeed, except for the lady Julia, Merza had not had conversation before with such a lady as this one. She was not one to be easily deceived. I shall have to study how to please her, thought Merza, or I will find myself on the streets, a slave with no owners and no identity I can prove. It is well nobody told this lady that Timothy anointed my abrasions. Do I dare tell her I'm starving? No. I will wait till that weeping person has made more bread.

Lydia said, "Niko, look among my clothes for something pretty. Merza, I believe you are tall enough to wear something of mine for today."

"I believe so, my lady," said Merza, and whacked off more hair. Now that it was beginning to dry, and was shorter, it was beginning to curl up around her fingers.

Niko's eyes were bright. "The russet chiton? You never wear it anymore, Lydia."

"Good! I gave up wearing chitons when I became a Jew. Bring the box with the fibulae. But first, the hairbrush. We must get the tangles out of this girl's hair."

"Thank you, my lady," said Merza. "When I have a brush I always keep it in order. But I have not had a brush since I left Ephesus."

Lydia said kindly, "When you are properly dressed, my child, you must rest for a while. We want you to be ready to meet the friends who will be coming at sunset. You have had a most interesting career as a clairvoyant, but now you must develop some other skill. We must each, in some way, earn our living. We must give some thought to how you are going to earn yours."

Merza laid down the hairbrush. "I have tried to think of something. Whatever I am to do, I will have to be taught. Oh, my lady, death is the punishment for slaves who try to elude their masters. I do not know what is to become of me." She added shrewdly, for she had to try to win the lady's trust, "Nor of you, if you help me."

Niko came down the stairs with clothing draped over her arm and a lovely blue-enameled box in her hands,

such as women use to hold their knickknacks. Merza followed the two of them into the room off the atrium
where she had slept. There she stripped, and Lydia examined her bruises and abrasions, saying only that they
seemed to have been properly cleansed and anointed. She
sent Niko for ointment, however, and used it on a bruise
behind Merza's ear, and on some others about her rib
cage and shoulder blades and hips. Then Merza put on
a shift of soft white linen, and over it the rust-colored
chiton. And when it was pinned at the shoulders with
bronze fibulae, Niko led her out into the atrium and over
to a tall mirror of polished bronze near the portal. At
sight of herself Merza buried her face in her hands.

Lydia touched her shoulder. "What is wrong, my
child?"

"When they find me, Zenon and Bias, now that I have
lost my vocation, they will sell me to be a tavern girl."

"That will not happen. I promise it will not happen,"
said Lydia.

Niko said reasonably, "All you need to do is stay hidden inside this house until they leave Philippi. They took
off your collar themselves. Timothy saw it done. Surely
you have a right—"

"Slaves have no rights at all," said Merza. Then,
"Thank you for the beautiful things, my lady. For the
chiton, fibulae—for everything. Niko, thank you for the
ribbons." Her hands touched the fibulae, smoothed down
the flowing skirt. "I've never worn anything so pretty."
Then she touched the ridged flesh at her neck, the pale
flesh which the collar had kept from turning dark in the
sun. "I'm so afraid."

Lydia said, "We will find you some better sandals
tomorrow. Now, Merza, sit here with me for a moment
and we will talk." And they went to the bench beside
the pear tree. "I do not care to break the law, yet I see
no justice in assuming your former owners still have a

claim. I must talk to Paul about that, and to Luke. Luke
has been a slave. He is now a freedman, well educated
and a physician. He probably knows much more about
the laws concerning slaves than Paul would know, or
Silas. But Luke is at the mine for a few days, and of
course Paul is not with us either just now. I have been
thinking, as we were dressing you. I believe the thing to
do for the present is simply this: You must remain se-
cluded in this house, and you must not attend the ecclesia tonight. I will ask those who know you are here
not to mention it to anyone. When the ecclesia begins
to gather you shall go to your room and stay there.
Niko, make her bed up in your room. You two will share
the room. Merza will be able to listen to as much as she
likes of the prayer service for Paul and Silas. We will
also discuss your situation with Rufus. He is in the dye
shed, Merza, if you want to go and talk to him now.
Tell him exactly what was done today to you, the re-
moval of the collar in particular, and tell of the threat
to sell you as a tavern girl. Rufus knows what slavery
and suffering are, and he is wise. He is good. And he says
that only a slave can understand a slave. So go on back
to the dye shed now and talk to Rufus, but don't let
him splash dye on this dress. Tomorrow we will give
you working clothes, and you might try to learn the dye-
maker's trade. Rufus could use a helper. You will not find
a better man anywhere to be your teacher. We are all
friends in this house, Merza, and Brother Paul taught us
the blessedness of all sitting at the table to take our
meals together."

Suddenly the house was permeated with the odor of
baking bread. The rich odor struck Merza with such
force she felt faint. "Please," she cried, "I think I will
never get enough bread to eat. I am famished."

"Niko, run and get a loaf from Erethrea. While you
are in this house, Merza, you will have bread enough."

Merza looked earnestly into the dark, Asian face of this woman who had so suddenly become the arbiter of her fate. "One other lady was kind to me. In Ephesus a lady called Julia, who is the wife of one of the Asiarchs, a man called Philologus, was kind and took me into her home while I was being delivered of a child brutally begotten upon me by Bias. I gave her my child. Timothy's grandmother was also kind, but I had told his fortune and he was very pleased with it. I do not know what to give you in return for so much kindness."

Niko came running with a fragrant loaf wrapped in a napkin. Merza began munching upon it happily.

Lydia said, "Niko, run up to your room and spread a clean bed for Merza beside your own." And when the child had gone she said, "Timothy tells me you have had visions of what is to happen to Paul in years to come. I do not know that he would care to hear about them, but I would be most interested." She smiled. "You are going to have to learn new ways of repaying kindness. But for now I will be well pleased to hear this."

Merza looked at Lydia carefully while she chewed and swallowed the bread in her mouth. "I will tell most of what I saw. I do not want to tell you all. The little preacher will not die in Philippi, my lady. I saw him suffer many hardships, travel many roads, cross the seas in various ships at various times. He will accomplish much of what he desires but not all. He will suffer arrests several times, and will be in several prisons. He has been stoned, and he will never be stoned again. He will suffer shipwreck, but will get safely to shore. When he dies, it will be by the hand of the Romans, after long imprisonment. When he dies he will be much older than he now is, with a bald head and a white beard. That is all I can tell you, my lady."

"Will he be—crucified?"

"No, my lady. He is a citizen of Tarsus and the Romans will not crucify him. He will die with words of love for the Lord Jesus upon his lips, and forgiveness for his executioners in his heart."

"I believe you love him too," said Lydia.

"I don't know about love, my lady. My grandmother sold me to Zenon when I was a little child. I don't remember about love." She turned away. "I will go and talk to Rufus now."

Lydia watched her go. I cannot tell when she is speaking the truth and when she is trying to manipulate me, she thought. But I think she told the truth about Paul.

13

MERZA HAD EATEN her fill of bread when she went to the room off the balcony which she was to share with Niko. She put on the sleeping tunic Niko brought, and laid a warm, woolen robe beside the bed. How good the bed smelled. How glad she was to be in this house. The lady is kind, though she still does not like me. Oh well, kindness is a habit with her, and if she cannot learn to like me she will send me away but she will never beat me or scream at me. I must learn to be useful. She will not send me away if I am useful. I would not mind working in the vat room. She giggled a little, thinking of herself all spattered and splotched with dyes as Rufus was. He is strange, for a slave. He can even tell the lady when she is wrong, and she just agrees with him and walks away. He is very strange but—I like him. I trust him and I like him. And Niko—my goodness, what a silly little thing she is. She would give away her last tunic and the food from her bowl if she thought some-body wanted it. She is surely a silly one.

The Christians were down there in the atrium, making enough noise to keep one awake. But it is best they don't know I am up here in this room. The best thing will be if Zenon and Bias just leave town and I stay right here inside this house till everybody has forgotten me. Then when I do go out on the street I'll be all stained with dyes, and if I eat lots of bread I'll get to looking all plump and different and when people see me they'll say there goes a dyer, not there goes that soothsayer.

Now they were singing down there. I suppose it would help if I learned to sing their songs, she thought. That might please the lady. And the singing made her think of Silas and the little preacher. They are in pain, she thought. I know they have been tortured and are in pain. Nobody had said much about that—just enough so that she knew. I didn't want to get the little preacher hurt, she thought. I just wanted him to change my life, and he has, and now he is in the prison, in the torture chamber, and I know he is suffering.

She rose and wrapped the warm robe about her and went softly out into the shadows of the gallery. The song ended, and it was Timothy who stood up to speak to the people.

"We must believe that God can turn every misfortune into glory. Silas has told me of a night when the ecclesia in Jerusalem had gathered to pray. You have heard Silas speak of the three who were closest to the Lord Jesus during his ministry—Peter, James, and John. This story is concerned with Peter and James, who had been arrested before the Passover by Herod, who was then king of the Jews. They were charged with plotting the overthrow of the Roman empire, and there were witnesses to testify against James, who had been preaching in Jerusalem, but no witnesses were found against Peter, because he had been preaching in Caesarea. James was beheaded, and Peter was held over till after the Passover, when a witness from another city would be brought in. On the night before Peter's hearing was scheduled, the Jerusalem ecclesia met to pray, as we have done here tonight. Midnight came and passed, and there was a knocking at the

door, and behold, it was Peter. Then they brought him
into their midst, rejoicing, and he told how an angel had
come to him in the prison while he slept, chained to his
guards. At the touch of the angel's hands his chains fell
away, and he arose, and followed the angel through one
locked door after another until he was in the midnight
silence of the streets.

"We must believe," Timothy concluded, "that God,
who delivered Peter from prison, so that he is still preaching after twenty years throughout Syria and Palestine,
is able also to deliver Paul and Silas that they may return
to us and continue their ministry."

He speaks very well, thought Merza, feeling a little surprised at the competence of the boy who had been so
helpless when he was alone with her. And he is right,
of course. They will be delivered, though I doubt an
angel will be sent to do it.

Timothy said, "We have wept for our friends today.
Let us not fail to praise God that they have this day witnessed to the glory of God and the death and resurrection
of our Lord Jesus in the presence of magistrates and
lictors. More townspeople have heard them today than at
any other time since we reached Philippi last autumn.
Without a doubt they are both still witnessing in the
presence of men who could never have heard them, had
Paul and Silas not become prisoners also."

Merza moved softly back into the darkness of her sleeping room. These were very strange people and none of
them stranger than Timothy. I don't suppose there is
very much money among them, she thought, but they
are certainly people of goodwill. Even Timothy, today,
when she stripped off her clothes and showed her body
to him, anointed her abrasions, and that was all he did!
Though he was out of his mind with desire for her, he
had turned away. He had given her his coat to wear and
gone away and she had not seen him again until the lady

and those others came home. Oh, she would have struck him and kicked him and clawed him if he had tried any tricks. Why did I treat him that way? What do I really want from him? She had no answer to the question. He had brought her here, in spite of all that was happening to his friends. Now he was down there talking like a real preacher to those people, and they loved him and took comfort from his preaching. I do not think they will take me to Zenon, she thought. Not unless they have to. They aren't rich, at least not rich like Julia and Philologus the Asiarch. But they wish me well.

She moved back out onto the balcony again, for down below they were breaking bread together and kissing one another, calling it the kiss of peace. She crawled back into her bed and pulled the sheet over her head to shut out their voices.

Her eyes closed. Scarlets, blues, russets—those are from vegetable dyes. Purple from the costly murex shells. Vegetable madder and indigo, the most ancient of all dyes. Rufus had told her all about these things today. In the indigo vat you use potash, lime, and grape treacle. It was a specialty in the House of Lydia. You put washed wool into the grape juice and sprinkle with powdered madder and leave all night, stirring occasionally. Ashes of wood or goat dung are added then, to set the color. A yellow is made of almond leaves. Pomegranate bark for black. Rufus—

She jerked wide awake. Rufus was making very strange sounds down there. She listened for some time before she realized this was what Niko had called the gift of tongues. She crept out to the balcony and looked down. It was a silvery, fluid sound, not loud but joyful. Near one of the burning cressets he stood, Rufus with the red beard and red hair, wearing a decent white coat and with upraised, blue-dyed hands. He held up those strangely splotched hands toward the sky—for he was in the peristyle, in the garden beyond the almond tree where there was no roof—and the lifted, red-bearded face glowed with joy.

Niko was beside him. "He says Paul and Silas will be with us in this house tomorrow. He says we will all be together with them at sunset tomorrow. He says, oh, he says praise God for His wonderful goodness to the children of men. He says, oh, we must hurry, hurry home now. There is no time to make your farewells."

The blue hands dropped. Rufus walked without a word to anyone to his own room off the peristyle, the one which was nearest to the dye shed. The people were departing in haste and the scene ended swiftly. Merza crept back into her bed, covered herself and closed her eyes. Then Niko was standing beside her, holding a little copper lamp with one wick burning, and Merza opened her eyes sleepily.

"Did we disturb you? Have you slept?"

Merza turned over, shading her eyes from the burning wick. "Niko, do you really think God will swoop down and take the little preacher out of that prison and set him down in this house?"

Niko said softly, "I do not know what God will do. I only know that what God wills to happen will happen. I know that when Rufus speaks with tongues and prophecies, that which he foretells will happen. Merza, I am sorry I left you alone. I was selfish, and it is the second time today I have treated you badly because I am selfish. I am the only one who can interpret when Rufus speaks with tongues; perhaps he speaks in a language I knew as a child. But still, I am selfish, and I am going to give you a gift, my most precious possession. Only for a few days, till you no longer feel strange among us. It is beautiful, and it will cover the ridges on your neck till they go away. It is my dearest possession."

She opened a small chest taken from a niche in the

wall. From it she took a strand of amber beads. "Wear them, dear Merza. See, you can wind them three times about your neck. Oh, they are pretty on you. I am too young for them, but they are my dearest treasure, and they are beautiful around your throat."

"You are giving me your dearest treasure?"

"Only for a while. Till your neck loses the pallor where the collar was so tight on it. Till you learn to feel at home and happy among us. It's a loan, not a gift. It belonged to my mother."

The child was embarrassed. Merza found her confusion charming, but amusing. Yet the beads felt warm and comforting against her throat, which had seemed all day strangely naked and exposed. The beads are costly, she thought. They are more costly than this silly child imagines.

She said, "Niko, I thank you for lending me the beads. I am starving. Can you bring me some bread?"

"It has all been eaten. Erethrea was making more bread during the preaching, and she put it in the oven to bake before I came upstairs. She will not go to bed tonight until it is baked and she takes it from the oven and wraps it in linen. Shall I go and bring you figs?"

"No figs, thank you. I've never learned to eat costly foods. Only bread. Good night, Niko. Go to sleep now. It is getting very late." She turned restlessly on her bed. "It is hard to sleep in such a quiet house. I have always slept in the midst of snoring and drunken rioting and all such things. The silence of this house is keeping me awake."

"Let me sing to you, Merza. I sometimes sing to the lady Lydia at night when she is restless."

Niko went out onto the balcony, where lamps burned beside several of the rooms. She returned presently carrying a lute. The somber little face was transformed when she plucked the strings. Her touch was sure, the

soft young voice true and pure. Merza lay still, astonished by the beauty of the child's performance:

My soul doth magnify the Lord
And my spirit rejoices in God, my Savior.
For He has regarded the low estate of His handmaiden.

Merza had encountered entertainers in the taverns. She
knew a fine performance when she heard one. "Who
taught you, Niko?"

"My mother. She taught me to play the lute and to
sing. But Silas taught me this song. It was sung by the
mother of our Lord Jesus when she learned that her
son would be the promised Messiah."

"Did your mother sing this song?"

"Oh no, Merza. Nobody in Macedonia ever heard this
song until Silas came here last autumn. He taught it to
me. Our beloved Paul brought Silas and Luke and Timothy to Philippi with him. Or perhaps it was Luke who
persuaded the other three to come. You do not know
Luke yet, but he will return to this house in a day or two.
He is a physician and is often called away when there
is sickness. There was an earthquake at the mine on the
mountain and that is where he is now."

Niko touched the strings and began another song. Suddenly the room fled away, and Merza was seeing and
hearing an older Niko with a richer, deeper voice. She
was singing in a great court, in a house finer than any
Merza had ever seen, for its courts spread away and
away, as only the court of a Caesar, or a governor,
might do.

When the song ended Merza was sitting on her bed.
She spoke in her public voice, the voice of the gates and
the agoras. "You will sing before kings." Then, in whin-
ing singsong, "There, I have told your fortune. Give me
the beads to keep."

The lute dropped into the child's lap. "They are my

dearest treasure. My mother—" Niko ceased on a ripple of soft laughter. "You cannot tell fortunes anymore! Paul has cast out your demon and you don't know what is going to happen any more than I do. You are only pretending. Oh, Merza, how funny you are!"

The vision had been true, as real and as true as any vision Merza had ever known. Pierced by disillusion, since her mystic powers had not, after all, been exorcised today, Merza exclaimed spitefully, "What do you suppose your mother gave in return for these beads? Was she a woman of the taverns? How many men of wealth gave her beautiful gifts?"

For some time then Merza lay quiet, listening to the muffled sobbing that came from Niko's bed. At first she felt only anger. That had been a true vision. Whatever had happened to her demon today, she was still clairvoyant, subject to being returned to Bias and Zenon to tell fortunes and follow the roads. But presently she thought, Whatever is to become of me, it is not Niko's fault. She has shown me only kindness. And if I am cruel to Niko the lady will kick me out of this house faster than she ever received me into it. I need not ever again tell anyone his fortune. Nobody needs to know the clairvoyance did not vanish with the demon. I must study the lady and learn to please her and make her love me as she loves Niko. I must be kind to Timothy, who brought me to this house. Most of all, I must be kind to Niko, for the lady will hate me if I am not.

Merza said softly, "Pay no attention to me, Niko. I was showing off. I have been telling fortunes as far back as I can remember. When I did not know what to say I made guesses. How else could I convince people so they would give coins to Zenon?"

Her hand went to her throat, touching the amber beads, which had taken on the warmth of her flesh. They were sensuous, responsive as if alive. The lady would hate

her if she took advantage of this child. Still, to wear the
beads about her throat would help her to forget the
binding touch of the collar. She desperately wanted these
beads!

The sobbing continued on the other bed. At last
Merza unwound the beads and leaned across to drop
them on the shadowy, hiccupping little figure.

"Here are your beads, Niko. I expect your mother was
given many gifts because of the beauty of her music. As
you will be also, Niko." And when the sobbing did not
abate, "Anyway, a slave cannot be blamed for obeying
her master. You are lucky to belong to a kind mistress
who loves you as if she were your mother and you her
own child, born of her own flesh."

The sobbing quieted. Niko gasped, "I wept because
I am so selfish. I wanted the beads for myself. I don't
want them now. Keep them, dear Merza. They are yours
forever. I wept also because you don't have even a memory of your own mother, but only of a grandmother
who sold you to be a slave. I wept for you, dear Merza."

Now it was Niko who leaned across to drop the beads
on the neighboring bed. And the smooth, responsive
ovals slid across Merza's hands once more. She fingered
them, loving their touch, while the breathing in the
other bed grew soft and even. Presently it was clear that
Niko slept.

It was a true vision, thought Merza. If these people
find out I am still clairvoyant—they follow such strange
rules—they will probably conclude that they must find
Zenon and return me to him. I have heard the little
preacher. Slaves, obey your masters! Wives, obey your
husbands! Citizens, obey your rulers! It was a true vision.
Niko will sing in Rome, perhaps even in the palace of the
Caesar.

She heard footsteps on the balcony and saw a lamp
with one wick go past the door. It lighted the face of

Erethrea. So the bread was baked and out of the oven and wrapped in linen down there somewhere—wherever the kitchen might be. At least, she thought, while I am in this house there will always be bread to eat.

For a while she slept. It might have been an hour or several hours later when she was awakened. How still it was. Last night she had slept in a noisy tavern and wakened to the snoring and muttering of many men. Tonight—how could one sleep in the midst of such silence? She could barely hear Niko's soft breathing nearby. From somewhere came the vagrant fragrance of bread baked only an hour or two ago.

14

MERZA ROSE, wrapping the warm sleeping robe about her. In the gallery a lamp burned beside the door. All up the gallery, outside each door, lamps burned in niches. And through the roof holes in atrium and peristyle moonlight sifted. How peacefully the household slept. How sweet was the perfume that drifted up from the almond tree. And with that odor again came the wispy drift, an aroma of recently baked bread. Softly, swiftly on bare feet Merza descended to the atrium. Yonder was the corridor down which Erethrea had disappeared today, the corridor which surely must lead to the kitchen. I want to stay in this house! I want to live here!

The kitchen had no roof hole to let in moonlight. Stone chimneys carried away smoke from the fireplace and ovens. There were slit windows under the roof's overhang which let in a slight glimmer of moonlight. The flicker from her lamp and the prospect of exploring a rich kitchen in a strange house lured her to move quickly across the floor. It was a big kitchen, big enough to serve a tavern. Maybe some day she would get to explore it fully by daylight, without Erethrea's hovering over her.

Her lamp was smoking. The oil would soon be exhausted. She held it high, staring about. On a table against the far wall were bowls filled with fruit and nuts and vegetables—bowls or baskets. Something was wrapped in linen—loaves of bread surely. Above the table a lamp stood in a niche. If she could get that lamp and light it from her own before it went out—she rushed across, stumbled against something heavy, and sat down abruptly, dropping her lamp, which sputtered and went out. The pain in her bruised toes made her want to cry out, but she must be still, be still. A brief exploration with her hands revealed that she had stumbled against a mill in which grain was ground.

Weirdly, the stones beneath her moved. Pans rattled on the wall. Something heavy and metallic fell clanging onto the stones. An earthen pot dropped to the floor, shattered, spilled oil that spread across the floor, fouling her nice, clean robe, draining into a crack between the stones. She screamed, "Be still! Be still!"

Terror was demoralizing. Madness was surely returning. She would be cast out from this nice house. It was only an earthquake! She had known earthquakes, the shudder of a hillside, the cracking wall of a smoky tavern. She had seen sections of cottages, of villages, of cities left desolate. Yet most earthquakes ended quickly, with little damage. The thing to do was get to the peristyle, into the garden, where there would be no roof to fall in on her, in case the quake returned. But she could not move. The mill was wedged against her leg and her clothing was pinned under its weight.

A man's clear singing was in her ears:

Surely he has borne our sins and carried our sorrows.
He was despised and rejected of men,
A man of sorrows and acquainted with grief.

The singing came out of darkness, a voice she had heard before, the voice of Silas. Silas was singing somewhere in the darkness, in the night, and another voice joined him, harmonizing, the voice of the little preacher. Then the singing was gone. A lamp was held high in the doorway, held aloft by Timothy. The tremor had ended. The danger was past.

Timothy said softly, "Merza! Are you all right?"

"Lift this mill off me. Get me out of here."

Timothy rushed toward her, slipped in spilled oil, dropped his lamp. It overturned, adding its oil to that on the floor and igniting. Fire ran across the floor, wherever oil lay on the stony surface in little pools. Merza yanked her feet away from the blaze. Timothy's coat caught. He rolled about to put out the fire but his coat picked up more oil and blazed furiously till Merza jerked it off his shoulders and flung it into the blaze. Now her hands as well as her thigh were burned.

Timothy rolled away from the blaze, bounded to his feet, turned toward where the mill had her pinned down. The stones moved again. A gap in the floor swallowed the burning oil and flame and again the room was dark. Timothy's groping hand found her, and he held her against him, there on the floor. The mill slid away, got caught in the crack, and held there. The stones were still again, and the only light came from the slits of windows under the roof. Timothy got to his feet and was offering Merza his hand to help her rise.

"You're safe, Merza. The earthquake is over and the fire is out and you're safe."

She said urgently, "The earthquake can return. Let's get out to the peristyle. It is safer there."

A light appeared. Lydia stood in the doorway, lamp held aloft. Erethrea, ghostlike in the dim flicker, held the linen curtain away from the lamp's flame. Niko came crowding between them.

"Hey, we had an earthquake!" she cried. "What are you two doing in the kitchen?"

Lydia asked calmly, "Are you all right? Has there been a fire in here?"

Her smooth, auburn hair was loose upon her shoulders. Her sleeping robe was a soft blue, bordered in white.

Timothy said, "There's a crack in the floor. Some lamps fell and oil got spread around, and we slipped in the oil. Merza, are you able to get up?" He twitched his coat, and it split up the back.

Merza said, "I'm able to stand. Do stop mauling me, Timothy."

Lydia looked at her strangely, and Merza realized she must be careful not to offend the lady. "I was scared to death," she said plaintively. "And the mill slid onto my clothes and pinned me down. My leg is burned a little. I'm not really hurt, though. Just scared. Where is the little preacher? Did he come home in the night?"

Niko took her hand and led her out into the passage-way. "Oh, Merza, you know where they are." Her voice caught on a sob. "I wonder if the quake was bad at the prison."

"But they were singing. I heard them—" She stopped, feeling the attentive regard of the others. It had been another vision. She had betrayed herself to the lady. "It —I guess it was a dream," she said hastily. "Everything is so strange—so quiet here, after the taverns." They had reached the peristyle now and she sank onto the bench near the almond tree. "I can't tell you how strange it is to waken in a quiet house, with the odor of new bread and the fragrance from this garden and everything so still."

Niko put an arm about her. "You woke up from a dream, and smelled the bread and were hungry. And after you got to the kitchen the earthquake came. I'd think you'd have been scared to death. And of course you are still hungry."

She darted away to the kitchen and returned and thrust a fresh loaf into Merza's hands.

The garden was illuminated by a brilliant gibbous moon. Merza sat alone, nibbling the bread (though she no longer felt hunger for it) while the women and Timothy, lamps in hand, explored the house, appraising the damage.

The dye-shop door flew open and Rufus called, "My lady!" Then, to Merza, "Run, girl. Find the lady. The quake cracked the new vat. Indigo is seeping into the fire pit. Tell her I must have some help."

From the balcony Timothy called, "I'll get her, Rufus."

Then Timothy, Niko, and the two women rushed through the peristyle and out into the dye shed. Merza trailed after them. While the women and Niko hovered about the great stone vat Timothy moved about, lighting torches from his lamp till the place was bright.

It was a long, low room, walled with field stone, partially roofed with rushes but with much of the length open to the sky. The vats in their fire pits stood under the unroofed section. There were three vats, two large ones set over fire pits and a third, for rinsing, which stood between the two.

Rufus was dipping dye into a large earthen vessel. Erethrea was examining an empty one. Meanwhile, Niko squatted by the oozing crack, catching the indigo drip in a small vessel.

Lydia said cheerfully, "The vat can be repaired with plaster. It was not a severe quake in this section of the town."

Erethrea said, "God grant that our friends are safe in the prison."

Merza wanted to say, "They are all right. I heard them singing." It would have been pleasant to tell what she knew, to remind them she was not like the common run of slaves. They had forgotten she was alive. Merza had always been in the center of every crowd, with everyone looking at her, gasping with admiration and excitement over every word she uttered. She crammed the last crust of bread into her mouth, chewing vigorously.

Erethrea said, "Not even prisons are safe from quakes. That mountain it backs into was cleft in half by a quake long ago. One side of it slid into the river Gangites. This formed the marsh south of the city where hunters go for birds. I gathered eggs there once."

Lydia looked up at the moon. "The night is almost gone. We won't go back to our beds—there is much to be done if, as Rufus told us, Paul and Silas with all the ecclesia will be with us at sunset today. Dear Rufus, it gave me such joy to hear you say that. Timothy, run over to Cheesemaker Street and learn how Syntyche fares. Erethrea, go make breakfast. Oh, Timothy, just a moment. Tell Syntyche we will be going to the jail at dawn. Not you. You must work today. You have missed too much time this summer and Clement is behind on his orders. Stay off the streets the Romans use, till this trouble has all blown over."

Suddenly everyone was busy, leaving Merza still standing, without an assignment, beside the cracked vat, now empty of cloth and dye. Rufus was stirring the blue yarns in the vat, lifting to examine them, then poking them back deep into the rinse, which by now was as blue as the dye that had been rescued from the cracked vat.

Rufus gave her a friendly nod. "You are looking much better, little lady."

The words burst from her. "What is to become of me?"

"You are in good hands. You have been set free of your demon. Have you no concern for what is to happen to those who did this mighty work for you?"

The words were spoken so gently that Merza gave the

honest answer they merited. "I have heard nothing but the troubles of all who came near me—since childhood, people have brought me their troubles—and most of the time I knew that either their troubles would destroy them and nothing could be done, or else their troubles would resolve themselves. Do you think I have spent my life fretting about the people who thronged the gates and agoras and squares? Moreover, during the earthquake I heard Silas singing, and the little preacher sang with him. They are all right. They will be all right. The little preacher will continue to live as he now lives, and some will listen and love him as your group here does, and some will seek to do him harm. He has many years of preaching in many places ahead of him. As for Silas, I think he will outlive the little preacher. But what is to become of me I do not know."

Rufus was dipping out rinse water, and Merza got a dipper and moved to help him. When he continued to work silently, she wrinkled her nose. "Something rank and stinking is in this shed."

"Goat dung. We use it to set the color. Some dyers use other acids, but this is available and costs only a little labor. Syntyche keeps goats for her cheese making and she is glad to exchange their dung for an occasional gift of cloth."

Merza said, "I could do well in the agora, selling cloth for the lady."

"The cloth the lady sells is not sold in the agora. It is sold only to people of wealth, and they come here to the house to buy, or she takes it to their houses to show. Moreover, it would be unwise for you to appear in the streets for a while. Your owners think you are dead. Let them continue to think so, until they leave Philippi. I believe Lydia will keep you inside this house for a time. Even so, if one of the people who come here—and many people come here, Merza—recognizes you, and the news spreads that you did not die in the street as your owners suppose, it would not go well for you or the lady. You are in danger to yourself and to whoever shelters you. There are laws concerning slaves."

"I know about the laws concerning slaves."

At that moment Niko came running to the shed to call them to breakfast. It was a hasty meal, but Erethrea had laid on the table the bread baked the night before, and so at last Merza was able to eat her fill of it. She saw Lydia glance at the dye stains on her arms and tunic. "How is the indigo turning out?" she asked Rufus.

"It is too soon to tell," Rufus replied, and rose to return to the shed.

Lydia said, "Timothy, when you have eaten, hurry on over to tell Clement we are ready to go."

Merza took one more loaf, and followed Rufus to the dye shed. "You are not going with the lady to the jail?"

"Clement will go with her. Someone must mind the vats. That is my responsibility."

"What is responsibility to a slave?"

Rufus was building a fire under the vat which held the salvaged indigo. Heat rose about him, and now the sun was beating down into the unroofed area. Sweat ran down the slave's face and body, dripped from the bushy, red brows, the curling red beard. "Slave or free, missy, a man is the child of God, a soul the Lord Jesus died to save. A man has responsibility, and I am such a man. Brother Paul says the secret is to learn to be content in whatever condition you find yourself. As well try to stop the ocean tides from rolling in as to fret about the condition to which God has assigned you."

Merza cried sharply, "Then why did God or the little preacher interfere with the condition I was in?"

"You forced Paul to do it. Your shrill cries distracted his hearers. That is one thing he could not tolerate."

"A lot of good it has done me! I still have visions. I had one during the earthquake. I heard Silas singing—I told you about it. Paul joined in at the end. And before that, when Niko was singing, I saw her singing in a palace. She will do that when she is a woman."

Rufus stopped stirring and stood very still. "I am sorry to hear that. Niko is happy with the life she leads. Still, she is a slave, as I am. The lady talks about setting us free, and I know she intends to do so. But I suppose she considers herself immortal.

"Now, Merza, back to you. I believe you are a natural clairvoyant, and have been all your life. The demon had no part in your visions. But keep all that to yourself, at least until your masters are far from here, lest they learn that Paul did not impair your value in casting out your demon. Someone may have informed them that Timothy carried you here. You are not yet safe from them, but you are at least safe so far as the lady is concerned. At the moment all her thoughts are of Paul and Silas, but be at peace. Nobody in this house will abuse you."

"I have never met anybody who would not abuse a slave."

Rufus twinkled. Under the red brows his eyes were as blue as the waters she had crossed to reach Greece. "I take my orders from the vats, not from the lady. While the scarlet boils, I am bound to stir. When the yarn is dyed I am bound to rinse. And when it rinses clear I must hang it in the shade to dry. And so must you if you are to work with me, Merza."

He swiped a muscular arm across his dripping face. "My wife had a demon."

Merza moved to the rinse vat and began dipping out the blue water. She felt a sort of kinship with Rufus. "Did your wife tell fortunes?"

Rufus dropped stones into the water to press down

the yarn. "She had a demon, but she was not clair-voyant. I do not think there is much relation between the one thing and the other. I told you that."

Together they dipped out rinse water. Merza began pouring in clean. You had to rinse the yarn over and over, endlessly, till the rinse water was clear. Merza said, "Tell me about your wife."

"She served the lady. When my master married Lydia, he gave me the maid as wife. The master was older than the Lydian lady, and he had lived in this house all his life, but the lady never liked the house. It was too big, too pretentious, too hard to maintain. Yet the master believed it good for business, since the customers come here to buy the purple."

"And your wife?"

"She was a good servant to the lady, a good wife to me, except for the demon. I do not speak lightly of her anguish. On a winter day, when rains were pouring into the garden and into the pool, the demon laid hold of her. She fell from the balcony there at the head of the stairway and died of the fall. She was a gentle creature when the demon let her rest. But she had no strength against the demon."

Talking with this red-bearded, red-haired slave was as reassuring as anything that had ever happened to Merza. She said, "I hated the life of the roads. I was always famished, no matter how many coins went into the leather purse Zenon carried. I was abused and beaten—not by Zenon, but Bias. I—I gave birth to a baby, in Ephesus. A woman called Julia took care of me, and I gave her the baby. She had a house like this one, but finer. She gave Zenon a gold coin and gave me clothing for the winter." Suddenly, with a cry, "Rufus, what is a demon?"

The slave took up a stained towel and wiped his steaming face. "I know only what my wife believed.

The lady Lydia was for a time a follower of the philosophy of Pythagoras. This was a philosopher who lived long ago, during the golden age of Greece. He taught that the souls of those who die enter into the newborn, to endure the discipline of another life, and another, until at last a life is so perfectly lived that the soul is finally released from the prison of flesh and taken up into paradise. My wife used to say that a demon is a soul whose life was so evil it is forbidden to enter the body of an infant newborn, but is sent to wander through the world, seeking its own place. I always thought the demon had so informed my wife, and I believed her."

"Zenon once told me something my grandmother said, about an evil woman, a neighbor, who died. It was believed she became my demon and entered into me, for my seizures began soon after she died. Yet my demon was not wholly evil. It helped me defend myself when Bias abused me. It gave me fortunes to tell. It tormented me sometimes, but it was not wholly evil."

"Perhaps it has become fit to enter into a child and live a better life. Perhaps at last it will find rest."

Merza said softly, "I hope so. Poor demon, it tried so hard not to leave me."

Rufus said, "Say what you like about the life on the roads. You had value. You used a unique talent to the profit of your owners. You had security. You are now in the hands of kind people but you have no value for them. You will not be secure until you have value. I have value with the lady. She relies upon me and upon Clement. Without us her business would flounder. She trusts us as she trusts her own hands. We are secure."

Merza exclaimed, "What kind of security is it which would lead that man to take away my identity and leave me to be given the burial of an ass?"

"Bias assumed that you had lost your value. He did not want to forfeit even one coin you had earned because he knew not where the next coins would come from. Christians would not have done what he did. Still, you will have no security even among Christians until you find some way to make yourself indispensable."

The intimate mood of the dye shed was interrupted by voices from the atrium. Paul and Silas had arrived, and Paul was saying, "The Christians must assemble at sunset. We must bid them farewell. We have promised the magistrates to depart before tomorrow's dawn."

15

TIMOTHY PAUSED in his weaving to twist the broken threads together. What could be keeping Clement away so long? Were Paul and Silas alive or dead? Or perhaps suffering such crippling tortures as did not bear thinking of? Horrid pictures came to mind, of crushed members, immobile in the stocks!

How well he knew Paul's pride. Paul could have saved himself and Silas all unusual and cruel punishment by showing his proof of citizenship when they arrested him. But Paul's way was to wait, let them do their worst (even chancing death, since he trusted that God would preserve him alive until his ministry was finished) in order afterward to say, "Look what you have done to me, and I a citizen by birth!"

"Perhaps they will learn to think twice before they abuse someone else," had been his explanation, after the stoning in Lystra, for this quixotic behavior.

If only Luke would come, thought Timothy with longing. And with that came the accompanying anxiety as to the extent to which the earth tremor lightly felt in this section last night had affected the Mount Pangaeus region, where Luke was, and the prison cave, where Paul and Silas were being held. These random quakes could be light, or severe, or totally nonexistent in adjoining areas. You could not even hazard a guess about such things.

There, he had broken another thread. He breathed the prayer, "They are in Your care, O God. They are Your servants." So praying, he felt quieter.

But only for a time. His thoughts veered to Merza.

On that day almost four years ago when he had first encountered Merza, the day when the dream was born, Someday I will become an evangel, and travel with Paul among the world's cities, he had vowed to Paul, "I will go with you. You have never married and I will never marry." Quite a promise from a boy fourteen years old!

Paul had replied, "The celibate life is not for every man. We Jews make much of marriage and family life. Wait before you decide that the life Barnabas and I have chosen is the life for you. I pay a great price for the gift I have given to the Lord Jesus. Perhaps no man ever enjoyed the company of women more than I do."

I don't want to marry Merza! all the prudent impulses within him were quick to protest. But his sexual nature clamored, I want her! I want her! Oh, he thought in profound self-disgust, I am no better than Bias. Yet that was untrue. I would never hurt her or abuse her. At least— God grant I never do. I do not understand her. She looks upon me as a bumbling fool, which I am not. I can only hope Lydia will know what to do with her.

He went round the cycle of troubling reflections, and back to the loved companions and their pain and danger. Clement was at the prison. He was staying longer than Timothy had expected. Come, Clement! Come soon!

The monotony of work at the loom lulled his mind to quietness. Shedding, shuttling, beating up the reed with the batten bar to firm the weft. Shedding, shuttling, the push to the batten and retraction, while slowly on the far side of the loom the beam settled lower, till it was time to reach round and wind it upward on the finished cloth. Today would see the completion of this coat. Already he was binding off at the underarms.

To fashion something of value, whether cloak to comfort the body or a script to inform and liberate the mind —this is my life work. If I never become a competent preacher—as Luke and Silas have—for I cannot aspire to preach with the power and persuasive insight of Paul —still, it is glory, a glorious way of life. O God, I implore, let them survive to return to us and to the mighty mission!

Clement returned at last, the wire-thin, hollow-chested, emotional weaver employed by Lydia to turn into cloth lengths the yarns Rufus dyed. Clement loved to tell a story and would never spoil one, not even today, anxious as Timothy was for reassurance, by telling the end before the beginning. Still, the brightness of his eyes, the contentment of his whole bearing, betrayed his great satisfaction with the day's developments. As soon as his wife had settled herself in the loom room, two children at her skirts and a third at her breast, Clement opened his narrative.

"At the hour when the earthquake struck the prison, Paul and Silas were in the inner room, where instruments of torture are used. You can imagine the pain of the posture, bodies aching from the rods, yet forced to maintain immobility in the stocks through the long, cold hours in the clammy damp of the cave. Yet during all those hours Paul exhorted his fellow prisoners, who were in cells encircling the central chamber, locked within them by bolted, slatted doors. Paul answered questions, expounded the Way, comforted the disheartened. Silas also did his part, for he sang the Christian songs, reinforcing both their own courage and the rising courage of those unfortunate and unhappy creatures. Exhausted, pain-wracked, they preached, they expounded, they counseled, they answered many questions shouted out from various cells. And they sang."

He is a vivid narrator, thought Timothy, even while his being yearned to leap ahead to the climax and the conclusion of the tale.

"Now when the earthquake shook the mountain with its noisome cavern, an amazing circumstance resulted. No harm befell any prisoner, yet every cell door was shaken loose from its bolts or its hinges. The stocks were also shaken loose, as were the chains which bound Paul and Silas at their arms, and they were free! Can you imagine! All the prisoners with whom they had been speaking throughout the night—and what a ragged, unwashed, hopeless crew they were—came stumbling into the great chamber, shambling unshackled across the stones to gather about Paul and Silas. Instead of seeking freedom in the street outside, they gathered about Paul and Silas! Is this not an amazing circumstance?" Clement relaxed against the wall, beaming upon his wife, his gaping children, and Timothy. "Think of it—no prisoner harmed, yet all unshackled, loosed, free!"

Clement's wife had finished nursing the baby, who had fallen asleep. She covered herself and went to lay it on its bed. And Clement continued to contemplate the wonder of his narrative, while Timothy, in nervous impatience, broke yet another thread. "Oh, Clement, do continue!"

The wife returned, needle in hand, and set to work on the seams of a finished coat from Clement's loom. "Continue, husband." Her eyes were bright with pride in her husband's dramatic powers. Timothy had twisted his thread ends together and again slammed home the batten bar.

"Picture them—perhaps a score of unkempt, unwashed, uncombed prisoners, moving freely about the great room for the first time in months—perhaps years. How good it seemed to them to stride about, to stretch their limbs, yes, even to embrace the wounded but courageous preachers who had made the long night unforgettable for them, releasing them from the torpor of confinement.

"Then a draft from the great door at the prison entrance blew out the lamp, and all discovered that they were actually free to escape into the streets, to get away perhaps to freedom in another city! But Paul stood between them and freedom, crying, 'Prisoners, be obedient to the sentence of the court and the laws of Rome. For when you have served your term it will be known that you are virtuous men, that on a night when you had a choice between obedience and escape, you chose obedience, and subjected yourself to the law. God will bless you and your rulers will hold you in respect.'

"Now this is hard to credit, yet true," Clement continued. "Not one prisoner left the jail. All, all remained with Paul and Silas. Then the jailer, a Roman whose name is Tullos, who also had been wakened by the earthquake, came and saw that the door stood wide open. Those within could see him in the bright moonlight, but the cave was in pitch-darkness, and he could see nothing beyond that open door. Assuming that his prisoners were by now scattered and gone, he drew his sword to kill himself.

"Then Paul shouted, 'Do yourself no harm, Tullos. We are here, all of us!' And Tullos called for lamps, and rushed in and threw himself down before Paul and Silas, crying, 'Masters, what must I do to be redeemed?'

"Then Paul said, 'Put your trust in the Lord Jesus, and you will be redeemed, with all your household.' At that late hour the jailer sent for ointment and for water, and himself washed their wounds and anointed them. Afterward Tullos and all his family were baptized. Then he brought Paul and Silas into his house, and seeing it was the third watch and dawn not far off, he set food before them, and they broke bread together and ate heartily."

Apparently Clement had concluded his narrative. He turned to his loom, removed his shoes, set his feet on the treadles, and took up the shuttle which waited, having been filled with yarn for him by his wife before his return. Timothy heard the familiar sounds begin. Shedding, shuttling, up with the batten bar, then retracting it. The sounds of the two looms reinforced one another, companionable, familiar. And he cried in frustration, for the tale was unfinished, "But where are they? Are they now free? Must they return to prison, having been bathed and fed and anointed and all that?"

Clement chuckled as his hands and feet continued their swift rhythms. "Oh, you see, Tullos had sent a messenger to the magistrates, explaining that these were virtuous men and, further, Roman citizens and deserved to be freed. And now listen to what followed. The magistrates sent word back by the messenger of Tullos, directing that Paul and Silas were to be released. Think of it. After such treatment, they were to be set out secretly in the anonymous darkness of the nighttime streets, to go wherever they would go. And Tullos broke the good news to them, saying, 'Go now, for you have only to leave Philippi and begone, lest questions arise which would embarrass our magistrates. Blessings upon you and upon your journey.'

" 'But,' said Paul—you know his pride, his stern sense of justice—'they gave us a public flogging though we are citizens and had not been found guilty of any crime; they threw us into prison, where we spent most of the night in the stocks. Do they think they are now to smuggle us out privately? No, indeed,' said Paul. 'Let them come in person to escort us out in the light of day.' Then the messenger returned to the magistrates to report Paul's words, and Paul and Silas returned to prison to speak fur-

ther with the prisoners, who by now had all been returned to their cells and must indeed have been in need
of consolation. Since they were to wait there for the
magistrates to come, I returned here, for I am in haste
to finish this garment, for it is to be given to Luke, who
has become quite threadbare during his months in Philippi.
We cannot send our beloved preachers on their way in
the filthy and bloodied coats they wore yesterday and are
still wearing."

"Why," exclaimed Clara, his wife, "then they are still
in prison. Who knows how long they will remain, or
whether they will ever be freed? I shall take this lad,"
indicating her eldest, a child perhaps half a score years
of age, "and go myself to the prison and wait there until
I see how this affair is concluded. You, Clement, and
Brother Paul are two of a kind, impractical dreamers! He
should have accepted freedom when it was offered! What
makes you think the magistrates will humiliate themselves
at his command?" And she was gone, holding the lad by
the hand.

She was scarcely out of the house when she bustled
back. She had seen Paul and Silas in their bloodied coats
entering the portal of Lydia's house.

At that Timothy rose, unable longer to contain his
impatience to learn how these two had survived, and
what they, and Timothy himself, would do next, whether
leave Philippi or remain—and what was to be done about
Merza. As he crossed to Lydia's portal he remembered
that Rufus had spoken in tongues last night, and Niko
had interpreted, saying that all the company would again
gather at Lydia's house at tomorrow's—that is, today's
—sunset. They will all come to bid us farewell, and we
will leave Philippi. And his heart was heavy, for this was
the first ecclesia in whose founding he had played a part,
and now he must say farewell to these beloved friends.
This was the meaning of their ministry, to be repeated in

city after city, but he was filled with sadness for it meant he would be seeing no more Rufus, and Lydia, and little Niko—and the many other beloved friends of the Philippi ecclesia. And what was now to be done with Merza?

He entered and found Silas in the atrium, and was told that messengers had gone to call the friends to come at sunset to bid farewell to Paul and Silas and Timothy.

16

"What is to become of Merza?" asked Timothy.

Paul had already ascended to the room allotted them off the balcony, and Silas sat as if too exhausted to move, his eyes rimmed from the pain-filled, sleepless night, his body bent with weakness and suffering. Paul had looked no less pain-and-exhaustion-wracked as he made his way up the stone stairway, shuddering with fatigue and the finally attained shelter from the challenge to courage imposed by the presence of his Roman converts at the prison. Now Timothy stood beside Silas, wishing he need not thrust this complication upon the exhausted companion of his travels.

Silas said, "Who is Merza?" Then he opened his eyes with notable effort. "Ah yes, the sybil. Plans will be made. The magistrates have ordered those two men, her owners, out of town. They are already on the road, I believe. We made it clear we did not want to leave Philippi in their company, nor encounter them. The magistrates agreed to get them well away today. Timothy, my boy, I must get a little rest before sunset. It was a long night, and a triumphant one, but if we are to speak to our friends at sunset—and be on the road to Thessalonica tomorrow— ah, it is painful to think of bidding all these dear friends farewell. Paul feels the pain of parting, and I know you also feel it." He arose and walked, more or less steadily, toward the stairway. "There is a special pain in parting from one's first ecclesia. Paul is an old hand at this, but for you and me, lad, it is our first time. This is the price we pay for the happiness we have had with these dear friends in Philippi."

Timothy said, "I must finish off the coat in my loom. When it is done I must talk to Lydia about Merza."

Silas did not reply. He was on his way up the steps, keeping close to the wall.

Timothy found Clement singing at the loom. Clara sat nearby, needle in hand, singing along with him. Timothy picked up the spindle Clara had refilled for him and left ready, the new threads already joined to the last hank of yarn. Presently Timothy joined in the song. "Praise be to God for all His wonderful works to the children of men!"

The third watch was well along when he finished the garment and took it from the loom for Clara to put the finishing touches with needle and thread. And Clement went to an inner room and returned with a purse of money. "Here are your wages for nine months of work." He smiled genially. "Lydia made up the purse, but Clara and I have also added our small contribution to your mission, and to the work of Paul and Silas."

From the curtained doorway of the dye shed, unnoticed, listening, Merza heard Timothy talking with Lydia. "She must be kept out of sight for a few weeks. Those men she traveled with have left town today. We cannot take her with us on the road, for we might very well encounter them in Thessalonica or elsewhere. If Bias gets his hands on her he will take her and sell her for a woman of the taverns." A spasm crossed his face.

"We are asking too much of you, Lydia, to leave you with this problem, but surely if you give them time to get well away, you can find a way to legalize Merza's position later on, or else I will return when she is safe and take her to my grandmother."

Merza could not see the lady's face, but Lydia said, "She had value in her former vocation. What her worth will be in an establishment like this I don't know. Rufus has found her helpful. He says she seems apt, quick to learn. Perhaps she will prove useful. Rufus is a patient teacher."

Merza faded back into the dye shed. "Nobody wants me," she said ruefully. "The preachers want to leave me here. The lady wants me to go."

"You must prove your worth," Rufus said cheerfully. "You have the makings of a good hand with the dye vats. You are capable of learning the hard part, which is color control. It is excellent news that Bias and Zenon have already left the city. You should feel very cheerful about that. You dare not show yourself on the roads for the present. So let us make a dyer of you. Weaving and dying are industries you will find in every city. You will have value when you have mastered a trade."

Timothy climbed to the room. Silas and Paul were arranging their belongings ready to roll inside their beds when morning came. Timothy had already arranged his own belongings for transport.

Silas said, "Paul, I think we might not have been rushed out of town so fast, had you been less proud."

"Proud? I, proud?"

"To demand a public acquittal from the magistrates. If you had just told them in the first place that we are Romans—or permitted me to do so. . . . These Philippians are not ready to be left, especially the jailer Tullos. Think of asking our loving and intimate little company who have been meeting together in this house to bring into their company after we depart a jailer and his family —all Romans—five prison guards and three converted prisoners, convicted of stealing gold from the mine. I shudder to think—"

"Do not shudder, Silas. We leave Luke with them. And we leave them in God's keeping. This ecclesia is fortunate. I have never before left a new ecclesia with such a man as Luke to be their pastor."

Silas said, "I confess that I am homesick for Bethany. Martyrdom I can endure if I must. But not a martyrdom that could so easily have been avoided. I will not silently submit again to being beaten, Paul. I will speak out. I will make it clear that as a citizen of Rome—"

"Brother Silas," said Paul, "not every man can bow his neck to the yoke of being my companion in travel."

"It is a form of enslavement," said Silas with a smile. "It is also a labor of love. But can you not occasionally trust my judgment, especially when my back as well as your own is to be beaten?"

"We are slaves of the Lord Jesus," said Paul.

"But I have two masters. You have only one."

Paul said, "I wish you had spoken sooner. I know my temper. I rush headlong, making decisions when it might be better to consult. I quarreled with the beloved James the day before he was arrested and beheaded. There are those among the Bethany Christians who will never forgive me for that. I do not want to quarrel with you or offend you, Silas. Next time—speak up, or at least nudge me."

Silas smiled. "I will. Providing the praetors are not pinning my arms. I would not want our enemies to see us at odds."

Paul said, "You were splendid in the prison, Silas.

You never sang more effectively. I was proud to be your companion."

"And I to be yours," said Silas.

Paul was alone in the room when, near sunset, Merza entered. His head rested on his hands. She busied herself spreading the three beds for the night, that the preachers and Timothy would find them ready when they came here after the ecclesia had departed. When Paul did not notice her she coughed softly. "Sir, what is to become of me?"

The face he raised from his hands was very sad. "Who are you?"

She smiled, pleased that he did not recognize her as the bedraggled girl of yesterday. "You laid hands on me and cast out the demon. I am the sybil."

"Lydia has done a good deal for you, my child. You will be in good hands in this house."

Merza flung herself to the floor, her hands clasped in supplication. "Take me with you. Take me where you go." Then, seeing denial and horror gather in the large, expressive eyes, "I can still tell fortunes, sir. I will be useful. I will earn money. Crowds gather to hear the fortunes, and then you can preach to them."

Paul took her hands in his. The large eyes were luminous with kindness. "My child, be at peace. Lydia will attend to all your needs. You in turn will receive her guidance willingly. The physician Luke will teach you. Open your heart. Repent your sins and be forgiven—"

Merza sat back on her heels, looking at him in confusion. "Repent? Of what should I repent? I am a slave. I do only what I am ordered to do. You can hardly call that sin in a slave."

Paul moved toward the door. "My child, you have much to learn, and I am needed in the atrium. The ecclesia is gathering. You are to stay here. Luke will teach you. Lydia will teach you. Niko—Rufus—they will befriend and guide you." Then, from the doorway, "Merza, the one place you must not go now is with us. Zenon and Bias have gone to Thessalonica, and that is where we are going. We start tomorrow morning, as you know. We will remain in Thessalonica and preach there until the Spirit leads us elsewhere. And that is the one place where you must not be found. Remain here. Let Rufus teach you the trade of a dyer. You could find no better teacher anywhere, and you must learn a trade, my child, having lost the only vocation you have ever practiced."

Desperately Merza cried, "I have seen visions of you. You will suffer again and again at the hands of Romans. You will be imprisoned in other cities. You will be scourged with whips, not just with rods. You will never again be stoned, but you will suffer shipwreck and dangers of every sort. I can stay with you, and warn you when these things are near, and you can avoid them."

"Peace, Merza. Be at peace. I understand that you are clairvoyant. But I do not require a soothsayer in my entourage. Nor is the life of an itinerant safe for you. Remain in Philippi. Learn the trade Rufus can teach you."

"I saw your death. In the end you will die of—"

"Merza, peace! In the end I will die. You will die. All mortal men will die, and only those redeemed by our Lord Jesus will go to dwell with him forevermore. Farewell, my child. Be obedient to your mistress."

He moved down the balcony. She heard him descending, sandaled feet on stone steps, into the atrium, heard the affectionate greetings come up to him.

He cast out my demon. I shall never meet another man with such powers. With such thoughts, ideals, beliefs, messages. They all love him. I love him. I do? Is that what they mean by love? I would die to win his acceptance, his approval. He did not want to touch me in the gate, yesterday. Was it only yesterday? He did not want to, but he did it, and the demon is gone, and nobody wants me, and I want only him, his approval, a chance to help him, to work for him at any risk. He did not rebuke me. He walked away, saying, "Obey your mistress." Oh, little preacher, I will try. I will truly try.

It was a large company which gathered in the atrium that sunset. They rejoiced that Paul and Silas had triumphed so dramatically over enemies in high places. They grieved that Paul and Silas and Timothy would be with them no more. But Timothy spoke to them of how the ecclesia in Lystra learned to love and serve one another, obeying the injunction of the Lord Jesus, "Bear ye one another's burdens." Then Silas spoke of them about the ecclesia in Bethany, on the Mount of Olives just across the Kidron Valley from Jerusalem, and of how they waited and waited for the return of the Lord Jesus, until at last persecutions drove them forth to preach and establish ecclesiae in other cities.

Then Paul spoke to them of the night when the Lord Jesus last broke bread with his disciples, saying, "This do in remembrance of me." And when all had partaken of the Lord's Supper together and had exchanged the kiss of peace with one another, Paul spoke to them once more.

"I leave my heart with you. You are my beloved friends, my joy, my crown. Now we press on, hoping to take hold on that for which Christ took hold of us. Forgetting what is behind, let us reach for what is ahead, toward the goal which is life in Christ Jesus. Let those who are mature in the faith guide those newly embarking in it. If you differ, take heed that you love one another in spite of differences, waiting the moment when God makes all plain. Stand firm in the Lord Jesus and in his love for you. Strengthen one another in the faith, for thereby you strengthen yourselves and the church in Philippi, ensuring that it shall continue until I visit you again. For I will come again, whether soon or late, at the time our Lord Jesus shall appoint."

Merza, in the shadows of the balcony, thought, He truly loves these people, all of them, even silly ones like Erethrea. And they all love him, even when he is sharp with them.

Merza saw that many of the people wept. Why should I weep? I am safe here with people who are too soft, too bemused with these strange ideas to do me harm. I have bread in plenty, a clean bed in a fine house, and beautiful clothes to wear.

She rubbed her cheek with the back of her hand, and wished that she knew how to weep.

BOOK III
Corinth

17

THE MARK of the best tent cloth is a weave so tight one rarely sees the warp strings. Paul slammed home the batten bar, snugging the weft strongly. With bare feet on the treadles he shifted the pattern of strings, opening a path for the great shuttle, heavy now and clumsy with the yarn wound around it, and again slammed home the batten bar.

Tentmaking gives wings to the mind. While arms and back exert their strength and hands and feet employ the timeless skills to transform the hair of the black Cicilian goats into durable, rainproof panels, the mind is free for reverie, for reaching out to God. Free to weigh the past and plot a future course, free to repent errors and follies, free to seek guidance, free to rejoice. Free, if one must, to weep a little.

Paul examined the pattern, took up the hand comb, and laboriously and meticulously tightened the weave where the batten bar had failed to snug it. His eyes rested with pleasure on the luster of the black cloth. These tents, he thought, are found in more lands than one man could traverse in a lifetime. If only they could cry out the Good News with an eloquence to match their durability. His feet shifted on the treadles. The cycle continued.

Slowly, slowly the panel lengthened, to be wound upon the lower beam while the upper beam released new lengths of warp. Such simple, age-old skills the work required, yet painstaking, for the man who is slack in the work of his hands will be slack in his responsibilities toward God and his fellow men.

And Paul's eyes rested on his agile, swift, and tireless hands, blackening again and coarsening—this was the badge of his trade—for these black tents left their mark upon the hands that made them.

Today, thought Paul, my pleasure is in the work but not in the reverie. The prayers I breathe seem to fall like drops of vapor to the ground. How they laugh at me, these strapping Roman soldiers in Corinth. How they squeak their voices and twist their faces when they pass by where I am preaching.

I have been driven from every Greek city where I preached save one. Jews drove me from Pisidian Antioch and Iconium. Jews and Greeks combined to stone me out of Lystra. In Philippi Romans "humbly requested" that I depart without a moment's delay, carrying with me the marks of the torture they had inflicted. In Thessalonica and in Beroea the Jews drove me out after only a few brief weeks, and the good Jason had to sign an oath promising I would not return. I departed, leaving Silas with them, lest those two ecclesiae perish stillborn from being left too soon without a shepherd. Luke I had left in Philippi. Timothy I sent back from Athens with letters to the three churches of Macedonia, and to bring me news of how they fared, all my newborn children in the spirit. And to bring Silas also if Silas sees fit to come. Ah, Silas, you should be conducting your own missions. You are ripe and ready in the faith. You participated in all the events of our Lord's ministry in Bethany. You sorrowed at the foot of the Cross, and you were present on the Mount of Olives when He was taken up into Heaven to be seen no more. You were in the upper room on the Day of Pentecost, the day when I, in my folly and my zeal, began to persecute the Christians. You, dear Silas, have not been called as I have to preach to the Gentiles. The congregations in Beroea and Thessalonica are Jews, either by birth or by conversion. Yet I have asked you to leave them and come to me. And there is a sweet reasonableness in your nature which assures me you will come. If you come, dear Silas, I believe that after the mission in Corinth is accomplished, the Spirit will permit us to return home and make our report to the churches who sent us out upon our mission.

In Athens—O Lord Jesus, you saw what a fool I made of myself in Athens. To be stoned, beaten, abused—these things I can endure, and have. But those Areopagites did none of these things. They did not even ridicule. They turned their backs. They conversed with one another about luncheon appointments and legal tangles. They walked away. Enmity I can endure. Ridicule I have borne. But to be treated as a bore!

I tried to appeal to them on their own intellectual level, to analyze, to show the beauty and the logic of the Good News, to clarify the mighty truths of the Messianic message. And they turned to one another, urbane and unimpressed, chatting of their own concerns. O Lord Jesus, I made such fool of myself! Teach me how to serve Thee in humility and wisdom. It is not for myself. It is for the Good News.

And after that came the sickness, the affliction You have seen fit to use to chasten my pride, to remind me that whatever blessings I enjoy, I am still only a man, while You are the Son of God. Forgive my complaints. Forgive, if you can, my pretensions to scholarship and wisdom.

Now I see why God drove me from Athens to Corinth, this most Roman of all Greek cities. Here I have found the crossroads between Italy and Asia, the city with two harbors, one facing east, the other west, the city of commerce, the city of travelers who will pick up the seed that falls here and carry it on and on, till indeed the Good News reaches the ends of the world. The feeling persists that here I shall preach as long as I care to stay, that from this city I will not be driven hence. Come soon, Timothy! Come, Silas! Bring me news of the churches from which I was wrenched all unready and unwilling!

In Athens I failed because I offered the cold fare of intellectual analysis. But faith is born in emotion. There is no other way. And I am a man whose fortune it is either to charm or to irritate. Men must love me or despise me. The Good News I bring is not conveyed through intellectual processes, however much I delight in them.

His hands dropped from the loom. He laid the empty shuttle on the low seat. He rose and flexed his shoulders. This is a decent house in a decent section of Corinth. When I can no longer sleep on the roof because of winter rains I must find a place elsewhere, for there is no second bedroom here. But God's hand has surely guided me from the moment I crossed the isthmus and set my feet on the streets of Corinth.

By what strange chance did it come to pass that the only Christians in Corinth are also tentmakers? I arrived here at the end of summer, feeble in body from fever, feeble in courage from my utter failure in the splendid and beautiful and intellectual Athens. Yet God had not abandoned me, for I carried a letter to Stephanas from the one Areopagite who had befriended me in Athens, to Stephanas the merchant with colleagues in half a score of cities. And Stephanas with his household became the first fruits of my ministry in Achaea. He gave me employment and sent me here to Prisca and Aquila.

Paul rose and went to the cottage to wind more of

the black yarn upon the shuttle. The house was a sturdy one, made of hewn stone with a court and a cistern in the fashion of Jewish houses, west of the city where the abrupt Acrocorinthus cast long shadows as the day waned. The ruins atop the citadel brought thoughts of peoples long ago who dwelt on its summit, drank from its springs, watched for the approach of enemies from either the Gulf of Corinth, which faced the west, or the Gulf of Aegina, which faced toward Athens and the east. Nowadays ships which entered one harbor were hauled overland on a made road and launched into the other, having thus escaped both the storms and the pirates which infested the Great Sea south of the Peloponnesus.

What happiness, thought Paul, it has been to learn to know these two Christians, and to hear them tell of the ecclesia in Rome. Not one apostle has ever preached to them! Ah, Paul, Paul, never doubt that God can raise up witnesses to replace you if some day an angry Jew or an angry Roman casts a stone or a spear that flies too hard and too straight, and you die of it.

Paul wound another load of the black yarn upon the shuttle. He dipped a cup of water from the cistern and drank and returned to the loom. Now at the end of summer the cistern was low, and left a taste of sediment. Paul's back still hurt at times from the beating in Philippi. I wonder if Silas also suffers still from those wounds, he thought. Oh, my dear friends, come soon, come soon. I long to see your faces. I long for the news you will bring.

Ah, Timothy, how I must depend upon you in times to come. On every mission one man must have authority. Such men as Barnabas and Silas sweat under my authority. Henceforth my journeys must be made with younger men, preferably converts of my preaching, who will not find it irksome when I make decisions. Do not fail me, Timothy.

The lusts of the flesh! O God, deliver that boy, for he is sick with love for the girl Merza. Whenever I lay healing hands upon someone, trouble follows, trouble for me, trouble for my mission. I was obliged to send Timothy back to Philippi if only to give him one more chance to drive his own demon out of his soul. Deliver him, O God, and return him to me eased of his anguish. If a time comes when he must marry, let him wait till he is older. Let him wait for such a wife as the little Niko will make. O God, bring back my son Timothy to me safe and heart-whole.

The spindle was heavy with yarn. The afternoon shadow of Acrocorinthus was moving toward the tree that sheltered the loom, toward the loom with its low bench and its bit of excavation for accommodating the weaver's feet. The street was dusty, but with winter rains it would become muddy, for the city fathers had not seen fit to pave the roads of the section where artisans lived—spinners, weavers, dyers, potters, millers, bakers, and the like. Back of the house was a spot of green where Prisca's goat grazed, and beyond this bit of pasturage, facing on the next street, was a house more commodious than this one, with at least four rooms on two levels and a roof reached by outside stairs. The two goats of Fortunatus, who owned the house, were nosing about on the platform at midpoint. Three of the children of Fortunatus were playing in the gravel beside the house while their mother sat on one of the lower steps spinning. Another neighbor was returning from the stream that flowed down from Acrocorinthus, carrying a bundle of washed clothes upon her head.

A voice from within him said, Paul, Paul, feed the heart-hungry. Do not torment yourself about Athens. Do not gaze after the retreating backs of those who walk away. Perhaps their time will come, in this life or another. Build solid foundations, Paul, and others will build the city. For if it is true, as the Essenes teach, that the souls of men return in another life, and yet another, they will thirst one day for the fountains of living water, and will drink at wells you have dug. From seed you sow, plants will spring up. On foundations you lay, others will build.

Find people who are athirst, Paul. You longed to dwell in Athens, with its splendid architecture, its philosophic wisdom. You found there a fitting habitation even for the Lord of Heaven, since beauty comes from God, by whatever name men call Him.

Paul slammed home the batten bar, shifted his feet upon the treadles. A cool breeze blew along the dusty street, touching his sweated face, stirring his beard. Long ago a Greek called Archimedes had said an astonishing thing. To dramatize the power of the lever principle, Archimedes had said, "I could move the world if I had somewhere to stand."

How I dramatize myself, especially my failures, thought Paul. The Athenian Areopagites did not scorn me. They merely walked away. And in my pride I reflected they would have done the same to Socrates. May God in mercy deliver me from the sin of intellectual pride. Socrates' message was an intellectual message, while I preach Jesus, the crucified Savior. *He* is my message, the power of God unto Salvation. Every man a sinner who can find forgiveness, peace, righteousness, and a new life through humble acceptance of our Lord's death as propitiation for evil done by ourselves in our own lives.

Again the terrible longing came, the longing that recurred many times every day which he spent at the loom, the longing to give all his strength, all his hours, to the ministry. Come, Timothy, he thought, for you can work for us both, and I can preach in this wealthy, sin-smitten city.

I have a place to stand, and I can move the world. This is what our Lord Jesus brought, and I am not alone.

Peter and James and Andrew and John and Silas and all the apostles, also believers we have never heard of—pilgrims like those who established the Church in Rome—all these are preaching and teaching. Mark and Barnabas are preaching, and Philip in Caesarea and others in Africa and Asia, preaching, telling the Good News, winning converts, establishing ecclesiae.

We have a place to stand. We will move the world, for we stand upon the love of God and the majesty of our Lord's death and resurrection. We preach the Good News, God's love for men; men's love for one another. We stand upon the injunction: Bear ye one another's burdens and so fulfill the law of Christ. There we stand, and we will move the world!

When our Lord departed into Heaven he left behind a few apostles, some seventy who believed His teachings. Now, after a score of years, we have founded hundreds of ecclesiae in Asia, in Greece, in Africa, even in Rome. We will all preach for years to come, and young men will come after us, of whom Timothy is one. Each of us lighting a flame here, a flame there, leaving to God to send the winds which will fan the flames we light, till they have swept through the world!

The panel was finished, and it was well made. Paul tied off the threads and unrolled it from the lower beam. He carried it into the house. Tomorrow he would deliver it to Stephanas and receive his pay, and wool for another panel, and so it would go until Timothy came to release him from the loom to the life of daily preaching and teaching in this wealthy and wicked city.

He dipped a cup of water from the pitcher beside the cistern. From the street he heard Prisca's high, clear voice calling, "Paul, Paul, they are on the road, your friends. Stephanas has had news of them from Athens. They went to Damaris to ask for you."

Paul stood in the doorway, looking anxiously up the

street whence Prisca and Aquila had come. "But why does the message get here before they do? They are overdue! They should have been here a week—two weeks—ago. I have counted out the time required—are they ill? Have they been wounded by robbers? They are long overdue!"

"Peace, Paul," said Aquila. "The girl who is with them required a night's rest in the house of Damaris. They will be here soon—tomorrow, or the day after."

18

THE PROMISE OF AUTUMN and grape harvest was in the air when Timothy knocked at the portal of the dyer from Thyatyra. He waited, eager, impatient, and when no sound of answering movement came from within, he remembered that he need not knock at this portal, and opened and entered. The atrium was empty of occupants. He caught a glimpse of himself in the great bronze mirror and shook out his skirts and reknotted his girdle, pulled off his headcloth and thrust it into his bosom, and beat out the dust from skirts and girdle ends. He started to call out, but heard an unfamiliar voice singing in the dye shed, and sped in that direction.

The garden was more bedraggled in late summer than at any other season, with seedpods cluttering the paths. He flung open the door into the dye shed. A sturdy figure in sleeveless tunic and long, leathern apron stood half averted, stirring the rinse pot and singing energetically. Her shoulders marked the rhythm of the hymn. Her short, chestnut curls were twined with white ribbons. The whole aspect was so expressive of energy and satisfaction that it took a moment to recognize the emaciated girl he had carried to this house in midsummer.

Who'd have thought that a few weeks could so alter her?

"Merza!" It was a cry of delight.

She turned, mouth open in midsong. She laid the stirring stick across the vat and threw her arms about him. The kiss of peace he had meant to give became something quite different.

He held her at arms' length. "I cannot believe what my eyes behold!"

He was kissing her again as Rufus entered, carrying a shovelful of goat dung. "Merza. The vat. You must keep stirring." Then, warmly, "Welcome, Timothy. What joy it is to see you after these months."

Rufus set down the shovel and came to embrace Timothy. Then, with a wry smile, "I haven't seen the kiss of peace given in just the style you bestowed upon Merza, Timothy. Did you come alone?"

"I came alone. I am delighted to see you, both of you. And I am astonished to see Merza. She is blooming. You have done wonders for her."

Recollecting his errands, Timothy continued, "I brought letters from Paul in Athens and from Silas in Thessalonica. Where is Lydia? Are all of this household well? And oh, there are so many, many questions, but then, there will be many days for those. I will remain with you over two Sabbaths. Where is Lydia?"

"With Clement. Merza, leave the vat. Run and tell them that Timothy has come."

"I will! The lady will be so pleased. Oh, Timothy, you are keeping some secret from me. Tell me!"

"You are right, Merza. You shall hear it all. Later."

Rufus watched the girl as she sped out the door. "Whatever concerns Merza concerns Lydia first of all," he said. "She accepted the responsibility, and she has not found it easy."

Timothy took the pole and began stirring, careful not

to stain his coat. "I am sorry she has not found it easy. I will keep Merza's news to myself until I have told it all to Lydia."

Why had Lydia found it difficult? he wanted to ask, but did not.

Rufus asked, "Have you seen her former owners in your travels, Timothy?"

"She had only one owner. Zenon. Bias was a hired bodyguard who got out of Zenon's control."

Rufus did not comment on his failure to answer the question. He was stirring dung into the indigo vat. "The girl was grossly abused by a man who desired her and took her. You also desire her, Timothy. Paul and Silas suffered fearfully for taking her out of the old life and giving her into the keeping of Christians. Do not trust your impulses, Timothy. They are likely to mislead you. Talk to the lady before you discuss these things with Merza."

Timothy said stiffly, "I have already given you my promise."

"Shall we wait in the atrium? Lydia is right next door and may be already at the portal."

Timothy led the way across the peristyle. "This ecclesia is the first which I helped to bring into being. Everyone in it is very dear to me, Rufus. Including yourself. Surely you know this is true."

"I know. Otherwise I would not have spoken to you as I did. It was presumptuous in a slave, but Merza and I have talked a great deal during the weeks she has worked with me at the vats. There is little about her life up to now that she has not revealed to me. Remember, Timothy, only a slave can know what a slave feels. With the best will in the world, you cannot understand what is in that girl's heart."

"What do you fear I might do to her?"

"I mistrust the hasty impulses of one who lusts for her,

even such a one as yourself. You lust for her. You do not understand her."

Timothy was silent. He had no defense and he had no answer. He was relieved when Lydia and Niko entered. He greeted them warmly and lovingly, as they greeted him, yet feeling self-conscious this time about the kiss of peace, till Lydia's warm embrace set him at ease.

"Are they well? Paul? Silas?" she cried. "Dear Timothy, this is such a happy surprise."

"Dear Timothy," cried Niko, throwing her arms about his waist. "Oh dear, you are much too tall." So Timothy bent to kiss the little girl and press his cheek against hers. When he looked up, Luke also was with them, his cool, scholarly face bright with pleasure.

"Paul sent a letter." Timothy drew the parchment from his coat.

The encounter with Merza and Rufus had left him preoccupied and confused. Lydia saw Merza lingering in the garden, watching them wistfully and curiously, and sent her back to her work. She sent Niko to prepare a bed for Timothy in the upstairs room Luke still occupied, and drew Timothy over to the bench beside the almond tree. "Now we will hear your news, Timothy."

"My news? You mean the letter?" He handed it to her.

She took it and glanced at it with a smile. "They never taught me to read. Business records I can keep, and understand—the Roman numbers are not difficult." She touched the letter as if loving its texture, then passed it to Luke.

Luke said, "We must call the ecclesia together, and you must read the letter to them, Timothy."

Lydia said, "It is too late to call them today. Tomorrow is the Sabbath, and the following day the Lord's Day, our regular time to meet. Are you willing to wait two days to meet with them, Timothy?"

Luke said, "We will be attempting our first meeting with the converts from the prison in attendance. I am delighted that you will be present, and it is surely fitting that you read Paul's letter to the congregation on that occasion."

"Your first with Tullos and the others attending?" Timothy asked in surprise.

"At first we did not meet together. Three of the prison converts were prisoners, convicted of stealing gold from the Panguitch Mine. Tullos and his family and the five prison guards who were converted met in the house of Tullos on the Lord's Day, to permit the converted convicts to attend. I met with them on alternate Sundays."

Lydia and Timothy were on the bench beside the almond tree and Luke had been pacing restlessly about. Now he sank to the pavement, knees akimbo, facing them. "The prisoners were charged with stealing gold. They maintained their innocence, even under torture. After their conversion on the night of the earthquake they continued to deny their guilt, and now at last Tullos became convinced of their innocence. He and I went to the mine superintendent on their behalf and learned that the thievery had continued after those three were sent to prison. We were able to persuade him at last to go with us to the magistrates, asking for the release of these men. But the machinery of justice moves very slowly, and only last week were the men officially freed. They have returned to their work at the mine, and this coming Lord's Day will mark the first ecclesia when all of this company who were converted by Paul and Silas on the night of the earthquake will become one with us here in the house of Lydia. It is a splendid occasion, Timothy. I am delighted you will be with us, and can report back to Paul and to Silas on how things are moving forward for us here in Philippi."

He glanced through Paul's letter. "May I keep it until

we meet? I want to make copies, that those who read may use them for family devotions. Shall I read it to you now, Lydia? It breathes of Paul's love and concern for his flock."

Lydia said, "Let it be fresh in all our ears when we hear it read to the ecclesia by Timothy."

Luke said, "I have errands back at the mine today. Do you want to go with me, Timothy?"

"Later. I will be here over two Sabbaths. We will find a time for me to visit the mine. Luke, it is Paul's wish that you spend a few weeks with the Christians in Thessalonica and Beroea this fall, and again in the spring. Possibly you can make the journey with me, ten days hence, and meet Jason and the others, and stay on for a while after Silas and I take the road to Athens."

Luke nodded. "If that is Paul's wish I will do my best. I have been making a record of Paul's journeys. You can bring me up to date, as we travel." He made his farewells and hurried away.

Timothy said, "How strange and marvelous are the ways of God. We were led to Luke at Troas as if God held Paul by the hand. We set out with the original intention of following the royal road straight across Asia to Ephesus. But we left the royal road. Paul had an injunction received in a dream not to pause to preach anywhere in Asia, and so we rushed directly to Troas, arriving just in time to encounter Luke at an inn to which we had been fortuitously directed. There Paul suffered a moderately light attack of fever, which drew Luke to offer us his services. And that night Paul dreamed the third dream of this journey, a dream which ordered us to go to Philippi. We had not enough money among us to buy passage, but Luke had money enough for us all. So we caught the last boat of autumn out of Troas and came here almost two years ago. Here we found you. Indeed, I had been sure we ought to go directly to

Ephesus, sure we would find Merza there. Yet it was here that we found her. So strange are God's ways with men."

Niko came running down the stairs from the balcony as Timothy concluded. Lydia said, "God's hand is upon Paul, guiding his steps. You know it and I know it, yet it seems to us marvelous. Niko, go to the kitchen. Erethrea needs your help. Tomorrow is the Sabbath, and the kitchen is a busy place, before the Sabbath."

Niko paused beside the bench long enough to touch her cheek lovingly against Timothy's, then ran off toward the kitchen passageway. When the child was gone, Lydia said, "Timothy, I must tell you," at the same moment when Timothy turned to her to say, "Lydia, there is a matter I—"

Each paused with a smile. Lydia said, "You first, Timothy. You are my guest."

Timothy's hand went to his scrip. From it he took a piece of parchment sealed in wax with a Roman seal. "Merza's deed of ownership. I got it from Zenon in Thessalonica." He looked at Lydia expectantly, but she was staring at him with a kind of horror. "It is for you, Lydia," he said. "It is in my name, but it is for you. You have done wonders with that girl. Rufus says you have not found it easy."

Lydia shrank from the deed as he extended it. "No, Timothy. I have been waiting to tell you that I—I cannot keep that girl. I have been desperate for weeks. I have discussed it with Luke, but found no solution. The moment I learned you had returned to Philippi, Timothy, I knew you must take her to Paul. She is yours, legally, and surely the hand of God is in it, for now you can take her anywhere in the empire, and no harm come of it to either of you. She is yours! God be praised."

"But, Lydia, this is incredible! You have worked a miracle with her."

"Only the outside is changed, Timothy. She is well fed and decently dressed. Timothy, she is a whited sepulchre. Within she is still full of evil impulses implanted during a lifetime of deception and abuse. All her life, Timothy, she has been rewarded and praised for saying whatever suits the need of the moment. The word *truth* has no meaning for her. She reads the hearts of us all, and uses what she finds to serve her own ends. She is a monster of evil."

Timothy protested, "But I saw her. She is working hard, and enjoys it. She is gay. She is handsome, happy —she was singing, alone in the shed, stirring the rinse pot and singing, when I arrived."

"Timothy, she is a mistress of deceit. No, I must say no more. She does not know good from evil. She is to be pitied. Luke tried to explain repentance to her, that she might become a Christian and be baptized. But she did not remotely grasp his meaning. You must take her to Paul. If he cannot reach her she is lost and there is no hope. At any rate, you bought her. She is yours."

Timothy put his hands over his face, shocked and desperate.

Lydia said, "Where did you get the money to buy her?" Then, when he did not reply, "Where did you find Zenon?"

"Lydia, surely there is some misunderstanding here. She worked so well and so happily at the dye pot."

"Rufus is patient. He knows how to win her cooperation. He is the only one she cannot deceive. She respects him. Timothy, she is absolutely brutal to Niko. And to Erethrea, poor, foolish soul. This is what I cannot countenance."

"I see that, Lydia. She is still a girl of the streets. The miracle of salvation has not yet come to her, even though the demon was cast out. Well then, Silas will talk to her as we travel, and I will do what I can to help. If Luke goes with us as far as Thessalonica and Silas is with us the rest of the way, perhaps the situation is not too perilous. Lydia, I am so enamored of that girl I could not trust myself to travel with her alone."

"You, Timothy? Oh indeed, I am bitterly sorry to hear it."

"From the first, when we were both children and she told my fortune in unforgettable words, from that day forward she has haunted my life."

Lydia laid her hands on his. "Now that I know you will take her away, I see her in better perspective. She is not herself a demon. She lived with a demon within her, and the devils who owned her and abused her and got their living from her affliction treated her shamefully. She is greatly to be pitied. God grant I may learn to feel only pity for her. God go with you, Timothy. You are very dear to me."

Timothy sighed. "I dread what Paul will say. Paul is unyielding in any matter which touches on his ministry." He sighed. "Merza is my responsibility now. I have made her so. What shall I say to her?"

"Tell her first of your encounter with Zenon. You will know how to proceed from there."

19

THEY WENT to the dye shed. Lydia said, "Rest a while, Merza. Timothy brings news which directly concerns you."

Merza dried her hands carefully on the towel at her girdle. She looked fixedly at Timothy, then moved slowly toward him. "You have seen Zenon." Then, "Zenon is dead." Tears washed her hazel eyes. "He tried hard. But Bias was too much for him. Was it Bias who killed him?"

Timothy had to keep his hands from touching her by the strongest physical and moral effort. Does she already know that Lydia is sending her away? Ah, no, she does not read her own future.

He said, "They had been at Thessalonica all these weeks. Bias got the purse Zenon carried, the day they left Philippi. Zenon, in his desperation, joined with a company of beggars. Twice Bias went among the beggars in the weeks that followed, robbing not only Zenon but others. They tried to set upon him in concert, to rid themselves of him, but he escaped, and preyed upon them when they sat alone in their appointed places. These things were going on while Paul remained in Thessalonica, and I with him. After a few weeks Paul was driven by the Jews of the synagogue faction to leave the city, and we went on to Beroea, where Paul preached. But the Jews of Thessalonica followed him, and he and I departed for Athens, leaving Silas to minister in the two ecclesiae of Beroea and Thessalonica. And all this while Zenon continued with the beggars, and Bias continued to prey upon them.

"But when Paul sent me back from Athens, to bring messages to the three churches of Macedonia, and to learn how they fared, I found Zenon. Silas had joined me at Beroea, and together we found Zenon, a pile of red and yellow rags huddled beside the city gate, and thrusting among the rags his gray beard. Even before I lifted him up I saw that he still lived, though he had been terribly beaten. His back—" Timothy paused, seeing the horror of both Merza and Lydia as his tale unfolded. No use presenting the shocking details. "We saw that he still breathed, and we, Silas and I, carried him to the house of Jason, who is our host whenever we are in Thessalonica. We bathed him and when we got a little broth into him he told us the things I have told you. Bias had been waiting that morning at dawn when he reached his begging place, and had beaten him once more and left him for dead."

Merza wept softly. "Zenon always feared him. Yet he feared still more to try to manage without him, especially when I was doing well and there was plenty of money in the purse."

Timothy said, "When Zenon first recognized me, he muttered, 'Where is she?' and then he said, 'Boy, you and those preacher fellows have been the death of me.' Then again he whispered, 'Where did you take her, that day? Bias has been after me all this while to tell him where you took her, and whether she lived.' So of course I realized that Bias had beaten him to make him tell where you were, Merza. And of course Zenon did not know any more about that than Bias."

"I think he must have," said Lydia. "He must have known where you were staying, Timothy. But if he had told that it was you who took her away, Bias could have returned and made trouble for us. We have Zenon to thank for sparing us that."

Timothy nodded. "It is true. Zenon had seen me pick you up and carry you away. He knew that you lived. He meant to outwait Bias in Thessalonica, and return here to find you and take you back on the road. You understand, he was not able to tell a connected story, but we pieced it together, Silas and I, afterward."

Lydia said, "I am surprised Bias did not kill Zenon long ago, Merza."

"Oh, my lady, Zenon was my manager. He planned where we would spend each day, and the best hours. He handled the money. He was very clever at knowing how much to demand from a man or woman, and the prices were different in the different cities, and in different parts of the cities. He was very good at managing me. Zenon was far more necessary to Bias than Bias was to Zenon."

Timothy said, "Silas and I talked to Zenon about what had been done with you. He was, I think, relieved to know you had fallen into the hands of a kind mistress. He made us promise to give him a decent burial. In return, he signed the paper—"

Merza cried, "He gave me my freedom!"

"Why, no," said Timothy, crestfallen. "He signed you over to me."

The climax of his story was gone, but he continued doggedly, "Jason made room for Zenon in his family vault. You can go there to see the place when you pass through Thessalonica, if you like. You and Luke and I will be going there, to meet Silas, on our way to Athens."

"Why should I care about that vault?" said Merza

coldly. "I am your slave now. What will you do with me, my lord?"

Lydia walked through the twilight over the cobbled streets with Niko prattling cheerfully beside her. "You need new sandals, child," said Lydia, as Niko bent to release a bit of pebble caught in a broken strap.

"So do you," Niko replied. "You give everything to others. You never used to do that. Before." She pressed Lydia's hand against her cheek. "When Brother Paul said, 'Bear ye one another's burdens,' he did not mean for one person to bear the burdens of a whole ecclesia."

Lydia only half listened. We miss you terribly, dear Paul. More than you can imagine. Luke is good with the sick, a good man among scholars, I suppose, if there were any scholars in our group. But he lacks maturity, warmth, experience. He isn't you, dear Paul. Merza was the cause of your banishment from Philippi. All the disasters of beating, imprisonment, expulsion—all were caused by that false, useless, deceitful girl. . . . Well, at least Merza would go when Timothy departed. She was Timothy's responsibility now. No doubt he would take her to Lystra before long. From all Lydia had heard of Lois, it seemed likely Lois could handle Merza. Meanwhile, perhaps Paul could make a Christian of her where others had failed.

I must advise Timothy to take ship from Thessalonica to Athens, she thought. If he goes by the highway the girl will find a thousand devices to delay them on the road. And her gluttony is insatiable. Erethrea did not complain of the extra bakings—she was flattered that Merza liked her bread. Somehow, Merza had wormed her way into the affections of Rufus, Erethrea, Niko. And she had done it by imposing on them, deceiving them, using them. Except in the case of Rufus. He was one she could not deceive.

At sunset the ecclesia gathered. Luke stood beside the

almond tree and warmly welcomed the newcomers to the company. He related the circumstances of Timothy's visit, told of the newly formed ecclesiae in Thessalonica and Beroea, and concluded, "If any of you have messages to send to Silas or Paul, Timothy will take them. He will be leaving us after the next Sabbath. Now before we partake of the sacrament of the Lord's Supper, Timothy will speak to you, and will read the letter he has brought to us all from our brother Paul. Timothy?"

Timothy stood beside the tree and looked about at the faces of these dear friends. "My heart overflows with joy to see you all once more. I marvel that in spite of the cloud of trouble under which we departed Philippi, all of you have remained faithful. Paul will rejoice, and Silas also, when they hear the good news I will give them, the splendid report of this Philippian ecclesia. My only sorrow is that Paul could not himself stand here, look into your loved faces, partake with you of the Lord's Supper, embrace you one and all and give you the kiss of peace."

He opened the scroll. "Now I will delay no longer, but read to you the message Paul has sent:

" 'From Paul and Timothy in Athens. We speak of you often, and of our sorrow that we parted from you so abruptly, leaving you with troubled hearts because of our sufferings. We are well, and the work we have set ourselves to do has prospered, both in Thessalonica and in Beroea.

" 'I pray for you daily, and my prayers are joyful because you have shared my labors and have abundantly proved that you care about the work I do. This is my prayer for you, that your love may grow ever richer, also your insight and knowledge and discrimination, that on the Day of Christ you will be flawless, reaping the harvest of righteousness.' "

Timothy's voice was warm with love as he felt himself lifted on the glorious exhortations. " 'If then your life

in Christ Jesus yields anything to stir the heart, any loving consolation, any sharing of the Spirit, any warmth of
affection or compassion, fill up my cup of happiness by
thinking and feeling alike, with the same love for one
another, the same turn of mind, a common care for unity.
Rivalry and personal vanity have no place among you,
but each must humbly reckon himself no better than
others. Look to each other's needs in everything. Be
even more careful of such things now that I am apart
from you than when I was with you. Work out your
own salvation in fear and trembling, lest you err on the
side of self-interest, remembering it is God who works
in you for His own chosen purpose. Thus you will be
my pride on the Day of Christ, proof that I did not run
my race in vain. Your faithfulness and love for one another are my crown of joy in this life and in the life to
come.

   " 'And now farewell, dear friends, for I write in haste,
to send this letter by the hand of my beloved son Timothy. I wish you joy in the Lord.' "

   Lydia's head dropped. Her hands covered her face.
The fault is in me, she thought sadly. Merza has suffered
the worst that men can do to her. If I cannot feel compassion for her, how can I love Syntyche, who is fault-
finding, self-centered, petty? How will we build a
community of Christians if we fail in love of such a lost
lamb as that girl? The Lord Jesus came to save the lost,
and Merza was lost and damned, a wretched, abused girl
until she came into this household. Rufus and Niko and
Erethrea have loved her. God give me grace to do the
same.

   They were serving the bread and wine when Lydia
uncovered her face. When the service ended and Luke
had spoken the prayer of blessing, Lydia moved among
the Christians, giving the kiss of peace to all, and espe-

cially the former prisoners, and the guards, and the Roman Tullos and his family.

Then she went to look for Timothy, to tell him he need not take Merza with him after all. But Timothy and Merza were talking, while nearby Niko mourned, "But, Merza, we do not want you to leave us."

Merza sent a sharp glance toward Lydia. Her mouth was hard, yet she somehow managed to make herself pitiful as she said, "Timothy owns me. I am his slave. Where he goes, I must go, and serve whoever he orders me to serve."

The purse Lydia gave Timothy in parting, eight days later, to be carried as a gift to Paul, was much heavier than Lydia had intended, heavier than she could actually afford. But it was not heavy enough to relieve her sense of unworthiness and guilt.

20

PRISCA, FATHER HAD CALLED HER, and Paul called her Prisca, though Aquila always said Priscilla, drawing out the diminutive form of her name in his gentle, caressing way. She enjoyed being called Prisca again. It took her back to the careless, abundant years when she and Aquila had lived with Father in Rome.

Prisca set the cakes left from breakfast in a dish near the doorway, in case the children of Fortunatus came dawdling past, looking famished. She put the washed dishes on a shelf and got the broom. For more than a year they had lived in this meager little house. The thought made her restless. Surely soon we can manage something better, something roomier. If Aquila doesn't speak to Stephanas soon about it, I shall have to, she thought. Paul had already made arrangements to leave them, and to take private quarters in the house of Gaius, next door to the synagogue, as soon as his friends arrived. There would be money from Lydia, then.

I am not an envious woman, Prisca reassured herself. But I hate poverty. I hate knowing that Lydia can give Paul money to help him in his ministry, and we cannot. I hate it that Gaius has a bigger house, where Paul and his friends will be comfortable, and we do not. Paul says I am not a good Christian, that a good Christian knows how to be content in whatever state he finds himself. How can he say that? I have been a Christian all my life! I have never known any faith other than the Christian faith! She put aside the broom, glancing at her blackened hands. I do not mind working at the loom. I do not mind what the black yarns have done to my hands. These hands are the badge of my profession, and I wear them cheerfully. But to be a slave to the petty round of housework as well—that I hate. I was a tent-maker in Rome, but in Rome we had slaves to bake and sweep and milk the goats and clean away after meals. I hate the poverty in which we live!

Father was a prosperous man. I have every right to ask my husband to become a prosperous man. But Aquila is a rolling stone, and he will never amount to anything until he is willing to settle somewhere and stay long enough to acquire property and become someone of consequence, someone with a house large enough to make a trio of evangels comfortable. Someone who could help protect Brother Paul from this strange quirk about preaching equally to Jews and Gentiles. He is a great preacher—I have never heard his equal—but in this one thing he is mistaken. We had no trouble at all with this problem in Rome, she thought. We merely converted all our Christians to become also Jews. We Roman Jews are Hellenists, as he is. Surely there can be no real quarrel between us.

When the Jews were driven out of Rome by the princeps, Claudius Caesar, it was Prisca's father who had cautioned Aquila, "Jerusalem is the place to go *after* you have made your fortune. Corinth is the place where a young couple can be sure to make their fortune. Go to Corinth, my son. Work hard. Corinth, the city of two harbors, will afford every opportunity. When you are ready to retire, bring your family and join us in Jerusalem. God bless you, and grant that the years are short till you can come to us."

Prisca could not even remember her family's momentous trip to Jerusalem in her infancy. Uncle Simon had been shut up in his great house, a leper, abandoned by his sons and most of his hirelings and left to die. Only his wife had stayed with him, and he had outlived her. All this was hearsay to Prisca, a tale told and retold as she was growing up. For the Lord Jesus had come to Jerusalem to the Feast of the Passover one spring, and had touched Simon and healed his leprosy. Father and Mother had taken the infant Prisca and some servants and gone to Jerusalem to learn at first hand of the marvel, meaning to stay on till after the celebration of Pentecost in the Holy City. They had learned after they arrived that the Healer had been crucified and entombed, and on the third day his friends had gone to the tomb and found it empty. Father had himself been present on a day when Jesus made his final appearance on Mount Olivet to his followers and had vanished in thick cloud, after promising, "I will come again. I will surely come again."

Father and Mother had waited, believing, and on the Day of Pentecost they had shared in the gift of the indwelling Breath of God, had seen the flames that danced above each ecstatic worshiper's head, had heard the many varied tongues in which the believers spoke, testifying to the blessedness of this unique experience.

So for a few months Father had remained in Jerusalem in the house of his cousin Simon. Then business had called him back to Rome, and the little company had set out, bringing the servants who had accompanied them and to whom also the gift of the Spirit had been given. Thus had begun the ecclesia in Rome, an ecclesia of which Paul was completely unaware until Prisca had told him the story. Now that the Jews were driven from Rome there remained only those Christians who were slaves and could not be spared. Among them were slaves belonging to Caesar's household, as well as a handful of other Romans.

Aquila, who had not been called *Eagle* without reason, had left his native Pontus on the Euxine Sea and had reached Rome five years ago. A tentmaker, he had found employment with Prisca's father. Within a year Prisca and Aquila were married. When the Jews were driven from Rome, Prisca and Aquila had come to Corinth to make their fortune, as her father advised, in the city with two harbors. Here they took employment with the merchant Stephanas, who exported goods of many sorts, including tents. Stephanas provided his tentmakers with looms and yarns and the sturdy string used for warp, then bought from them the finished products.

Piecework is what it is, thought Prisca restlessly, as she finished drying the breakfast dishes and put them on the shelf. But Aquila was a man without roots or capital. There were men in plenty who would have taken advantage of the Jews who were banished from Rome. Prisca acknowledged that they had been fortunate to find such a man as Stephanas, who treated them with strict justice.

But Aquila had begun talking of moving on to another city, Ephesus, the capital of Asia, or Antioch in Syria, or even Alexandria in Egypt. If she did not keep a firm grip on the situation Aquila would pull out of Corinth when Brother Paul finished his ministry here and moved on. If she did not learn to manage her husband as skillfully as Father had managed Mother, they would spend their lives hopping from city to city, and finding piecework to do in each city in turn, a pair of rolling stones without a single possession with which to bless themselves.

If we cannot prosper in Corinth we cannot prosper

anywhere. What we must do is get together a little capital, enough to buy a loom and some yarns. Then our
labor will bring in more income. We could then save
more money and hire weavers and in the end build such a
business as Father built in Rome.

She spread a linen cloth over the clean dishes on the
shelves to keep the dust of the road from settling on
them. She heard the bleat of the goat. Fortunatus' children were at her again. Milking the goat was a menial
job. There had been servants in Rome for sweeping and
washing dishes and making fires and milking goats. I am
worth far more as a weaver of tents than at these pid-
dling tasks, she thought, feeling restless. Still, she had
best get out to the goat while there was still milk to be
got from her.

Prisca took up a pitcher and a bit of clean linen and
went outside. Remembering Aquila's easy-going way
(better to warn them off, my dear, than to confront them;
they are our neighbors, and only children after all) she
stooped and gathered pebbles and tossed them out beyond
the corner of the house, toward the grassy patch where
the little goat was tethered. She heard the scuff and
scramble of a startled child, the plaintive bleat of the
abandoned goat, but waited still, giving whichever child
it was time to escape before showing herself.

The two goats of Fortunatus were at their favorite
spot, on the platform at midpoint on the stairway which
rose to his roof. The family oven was on this landing,
and here the family gathered for meals in fine weather.
That house was much larger than the tiny cottage of
Prisca and Aquila, and the goats had obviously been
milked earlier this morning. But Fortunatus had seven
children and an ailing wife and a bustling sister-in-law
who kept up the house and the cooking and all that. The
children, however, got less attention, and Prisca had never
seen them when they weren't scrounging.

Prisca patted the little goat, who nuzzled her skirts before resuming her grazing. Then Prisca knelt and reached between the legs, found the udder still reasonably firm. She wiped the teats and bag with the linen. As she listened to the pleasant ping of milk streaming into the pitcher she reflected on the arrangements Paul would be making today. He had been aghast, at first, to learn that a girl was coming with Silas and Timothy. And Prisca's first thought had been, There is one thing he expected of Lydia and was disappointed in his expectations.

Then he had said, "She is an unfortunate girl, and Timothy probably wants to take her to his grandmother in Lystra. Now, Prisca, I appeal to you. There will be no place in our bachelor quarters at the house of Gaius for this girl. Can you squeeze her in here somehow, and give her work to do to pay her way?" He had added, "It is only until we take ship for Ephesus. Perhaps Timothy can help out if the girl doesn't earn her keep."

"I need a girl's help," Prisca had assured him. "If she will keep the house tidy and cook the meals and milk the goat, I'll be very glad to have her." I'll be very glad to succeed where Lydia failed, she thought. Indeed, the girl will be very welcome in this house.

Aquila had also been pleased. Paul was relieved, and Prisca was glad to think that for a few months at least she would have more time to work at her profession. In this one thing I will show I can manage better than Lydia, she thought. Another pair of hands—a soothsayer to help me persuade Aquila to forget his roving. . . . She has probably been in all the cities he yearns to see. It sounded very good to Prisca. Who knows, she thought, how it will all turn out?

It is possible, she thought, that by the time Aquila grows too restless, so that I cannot keep him settled here longer, we may have a bit of money put by, and can start in another city on a more profitable arrangement.

Prisca rose, took the pitcher of foaming milk into the house and laid a cloth over it and set it in as cool a corner as the kitchen afforded.

She went out and moved the peg which tethered the goat, to give her more shade and deeper, greener grass for the day's grazing.

I do not really like this city, she thought. I do not like a city where Aphrodite is worshiped above the other gods. Corinth was famous for many things—for the Isthmian games held every two years; for the two harbors which gave it ascendancy over other seaport cities; for the forty-nine taverns facing on the great Roman forum; for the beauty and perfection of its theater, the excellence of its hospital, the two paved roads which led, one north, the other east, to its two harbors; for the abundant waters of its Pyraean Spring; for the thousand prostitutes who served that lovely, glowing little temple that stood on the highest and most conspicuous spot on the Acrocorinthus; for the excellence of its Roman governors, who rotated in such a manner that not one of them ever served longer than two years. But most of all for its wealth, for the name of the city in the mouth of the world was Corinth the Rich. If we grow prosperous, she thought, perhaps Aquila will be content to stay on here.

She took a pitcher and went to the aqueduct that flowed from the Pyraean Spring out through this section of the city. She drank a cup of the delicious, cool and sparkling water—the hospital was built beside the spring, because of the water's remarkable healing properties—and now at last she was ready to go to the forum, to the shop of Stephanas. Aquila and Paul were there today, as were a score of other tentmakers in his employ. Today everyone was sewing—attaching the wooden rings to the black panels, to accommodate the ropes which anchor tents to their poles. Stephanas had a very large order from Libya which must be filled and the tents stowed aboard ship in Cenchrea, the eastern harbor, today.

Prisca washed her hands. It was time to get down to the forum. She had delayed too long. She looked at her roughened, blackened hands as she dried them. They were the badge of her profession. She was proud of them. In a city of strangers, they were her protection. Anyone could tell at a glance that she was a tentmaker. She would never be mistaken for one of the temple prostitutes who thronged this city.

21

MERZA LAGGED as they walked the long miles. This was the third day since they had left Athens and the comfortable house of Sister Damaris. Silas promised they would be in Corinth well before sundown.

"We would have been there in two days," he had said last night when they took lodgings in a village about midway of the isthmus. "Timothy and I could have made it in two days, and you are just as sturdy a traveler as we. You delayed us for no reason except your whims, which you used to slow us down more times than one can reckon. We must reach Corinth today well before sunset, for after we enter the city we must find Paul. If there is no room for us where he is lodging, we still must find a lodging place before we can rest. Now if you love Paul at all, or feel any gratitude that he delivered you from the life of the roads with Zenon and Bias, do not dawdle."

"I am grateful to the little preacher," she said reasonably. "If you want me to keep up, put a collar and a leash on me. But why are you giving me orders? It is Timothy who is my lord and master." And she looked up insolently at Silas.

Timothy was furious, but what did it matter? If just once he would beat her she would know where she stood with him, with the world. He could not possibly feel as bewildered and wretched as she. The little preacher wanted him. Nobody wanted her, the little preacher least of all. As for this journey, it had been bad from first to last. *Somebody* has to be the boss when a group travels. They had lost plenty of time because nobody made the right decisions, or if decisions were made nobody enforced them. When one or the other of them dropped back to walk with Merza, thinking thus to hurry her, she wanted to scream. It was not her custom to walk with the men she traveled with. She walked alone. she looked, she listened, she savored the thoughts and impressions as they came. How can you walk with someone who chatters at you, while you are drinking in the message of the earth?

Yet often as not, it was their talk she was drinking in. Silas—what a feeling he had for the country. What information he acquired, and passed on to his companions. And Timothy knew old legends to match the places where they walked. This isthmus was full of dark tales. Blood had been spilled on this earth. The earth had drunk deep of the blood—blood of heroes and blood of evil and infamous men against whom they had struggled. Sometimes the awareness of old evils and old anguish was almost more than Merza could bear. She could have told Timothy and Silas about evils as fresh as tomorrow. But what would be the use? Tomorrow would bring its own evils.

Her feet had a life of their own upon the paving blocks. She never stumbled, though she never watched her footing. These were roads the Romans had built to last forever. Merza had supposed till now that the Roman roads were built by slaves. But Silas said the legions built them, that after victory the soldiers were not idle in camp. Oh no. They went out into the conquered land to bind it to Rome with the eternal network of Roman roads.

Armies come and armies go, but the people who dwell in the land continue, generation after generation. Governments change. Taxes are paid. Armies march and blood is shed. But the people remain, and seedtime and harvest, rains and drought, earthquakes and windstorms, clouds and beating sunshine, birth and death, and the crowding spirits who ever hover, longing to speak their wisdom but finding few souls in the earth who can hear their breathy voices. Beware, Merza! Do not invite them, lest the demon enter you again!

Sometimes the road came down near the sea, the blue, blue sea of these Grecian lands. Sometimes the road wound round behind the little hills and the wooded bluffs that shut off the sea. Silas and Timothy had much to say to one another, and this journey was nothing whatever like following the roads with Zenon and Bias. Silas had a beautiful way of telling things. Indeed, so did Timothy. Early today Timothy had been telling tales of the hero Theseus and his bloody but triumphant crossing of the isthmus, on his way to Athens, to make himself known to the king, who was his father.

Now Timothy was narrating a dreadful story of a queen called Medea who had once dwelt in Corinth, who there murdered her own little children out of hatred for her husband. She must have been possessed by a truly dreadful demon, thought Merza. And she thought, feeling virtuous, I only turned my face away from my child, in my hatred of Bias. But something cold seemed lodged within her, crowding her breathing. I did not injure my child. Actually, it is far happier where it is than would be possible anywhere else in the world.

Yet the coldness remained. You could at least have looked upon it with pity—with—tenderness.

Oh, what a horrid thought. How would I know about tenderness?

What but tenderness have you been hearing about, yes, even witnessing, ever since Timothy picked you up in the street and laid you down on a clean bed in the house of Lydia?

It was the demon, she thought. The demon was to blame for what I did. The explanation was simple and required no further consideration.

They had come out upon a stadium, and Silas and Timothy stood looking downslope upon the vast array of seats, with a racing track below. Across the open space rose another hill, topped by a temple to Poseidon, the deity honored in the games.

"It has been a pleasant journey," she said, and smiled at Timothy. "Except that you have kept me starving all the way. Oh, Silas, look. Yonder lie the remains of those old walls you spoke of."

"The walls to the north harbor, like the Long Walls of Athens to Piraeus," said Silas, "except that the Corinthians built two sets of long walls, one to each of their two harbors. They are thick with vines now. I suppose they served as a stone quarry for the soldiers of Julius Caesar who rebuilt Corinth three or four generations ago."

"Oh, let us hurry," cried Merza. "The little preacher is impatient for our coming. He is eager to hear the news we bring."

Silas looked at her with lifted brows. "Indeed he is, missy. And he shall be told who delayed us."

They came out onto the road guarded by the vine-covered heaps of stones. They are nice men to travel with, thought Merza. But I do not think the little preacher will want me as a companion when he takes the road from Corinth.

As if he had read her thoughts, Silas said, "When next

we journey it will be by ship, for our plan is to go from Corinth to Ephesus, and again by ship from Ephesus to Caesarea and Jerusalem. Timothy meanwhile will go from Ephesus by the royal road to Lystra, for our journey is nearing its end."

Merza said, "I shall go with Timothy. And of course I shall have to make the journey to Lystra on only two loaves a day." She resolved, though she did not say so, that in Ephesus, after Silas and the little preacher took ship for home, she would tell fortunes until she had earned enough money to feed herself, and bed herself, comfortably on the journey to Lystra. Yes, and clothe herself in something better than the unbleached homespun in which she was making this journey. And she thought with anger and longing of the lovely clothes Lydia had let her wear on special occasions but had never considered letting her carry with her when she went away.

"Vanity is a besetting sin in you, my child, and I will not contribute to it," she said, but Merza knew better. The lady liked to pretend that she cared for Merza, but she hated her. The lady would never forget or forgive Merza because on her account the little preacher had suffered at the hands of the Philippian jailer, and on her account the little preacher had left Philippi.

Merza's fingers reached for the end of her girdle, touching the place where she had sewed into a fold of cloth the three silver coins. Rufus had earned those coins, working at night after his day's toil for Lydia was finished, in the dye shed of a neighbor. Rufus had given her the coins, had closed her hand over them.

"Save them till you desperately need them," he had said, and kissed her cheek. "I will surely miss you, my girl. And I think you will miss the Hibernian helot with his red beard and his body discolored with dyes. Say to yourself, if trouble comes, 'Rufus prays for me. Yesterday, today, tomorrow, Rufus remembers me and sends kind thoughts and prays for me.' "

Timothy cried, "Look how the sun strikes that little building on the mountain yonder."

"That is the temple of Aphrodite," said Silas. "It is said that a thousand prostitutes serve that temple."

How many times had Bias threatened to sell Merza into a brothel! That is something I need never fear now that Timothy owns me, she thought, and giggled softly, thinking how silly it was for Timothy to be her master. I can do anything I like with Timothy, she thought, after Silas and the little preacher go home to Jerusalem.

What do I really want? she wondered. I wanted to leave Philippi and go with the little preacher two months ago, but it was not safe then. Now it is safe, and Timothy has the paper that says I belong to him. And soon we will see the little preacher, and that is what I want.

So this is what I want, so now I am happy, she thought. Except for Rufus. I did not want to leave Rufus. He really cares about me. Why do I care who likes me and who hates me? I know many things they do not know. I know more about all of them than they know about themselves. It is only myself I do not know about— what will become of me. I did not want Lydia to hate me. I wanted her to like me, but she did not.

Merza paused to take a pebble from her sandal. When she looked up, Silas and Timothy were out of sight beyond a bend. A squad of Roman legionaries had overtaken her, marching hup, hup in brisk rhythm along the road. As they passed her, the last man in line, the one calling the cadence, seized her arm and linked his through it, forcing her to match their quick pace.

"Come along, sweetheart!" He fitted the invitation to the cadence.

> "Where did you get—hup, hup—
> That pretty curl—hup, hup—
> Give us a kiss—hup, hup—
> You darling girl—hup, hup."

She screamed, "Silas! Timothy! Help!" But they were out of sight. They had rounded a corner where the road turned to avoid an ancient temple. She started screaming in earnest, but the screams were drowned in the laughter of the soldiers, who were now gathered round, admiring the fish their corporal had captured in his net.

Off to the left came the grinding noise of wood and metal heavily rubbed together. Over the land came a boat laden with grain, pulled upon a road of crushed stone by a score of men, while others ran with the rollers on which it moved, carrying them from the back of the boat to the front, to be used over and over. These were sturdy men with bunched muscles in arms and thighs and shoulders, men who wore pads of leather over their shoulders on which the ropes rested by which, bending almost double, they tugged the boat along.

The boat was squarely across the highroad now, and the soldiers halted, still marking time, and all joined in the cadence:

"Give us a kiss—hup, hup—
You darling girl—hup, hup."

The corporal, meanwhile, was using the time to kiss and fondle Merza, while her screams for help were lost in the grinding of the boat and its rollers.

Then Merza used her wits, the only real defense she had ever possessed. "You fool! You fool! Soon your arms will be leprous. Soon your mouth will rot with leprosy. Can't you see that I'm a leper?"

When he jerked back to take a look, she got free and ran to the rear of the boat. She got round behind the toiling men and the groaning of the rollers and came up on the other side. There Silas and Timothy waited. They had turned back to find her till they found the boat blocking the road.

Intensely relieved at sight of her, Timothy said firmly,

"Hereafter you walk between us, or you'll get no bread at all. You could have been kidnapped and sold to one of the brothels Corinth is so famous for!"

"All right, Timothy," she said meekly.

Soon they were in the midst of small houses. The odor identified it as the district of tanners. Merza walked demurely between the two men, and Timothy was proud to see her so biddable, at last. Merza also was content. She had been frightened. Now she was safe. When the soldiers passed them still chanting the "hup, hup" of the cadence, both they and Merza kept eyes front.

They left behind the streets of the tanners. Presently the houses became larger and handsomer. They were upon the Lechaeum Road, one of the great avenues of Corinth. Called the Straight Way, it was made of stones cut in octagonal blocks, very handsome and impressive, and once they were within the city's precincts the buildings on both sides were equally impressive. The synagogue faced upon this avenue, and there they would learn where Paul was to be found.

On they went, and the buildings grew larger and more opulent, temples, public buildings, great houses. "Corinth the Rich," murmured Silas. "It is aptly named. Oh, I will be glad to learn how Paul has fared in this city."

Then they saw the synagogue, massive, rich with marbles, but with no ornaments visible save the beauty of the stone and the handsome Hebrew lettering carved over the massive doorway, Synagogue of the Hebrews. There their journey ended, for Paul had moved into private quarters in the house of a Greek named Titius Justus. The house stood adjacent to the synagogue.

Now the men were embracing one another with joy, while Merza tried to make herself invisible behind the bedrolls they had dropped just inside the door. The little preacher had been ill since last she saw him. Also he had been working at his trade, for his hands were black from the yarn. At first he was so overjoyed to see his friends he did not even glance in her direction.

"Welcome! Thrice welcome! Are you well? Oh, to be sure—that is quite evident. Tell me the news of the churches. Oh, I yearn to hear everything about everyone. My children in the faith. How do they fare?"

Presently he noticed her. "Why are you here, child? You were told to remain with Lydia."

Merza shrank into herself under the disapproval of the little preacher. I have no value for him. I have no value for Timothy. I must say something, but what can I say? I have no value for Lydia. She lifted pleading eyes to Paul. "The lady sent me to you to be taught, for I am —slow to learn the Christian ways. The lady—the lady believes I am such a difficult case that only you can make a Christian of me."

It was as good a reason as any. Then it struck her. It was a better reason than any. It was an excellent reason. Maybe it is the real reason, she thought, and breathed deeply. She said, "Dear Paul, I will try not to be a trouble or a burden. I will try to be—useful."

Silas said, "Come, Merza. Bring water and towels. You must wash our feet and then attend to this luggage. You must tell her where things go, Paul."

Merza was kneeling to wash Timothy's feet when the blow came. Paul said, "You and Timothy, Silas, will live with me here. I have rented the one room from our convert and friend, Gaius. Merza cannot share these quarters with us—they are too crowded for that. She will live with Aquila and Prisca. My child, you will be useful to Prisca, for both she and her husband are tentmakers. You will help with the housekeeping chores, and once a day you can come here and attend to our needs as well. Oh my friends, I have so much to tell you. Timothy, did Lydia have any—special message for me?"

"Indeed she did. I had forgotten in the joy of seeing you, Paul. I have saved some silver from the travel money." He dropped a small handful of coins into Paul's open hands, the rough, blackened, tentmaker's hands. He continued, "There is also gold. It is in a belt under my tunic. Enough gold so you can cease weaving and spend all your time preaching."

Merza bent low, drying Timothy's long, narrow feet on the towel. She was so angry, so wounded and so angry, she longed to beat them with her fists. Instead she took the basin and towel and went to wash the feet of Silas. Two loaves a day! she thought in an anger that was more like despair. He had all that money, and he gave me only two loaves a day.

They reject me, all of them, she thought, as she poured water over the sturdy feet of Silas. Lydia has kicked me out of her household, and the little preacher has farmed me out to a woman who needs some menial help about the house. If it weren't for Timothy—I wonder what I will do when we get to Lystra and Timothy's grandmother kicks me out into the street?

22

From the northeast corner of the agora the stately Propylaea Gateway led down onto the Lechaeum Road, which was the famous Straight Way connecting Corinth with her northwest harbor. The house of Gaius faced on this road and was spacious enough to accommodate the growing congregation of Christians—the largest congregation Timothy had as yet encountered, for Paul had had excellent success in his fifteen months' preaching mission in the city with two harbors.

This congregation was not only the largest, but the most diverse, ranging from Stephanas, the merchant with worldwide connections, through Erastus, the city treasurer, and Titius Justus, whose wealth came from his tavern in the agora, to Crispus, who had resigned his responsibilities as ruler of the synagogue when he became a Christian, and down through every stratum of society. There were men whose bulging muscles testified that they were employed in the heavy labor of moving boats over the isthmus, from one harbor to the other, including a number of slaves. A score of the slaves were called Chloe's People. Chloe was the supervising housekeeper for the prostitutes who served Artemis in the temple atop the Acrocorinthus. Her slaves served in every menial capacity. Racially they were a mixed lot.

The congregation included also patients in the healing sanctuary of Asklepios, built beside the Pyraean Spring, which emerged not far from the Propylaea Gateway. On a day in Paul's second winter in Corinth, Timothy sat beside the bed of a man who was at the very nadir of life. He was undergoing the standard Greek treatment, whereby men with profound internal infirmities were slowly reduced, through sweats and purges and starvation, to the lowest possible ebb short of death. Having thus rid them of their infirmity, the physician began rebuilding through strict diet and liberal doses of the medicinal waters of the spring.

The patient was barely conscious, silent, unmoving, comatose. Nearby a third man, a sculptor-in-residence to the hospital, was at work. A grateful patient had commissioned him to create a leg of terra-cotta showing where the compound fracture in his leg, of both the tibia and the fibula, had been mended. This work of art would be added to the shelves of such terra-cotta mementos that ornamented one entire wall of the long dining room. These items included heads, hearts, hands, arms with and without hands attached, lungs, stomachs, jaws, even a spleen or two. Kitibo had earned his livelihood for a number of years fashioning these articles for the beautification of the hospital's public rooms and the inspiration of incoming patients. Kitibo was also one of the Corinthian converts.

As the two of them, Timothy and Kitibo, sat companionably near the torpid patient, in the loggia just outside the dining room, suddenly the street was loud with hurrying men. Among them was Paul, in the grip of Sosthenes, who had succeeded Crispus as ruler of the synagogue. Paul was angry. His voice was heard as he approached and even after he had passed by the hospital.

"You Jews! You cannot believe without miracles. What are miracles but the contravention of natural law? Do you think a greater power is employed to contravene natural law or to conceive and establish it? Who do you think set natural laws in motion? Why do you ask for miracles, seeing they are all around you? You are a fool, and I refuse to turn mountebank to win you, for that kind of conversion would not endure."

Sosthenes was still gripping Paul's arm and rushing him along when they passed up the steps and through the Propylaea into the agora.

Timothy and Kitibo, hurrying along after the cluster of agitated Jews and Christians, soon understood that Sosthenes was taking Paul before the governor of Achaea, a Roman named Gallio, then resident in Corinth.

"On what charge?" mourned Timothy, filled with despair. For all these months they had dwelt peacefully in Corinth, preaching to crowds, winning converts. At worst it might mark the end of Paul's life, or at any rate his liberty. Certainly Paul would see in it the signal to terminate his Corinth mission. What kind of man was this governor Gallio? What would he do with Paul?

Gallio dressed with care. His appointment to the governorship of Achaea had proved quite as disappointing as expected. If Athens were the capital instead of this brassy, buoyant city, he could have expected to find friends among the Greeks he was appointed to rule. It became increasingly evident each week that when they called Corinth the most Roman of Greek cities they were not flattering the Romans. One came to Greece expecting to find poets and philosophers. In Corinth one found hustlers, or at best able and aggressive business men. And the theater! Obscenities and belly laughs. Who would have believed that Greek taste could have sunk so low? Two of the Latin plays written by his brother Seneca had been produced in his honor when he arrived in Corinth last summer, but since then, nothing worth seeing. The Corinthians preferred their entertainment in Greek, and the theater was half empty for the Latin dramas. Ah well, Seneca had only paraphrased the Greek classics into Latin, and did not pretend he had done more.

Well, at least Corinth was better than exile in the cold, windy mountains of Corsica. Seneca had been a fool to ridicule the pretensions of Claudius to divinity. Claudius was a clown. But when you have a clown for princeps you don't point your finger and snigger. Gallio and Seneca had been lucky to get off with exile. Had they been less than the sons of the philosopher, Seneca the elder, they would have died instead. Two more of those mysterious poisonings that haunt the reigns of the mighty Caesars.

The brothers had suffered a decade of exile, ending when Seneca was called home to become tutor to Nero, whom Claudius had finally named as his heir. Gallio returned from Corsica with rotten lungs and a disgusting cough, and Claudius showed him kindness in giving him this southern province to govern. But it was doing him no good. If Gallio did not get better soon he would have to resign and go to Egypt. I would like to live long enough, thought Gallio, to see how younger brother adapts himself to the task of tutoring Divinity.

I no longer fear death, he reflected, since my sojourn amongst the followers of Pythagoras. I do not shudder when I feel her clammy fingers clutching at my lungs. But I cannot hope for so remarkable a collection of relatives in the next incarnation as in this one—a philosopher for a father, and poets for brother and nephew. I do not want to depart this life before I must.

He nodded dismissal to the young Greek who was his dresser, and strode out into the wintry cold of the porch, where his chair of judgment stood some nine feet above the cobbled pavement of the forum.

The Jews were in an uproar again. Gallio was reminded of his father's admonition when he had received his first political appointment to a province. "Beware the bickerings of the Jews. Remember Pontius Pilate!" For Pilate had let himself be drawn so far into the affairs of zealots in Jerusalem as to sentence to crucifixion a man who was patently innocent. He had gone a little wrong in the head thereafter, and wound up with an appointment to a high mountain district in the great, snowy ranges which protect Italy on the north from the barbarians of Gaul and Germany. There Pilate died. And the senior Seneca had warned, "Never touch a zealot. Let the Jews be Jews—you cannot change them—it is their nature. You come from a family of philosophers and poets. Govern as a philosopher, with wisdom and tolerance."

Gallio took his seat on the bema. His guard ranged in their places all about him, where they could watch the agitated people on the cobbles below. A thrown knife was the worst one had to fear, but the Roman guard had been trained to watch both the faces and the hands of subject peoples, and were skillful at spotting troublemakers.

Gallio spoke strongly, though the effort rasped his vocal chords. "Who is spokesman for this affair?"

The man who spoke up was known to Gallio, an honest man and respected, the ruler of the synagogue of the Jews. He was called Sosthenes.

"If you please, your honor, Governor of all Achaea," and he bowed slightly, after the manner of his people. "This man is Paul, a citizen of Tarsus. He has broken the law, in that he induces people in this city to worship

God in ways repugnant to Jews, ways that are an offense, a breach of the law, a cause of rioting."

Gallio asked mildly, "Be specific, Sosthenes. What law does he contravene?"

Someone shouted, "Your honor, this man Paul is a citizen born, with all the rights inherent to Roman citizens."

"Your name, sir? Present yourselves properly when you address me."

"I am Kitibo, a sculptor, employed for more than a decade in the hospital." He held aloft one of those painfully undecorative objects used to ornament the walls of the hospital. This was a leg, from knee to toes. Unfinished.

Gallio coughed into the cloth he always carried. There was a trace of blood in the sputum. I must learn to delegate all this shouting to an assistant, he thought, and rebelled at the prospect of publishing to the world that he was less than a man. He said, "Sosthenes, continue."

"This man, Paul of Tarsus, has been arrested, or stoned, or imprisoned, or driven thence from every city where he has preached in Asia and Macedonia. His views are repugnant to Jews, yet he continues to attend synagogue and preach to pious Jews on every possible occasion. He speaks contrary to the ancient and holy Law by which Jews have lived and ruled themselves for two thousand years."

Now the accused was preparing to launch his defense. He looked quite impressive in spite of his slight stature. Gallio had heard him harangue—actually he was an excellent speaker so far as his voice and delivery were concerned. Gallio had not troubled to follow the gist of his arguments, but one learned to recognize the spellbinders, and this one was good, of his sort.

I will not let him get started, thought Gallio. There is rain in those clouds and I do not care to sit here in the bema coughing. He leaned back comfortably in his

chair, smiled down at the spellbinder who was trying to
get himself free from the grip of Sosthenes before he
began.

Gallio said pleasantly, "You Jews make much of your
differences. Your quarrels over Jewish legalisms do not
concern Rome. They are your affair and yours alone.
Go! Get hence!" He made a shooing motion with his
hands.

His father would have been pleased with him today.
"The Jews can entangle you with their specious logic. A
man not trained to fiddle and dabble and quibble as they
do will get into all kinds of trouble if he lets himself
become entangled. Beware of the Jews."

I must write a letter to Father, thought Gallio.

Below him the sculptor from the hospital raised the
terra-cotta leg and brought it down on the shoulder of
the complainant. Gallio glanced at his captain of lictors,
raised his brows, nodded toward the rioting Jews. It was
apparent that the party which supported the man from
Tarsus was giving Sosthenes quite a drubbing.

"Keep an eye on them. Follow them, but at a distance.
If they do serious bodily harm to the ruler of the synagogue we will have a case against the man Paul." He
coughed. "Report back."

Gallio was resting near the fire in a warm room when
his captain returned. "They talked," he said. "They were
more or less peaceable by the time they reached the synagogue. The man from Tarsus did most of the talking, and
the other one, Sosthenes, grew peaceable and attentive.
Presently they were weeping on one another's shoulders.
The last I saw of them they were chums. They wept as
they talked over old crimes, old crucifixions, stuff like
that. Then someone brought water and the man from
Tarsus bathed the wounds of the man from the synagogue. It appeared to me the accused has made a Christian of his accuser."

"My father is right," said Gallio. "The Jews are strange, unpredictable people."

Paul's encounter with Gallio was the signal to the three apostles that they had stayed long enough in Corinth. They resolved to take ship for Ephesus when spring brought sailing weather.

"Ships bound for Ephesus," said Silas, "are bound also for Caesarea. The time has come, Paul, for me to return and report on this journey to the church in Jerusalem which commissioned me."

Paul felt a deep stab of homesickness. "I may go with you, at least as far as Antioch," he said. "However, I shall await the guidance of the Spirit. It is much in my mind that Ephesus is central to the churches of Asia, of Macedonia, of Achaea. It is much in my mind that a mission to Ephesus could not be brief. I may go home to Antioch to report, spend a winter with my mother in Tarsus, and set out next spring when the Gates open to make the journey to Lystra, pick up Timothy there, and proceed to Ephesus. I must speak to Prisca and Aquila. He has talked of making his home in Ephesus rather than Corinth. Ephesus is to be central to our churches in Asia and Greece. Those two should proceed at once to establish themselves in that city. They are no longer needed by the church in Corinth. I shall speak to Prisca about this. I am confident they would be of the greatest assistance to our purposes in Ephesus. As for you, Silas, I would like you to escort our brother Peter on a journey to all the churches where I have preached. He can enrich them as no other living man could do."

"The last time you talked with Peter you called him hypocrite because he gave over eating with Greeks when a group of us came up from Jerusalem to Antioch."

"So I did," said Paul with a reminiscent smile. "And Peter understood what was in my heart, and set the wheels to moving which led to my commissioning, with Barnabas, for the first missionary journey. This is how Christians settle their differences."

"It is indeed," said Silas. "It is indeed. And you, Paul of Tarsus, are the one apostle who thinks always in terms of the grand design. The rest of us are so full of the past, the years when the Lord Jesus was among us, that we overlook the injunction, Go into the world. Preach to all people. We were followers while he lived among us, and we are followers still. But you, Paul, are carving great, bold pathways through the world. Sooner or later all the other apostles will follow you."

"Perhaps it was for this," said Paul, deeply moved by the tribute, "that I was born out of season. I do not have your memories. I have never been tempted to dwell in the past. For me it comes naturally to think in terms of the future."

Two months of winter storms remained before the spring sailings would begin. Paul wrote letters to the churches in Macedonia, which Stephanas undertook to have delivered overland by associates who delivered merchandise in the north country.

When the storms ended and the skies smiled and the seas grew favorable to shipping, Paul set out for Ephesus, and with him were Silas and Timothy, Prisca and Aquila and Merza.

BOOK IV
Ephesus

23

TIMOTHY STOOD between the deckhouse and the rail as the *Swan* passed through quiet water between the island and the mainland and entered the Caÿster River. Soon she was sailing upstream before a fair wind, buffeted by the turbulent spring current.

The *Swan* was a splendid little ship, clean, fairly new, and freshly painted for the spring sailing, in olive green with a dark red trim, the color called Cretan red. She was in ballast, having sailed from Italy with very little cargo. She had been dragged over the isthmus from harbor to harbor, had taken on cargo and passengers in Cenchrea and in Piraeus, would take on more cargo in Ephesus, and move around the eastern end of the Great Sea. When she reached Alexandria in Egypt she would have delivered most of this local cargo. There she would fill her holds with early grains, then sail directly across the Great Sea to deliver the grains to Rome, for Egypt was the granary from which the great city of Rome was fed.

The *Swan* would spend only three days in Ephesus, discharging and taking on cargo. When she proceeded on her way Paul and Silas would be aboard her. I may never see Silas again, thought Timothy with regret. If he brings Peter on a journey to the churches of Asia, I will no doubt be off somewhere with Paul. The future and the past were at his elbows as he stood at the rail, watching the glittering marbles of Ephesus draw nearer in the morning sun. Prisca and Aquila would leave the *Swan* at this port. Their household goods were in the hold, to be unloaded at dockside. Aquila would find a donkey to carry his belongings to the address of an associate of Stephanas who would provide them with employment and a dwelling.

Timothy and Merza would leave the ship at Ephesus also, their belongings rolled into their beds. In a few days—after the *Swan* sailed with Paul and Silas aboard her—Timothy and Merza would set out along the royal road for Lystra.

The great hills of Asia, so green, so near, tugged at Timothy's heartstrings. He was homesick. Grandmother, Mother, Lystra, home! A few days' swift travel down the royal road, ten at most if Merza cooperated, would bring them to Lystra. There would be delays in Antioch of Pisidia and in Iconium. Timothy would meet with the ecclesiae there and speak for Paul, reporting on their journey, enumerating the new churches, giving names and addresses of Christians in Greece to Christians in the Galatian churches.

Paul had dictated a general letter to the churches of Galatia, and Timothy had made four copies, with greetings added to each, personal greetings dictated by Paul to the elders and deacons of each city, and to women who had given him hospitality. And in each city Timothy would gather up a report to be transmitted to Paul, adding his own notes on the situation in each ecclesia as he observed it. All these notes would be copied into a letter which Timothy would transmit to Paul during the summer by the hand of some merchant who was making a journey into Syria and would undertake, for a fee, to deliver the scroll to Paul or leave it for him at a local synagogue.

The harbor of Ephesus was not far ahead. The great buildings of the city gleamed white against the green hills, with the tall, swaying masts of ships at anchor in the immediate foreground. Four ships were in line, waiting to enter the inner harbor, and the *Swan*'s mainsail dropped with a whoosh and a clatter as she took her place as fifth in line. Two topsails still billowed, filled with wind, but they were small, triangular affairs, and the wind they caught served only to maintain the ship's place in line against the strong downstream current of the spring freshets in the river. Depending from the slanting, forward mast was a large, square sail called the artemon. It was being gathered up and bound under its spar.

Bumpers were fastened along bow and stern to protect her beams and her paint against rubbing too harshly against neighboring ships, for the harbor was an exceedingly busy place on this beautiful, bracing spring day. Sailors with poles were also stationed both fore and aft to fend off collisions with river traffic, and to keep the *Swan* in her correct place in line. The captain, meanwhile, had departed in the ship's dinghy to register his turn in the line. The *Swan* was now third of seven boats waiting to use the dockside facilities. So many vessels lay at anchor that one saw in every direction the tall masts swaying against the horizon, and beyond them green hills and blue sky, with a scatter of soft clouds such as follow the end of the rainy season, undecided whether to dump their moisture or move on until they were blown clean away.

Home! Grandmother, Lystra, home! He would tell his dear ones of all the events of the journey. He would learn how they had fared. He would tell Merza's story to Grandmother, and God grant, he prayed, that all would go well in that quarter. Ah, Merza, he thought, this time I pray you will not dawdle and delay us on the road, for I long to fill my eyes with the dear sights of Lystra.

Merza emerged from the hold, where she had been helping Prisca count over once more all the parcels of her household goods, preparatory to carrying them ashore. Timothy asked, "Is Prisca packed and ready?" Prisca had brought with her what seemed to Timothy a ridiculously extensive array of goods—linens, pottery, knickknacks such as women treasure. The others had only what could be rolled within their beds.

Merza said, "Prisca is packed. I doubt she is ready. Her heart is still in Corinth. She might never have agreed to come had the little preacher not joined Aquila in persuading her. He seems to think that Ephesus will become the center for all the churches of Asia and Greece."

Her hand tightened on Timothy's arm. Her eyes were on the gleaming towers of the city which spread before them. Her voice deepened in a sort of mechanical singsong.

"You will dwell in this city. You will grow old here. You will have oversight of twoscore churches, and their elders will come to you for guidance. You will be happy in Ephesus, for churches will flourish and multiply, and you will speak with authority, for you will inherit the mantle given to you by the little preacher when he ascends into Heaven. Your wife, your sons, and daughters —elders and deacons from Asia and from Greece—all will honor you, First Bishop of Ephesus, the mother of churches."

Timothy smiled into the girl's tense face, and his hand closed over the hand which gripped his arm so tightly. "So now once more you have told my fortune. Do you want to see the color of my penny?"

Merza turned away. "I will go and see if Prisca needs me."

"No, no. Stay with me. What's the matter, Merza? Have I offended you? Surely you do not think me as gullible as that child in Lystra?"

"Why not? Oh yes, I am menial now, milker of goats,

floor-sweeper, pot-washer, clothes-mender. I no longer wear the leather collar." She touched the amber beads at her throat. "When you go to Philippi with the little preacher next year you must take these back to Niko. I rarely wear them. They are not suitable for so menial a slave as I."

"When did you decide that you are not worthy of the beads?"

"Does it matter? I told your fortune a few years ago, when we were both children. You believed me and it changed your life. This that I told you today is a true fortune, and the vision is the first I have had since I left Philippi. And you laugh at me. Oh, Timothy, life for me is dull. I wish I were on the road with Zenon once more. Look at my hands. How many hours of labor does it take to form such calluses?"

Timothy's eyes narrowed as he stared out over the glowing, marble city. "You surely do not expect me to believe that all that glory is for me?"

Her mouth tightened. She said nothing, but she did not meet his probing glance.

He said, "Merza, over and over you have told me how you invented fortunes. Why should I believe this—this tale of a glory to which I have never aspired?"

"Because it is a true fortune. And I do not want your penny nor would I take even a gold piece if it were offered. There is no price upon the fortune."

"Merza, I would like to understand you. I have seen your patience. Prisca has appreciated your help. It troubles me that you have found life with Prisca degrading. Do you think living with Grandmother on the farm will be different, or easier?"

"I think we will work together on the farm. I will not be doing all the menial work while others practice their skilled professions. I do not mean to make a fuss, Timothy. I am trying to learn to be a good slave."

"Very well. When we take the road to Lystra I shall

expect you to be obedient, and walk beside me and keep up with the pace I set."

"If I do not, you can of course beat me." When Timothy did not reply, she said, "The hills of Asia have made you homesick for Lystra."

She was reading his thoughts, but he refused to admit it. He said, "How green are the hills—like the hills at home in early spring. And how beautifully the city nestles among them. This is a splendid city, fitted in all ways, but especially in its location, to become central to all the churches of Asia and Greece. That wide avenue yonder is like nothing I have ever seen. It runs straight through the city, from the great arch over the harbor to the double arch at the other end, with the green park beyond. I suppose that must be the great Temple of Diana we have seen on Asian coins."

"The Temple of Diana is at the far end of the Avenue Arkadiane, facing on the green park. Opposite it, nestling into the side of the mountain, is the great theater. They say it seats more than twenty-five thousand persons. It is a well-planned city, with the avenue marching up the center, lined with shops like a vast agora, and the city streets branching from it on both sides into the hills. The avenue is paved with marble and almost twoscore feet in width. I heard all this while I dwelt in the house of the lady Julia and her husband, Philologus the Asiarch. The length of the avenue is three stades. The theater is used oftener as an arena where men fight with beasts than as a place where dramas are performed."

"Come soon, Lord Jesus," Timothy murmured, and remembered that his mission in life was to hasten the coming of the Lord Jesus and his kingdom, bringing an end in the earth to the cruelty of men toward one another.

He asked, "Are you also homesick to see Grandmother Lois?"

Her eyes no longer met his. "I am afraid. I am afraid she will send me away, as Lydia did, or make me into a beast of burden, as Prisca has done. I am also afraid she might keep me out of charity, not really wanting me. Oh, Timothy, I was once a slave of great value. Nobody wants me anymore, nor do I feel content doing menial work when I have one skill at which I excel, but which I am forbidden to use. To you I am a burden, nothing more. You ought to find someone who wants a fortune-teller, and sell me. You could get enough money for me to finance many missionary journeys."

"I will never sell you."

"Then take me into the agora, here in Ephesus. Let me tell fortunes here. The money I earn would pay for our journey to Lystra even if we stay in the best taverns, and leave you with money to buy presents for Eunice and Lois."

The boat had been edging ever nearer to the wharf, as the ships ahead discharged passengers and cargo and turned into the broad anchorage. Now the *Swan* was second in line.

Timothy said, "Merza, I respect your talent as a clairvoyant. This is a remarkable gift. But when you set yourself up to tell fortunes in the agora you depend on fortunes you invent. It is cheating to take money for such stuff. Nor do I think it right to ask money for even the true visions. You have a great gift. When it is honestly used it should be freely used, for whoever will benefit from it. You received this gift without price, and should use it without price, as Paul uses his gifts in spreading without price the Good News."

"I wish you had explained all this before. Timothy, why didn't you say all this to me long ago? You are quite right—my fortunes are, most of them, built on—imagination. Call it lies if you like. I was proud of my quick and ready wit. I am proud when I look into a face and read something there about the person—his habits, his desires, his dreams. I did that very well. I was proud that people would wait for hours in the heat or the cold hoping I would tell them what they wanted so much to hear. It did not seem important to me that much of what I said was sheer invention. But you are right. It is false to offer the fruits of one's imagination as if there were some kind of magic back of them."

Timothy watched her face, listening intently. She was not the girl who had dawdled along the Greek roads. She had changed. Her eyes were clear, her mouth was firm. Her hands were strong and sure, no longer restless, groping. The curling, chestnut hair was clean and disciplined, the hazel eyes direct. He said, "You ought to keep the amber beads, Merza. They become you. You are a very pretty girl. I wish Lydia had given you the russet chiton to wear. That, with the beads and all, makes you look very handsome and attractive."

She smiled. "You are growing handsomer also, Timothy, now that your beard is grown so thick and soft about your jaws. Anyone who had ever seen those blue eyes with the yellow hair and all, and the dark skin coloring, would never forget you. You will make a wonderfully handsome bishop of Ephesus someday. Oh, Timothy, I want to give you something in return for all your kindness. Perhaps, when we are on the road, just the two of us, we can find a way for me to repay your goodness to me."

Timothy's face was flaming. "You know that is forbidden to me—if I am to be Paul's companion."

"Nonsense. I am your slave. How can anyone remain so ignorant about the rights of slave owners?"

"Merza, Merza, what am I to do with you?"

"I owe you a great debt. If I changed your life, long ago—well, you also have changed mine. And I have no way to repay you."

The ship was now first in line, and Paul and Silas were coming to join them. Prisca and Aquila came from the hold and together they settled upon how they would use the day, and where they would meet when their errands in Ephesus had been accomplished.

Paul and Timothy and Merza set out up the Avenue Arkadiane. Silas had remained with Prisca and Aquila to help them with their baggage, and with engaging a donkey to carry it to the house which would be provided for them by their prospective employer.

Paul was full of hope that messengers would have arrived from Macedonia with news of the churches of Philippi, Thessalonica, and Beroea. They were to meet him at the synagogue, or leave word there where they could be found.

All directions in Ephesus were relative to the Avenue Arkadiane. The synagogue, the agora, and the business establishment of Stephanas' associate were all relative to the avenue, and of the three, the synagogue was nearest to the harbor. The three of them, walking on marble pavement, moved rapidly in the general southeasterly direction toward which it pointed, moving ever closer to the towering Doric pillars for which the Temple of Diana had become famous throughout the world.

They turned right at the street of the synagogue, away from the Caÿster River, toward the green hills among which most of the dwellings of Ephesus clustered. Paul was in deep reverie, anticipating the messengers from Philippi and the other cities where he had established ecclesiae. Timothy half-listened to Merza's chatter about this building or that. Suddenly she clutched his hand.

"This is the street where the lady Julia lives. Two squares beyond the synagogue. I had forgotten about that until now. She lives in such a splendid house, but after all, why not? Her husband Philologus served his term as Archon of all Asia only a year before I was in that house. Oo-oo, Timothy, I do not want to see her."

Paul said, "Here is the synagogue. They do themselves well in Ephesus, these Jews. Their number must run into hundreds in such a great city, built on the crossroads of sea and land traffic."

Timothy said, "Merza, I think you must see the lady Julia. She will be glad to know of the change in your fortunes. Moreover, you owe it to Paul to tell these people what he has done for you. He may someday need the help of an Asiarch in Ephesus. You must go to visit Julia and take us with you."

Paul turned upon the unhappy girl. "Why don't you want to visit the lady Julia?"

Merza ducked her head, unable to meet his sharp, examining glance. "When she knew me I was a sybil. She respected my talent, and pitied me because of the abuse I had suffered. Now I am fit for nothing but to milk goats and carry clothes to the river to be washed. Nobody respects my talents anymore. I am ashamed."

"Spoken like a fool," said Paul, and entered the synagogue.

The messengers from Macedonia had not yet arrived. Paul left word that he would return before the third watch. He asked the bent little Jew who served as custodian to request the messengers, when they came, to wait at the synagogue for him. "Have you a room where they can wait for me?"

"There is an anteroom. May I tell them where they can find you?"

"I will be at the house of Philologus, the Asiarch. But do not send them there. Ask them to wait for me here. Or if they do not come before I return I will wait here for them."

24

THE HOUSE of Julia and Philologus was larger than Lydia's, larger than the house of Stephanas in Corinth. The portal was ornamented with statuary and a plaque over the door showing twin boys suckling a wolf—actually it was the identical scene that was sewn in appliqué on the great sail of the *Swan*. The pagan statuary meant nothing to the little preacher, though Merza saw Timothy eyeing it with a certain interest, and knew he had recognized the two male figures. One she knew to be Apollo of the Python—Pythian Apollo was lord of the fortune-telling shrine at Delphi—she recognized it easily. The other figure held a sword and shield. Timothy would recognize it no doubt, but Merza did not. Nor was she in a mood to speculate on these matters. She shivered in nervous dread in the sheltered entry.

"Philologus can do anything he likes with me. He may accuse me of evil intent and cast me into prison. He is an Asiarch. He has the power."

"Peace, girl," said the little preacher impatiently. "Good will come of this visit. Do not doubt it."

A pretty maid with fair complexion and blue eyes answered their knock, but not until it had been twice repeated. Paul made ready to speak. But the maid stared hard at Merza, and cried, "You! Go hence! You are not wanted in this house." Then, with a look at Paul and Timothy, "These are not the men who came with you before. Wait a minute. I will speak to the lady."

She left them outside the portal. In a moment the lady Julia appeared. She was panting, from apprehension perhaps, or from haste, for she was heavy with child. Even with the blue mantle over her head Merza saw that her black hair was streaked with gray. Nevertheless, she was still a woman of dignity who carried herself well in spite of the burden of pregnancy.

Whatever she had come to the portal to say to them, their manner and presence softened her. "Come inside, if you wish," she said coolly. "Really, Merza, I don't know what your game is. You certainly look better than when you came here three years ago. But I have already told your accomplice that the child died in her first year. You need not expect anything from Philologus, or from me. Who are your companions?"

Paul said, "Madam, I am Paul, a citizen of Tarsus. This youth is my traveling companion, Timothy of Lystra. Merza is now his slave. We are sorry to hear of the death of the child. We called to inquire as to her well-being, as well as your own."

The lady listened, her eyes fixed on the little preacher. She said, "Sir, I well believe you mean no harm to any in this house. Come into the reception room and be comfortable." And the maid drew back the curtain of a small room which opened off the passage.

It was a warm and colorful room. The floor was thick with rugs. On a handsome, carved chest along the wall were ornaments Merza remembered from her previous visit to this house. When they were seated on the rugs, Merza dropped her face into her hands, confused by the strange sense of loss she had felt ever since hearing that her child was dead.

The lady Julia motioned to the maid, saying, "Bring wine. Will you have cakes, sir?"

"Nothing, madam. We are rather pressed for time."

Merza said softly, "She died, the little girl. And all this while I thought of her as my gift to you, my lady, in return for your great kindness." There was a kind of soft gentleness in her manner which struck Timothy as remarkable.

Paul said, "Madam, if I understand you correctly, the man who recently came to you and threatened you concerning that child is a person called Bias. He was never Merza's owner, nor was she ever his willing companion. He is by no means her accomplice. Merza has been with us in Corinth for a year and a half, and before that she was with our friends in Philippi. We have just this day arrived in Ephesus by ship. The man Bias formerly traveled with Merza and Zenon, whose slave she was. Zenon was murdered by Bias in Thessalonica more than a year ago. Three witnesses heard Zenon's dying accusation of Bias. One is this young man Timothy, who is my companion in travel. Another is also with our party, but still at the harbor. The third witness is a resident of Thessalonica, where the murder occurred. Zenon and Bias abandoned Merza in Philippi eighteen months ago, after her demon was cast out by the power of God, whose ministering servant I am."

The maid had appeared with wine. The lady said, "I am glad to see that your situation has so greatly improved, Merza. You are looking very well—extremely well. I was sad to send you on your way three years ago in the company of that brutal creature Bias. He said, when he appeared here last month, that he was father to the little girl you gave me. You will not be grieved to learn that this ruffian is now among the criminals who will fight with beasts in the arena during the spring festival of Diana."

Merza drew a deep breath and expelled it. "Then we will not encounter him in the streets. When you mentioned that he had been here it filled me with such dread, my lady. Still, evil as he is, I cannot believe that even Bias should be punished so barbarously."

"No punishment is too harsh," said the lady fiercely, "for a man who would try to steal my child!"

Merza looked at the lady through narrowed eyes. She said softly, "You are going to be delivered soon of a child. I am very glad to know that the fortune I told you is being fulfilled."

The lady's dark face grew warm with happiness. She pushed back the blue mantle. "This baby will be my second, Merza. I was with child when you were here, but did not know of it. My firstborn is only a few months younger than the little girl you gave me."

"That is the way I saw you." Merza's face had taken on a shine of happiness. "There were three children, two of them much of a size, and the third somewhat smaller, an infant. You are very wise, my lady. You told Bias the child had died. You were protecting both children, the one you had borne and the child I gave you. That one has given you happiness for three years now. I am so very glad to see that this is true."

Paul said abruptly, "Madam, it is evident that you have two children. I am a servant of the Most High God, as Merza publicly testified more than once. I have an urgent desire to bless both the children of this household."

"You are a good man," said Julia. She clapped her hands, summoning the maid. She said, "Bring the children, Philomena—both of them."

Merza began weeping when they left the house. "What is wrong with me?" she sobbed, as they turned down the street toward the synagogue. "I have not wept since I was a small child. I cannot remember when last I wept, it was so long ago. Tears angered Bias, and I learned very young not to anger Bias." And she sobbed into her white linen mantle as she walked along the street between Timothy and Paul.

Paul said, "We will soon be in the shelter of the synagogue. Your tears are beautiful, Merza. Tears can cleanse away much evil from the soul."

Timothy put his hand on the girl's shoulder, guiding her along the cobbled pavement.

They reached the splendidly massive synagogue with its deep-carved Hebrew lettering across the lintel. In the shadows of the entry Merza sobbed aloud. "Paul, ah, Paul, you make me so ashamed. You are all goodness, loving and caring. Isn't she beautiful, my little daughter? When you laid your hands on her to bless her, I remembered the ugliness of her conception, the hatred in me because she had meant to me only pain and anger and helplessness. And when you blessed her, all the ugliness, all the evil seemed to wash away. I saw her, a gay, pretty child with no trace of the hideousness of her begetting. Now I know what you mean—God can separate our sins from us, as east from west. Dear Timothy, isn't she beautiful, my little daughter? I thought she would be ugly and hateful, like Bias. But she is not."

They had entered the synagogue and were crossing, following the bent old custodian, toward a smaller room where, it seemed, someone was waiting for them. But Paul halted in the big, shadowy room where Jews came together to worship. He gathered Merza into his embrace.

"Put your head on my shoulder, dear child. When I think of the hideous experiences you have survived in the few, short years of your life I want to weep with you."

Merza sobbed against his shoulder. "You are kind and good, so wonderfully kind and good. You also, Timothy." She reached out blindly to touch Timothy's face and caress it. "And when I think of Lydia! She could hardly bear the trouble and pain I brought you, Paul, yet she tried hard to be kind. But I deceived her and lied to her. I was cruel to Erethrea and Niko, because the lady loved them and could not love me. And you, dear Timothy—" She turned from Paul to take Timothy's face between her two hands. "Ah, Timothy, how could you love me when I treated you so shamefully?"

Paul said, "Merza, dear child, this is repentance—sorrow for sins committed and the resolve with God's help to go and sin no more. Accept the gift of forgiveness in Jesus' name. Repentance is the first step. The second step is learning to live as a Christian. First one must get right. Then one begins to live a righteous life."

"I know, Paul. The Good News—I have heard you preach it, many times. It is all clear now. I have been so blind to the hidden meanings of your message, but it is clear to me at last." As suddenly as it had begun the weeping was ended. "Will you baptize me, Paul? Before you sail for home?"

"Timothy will baptize you, Merza. It is fitting that he do this."

The custodian still hovered, bewildered by this scene of high emotion. Now he said, "Come, sir. Your friends are waiting. They are in the anteroom yonder, both of them."

Merza said, "Timothy, I will be a good slave. I promise."

"Come," said Timothy. "Rufus is here, Rufus and Sopater, the scribe from Beroea. They are waiting to greet us."

Merza turned with a cry to where the two men stood in the curtained doorway of the anteroom. "Rufus? Are you really here, Rufus?"

While Paul was greeting the scribe from Beroea, the

girl was suddenly gathered into the close embrace of the red-haired, red-bearded master of Lydia's dye works.

"God be praised," said Sopater, embracing Paul, then Timothy. "You left us in such haste, at hazard to life and limb. How glorious to see you looking well. We have heard that your mission in Corinth has prospered splendidly. You arrived ahead of us by a few hours. Our pilot had a fearful struggle against the Caÿster's current. Paul, Paul, you look well! I have so much to tell you."

Rufus held Merza's arms between his dye-stained hands, looking joyfully into her radiant face. And Timothy acknowledged with a wrench of joy mingled with pain, Those two belong together.

Sopater exclaimed, "Dear friends, what a joy this is. We bring nothing but good news."

Rufus held Merza against himself. "I also bring good news. Our ecclesia flourishes. Luke is an excellent pastor, both in Philippi and in the other churches of Macedonia, as Sopater will agree. Lydia has commissioned me to bring Merza back to our dye works. She will not be content till this girl is again one of our household. Nor will I, as the lady now knows. Timothy, I have Lydia's consent to make this girl my wife. Has she yours?"

Close in the shelter of his loving embrace, Merza said, "This is where I belong." She reached for Timothy's hand. "With your permission, dear Timothy?"

"You have my blessing." Timothy thought his heart had not been so light in many months. This was the right ending to the story of Merza which he would carry home to Eunice and Lois. Merza would be where she belonged, and Timothy now knew that was all he had ever wanted for her.

Paul said, "Come with us to the agora. We have friends there I want you to meet—tentmakers from Corinth. Aquila and Prisca, whose father founded an ecclesia in

Rome. Come along. The letters can wait until they can be read to Silas and Prisca and Aquila. Ah, Sopater, did you know that there is an ecclesia in Rome? How long have you before your boat sails? Oh, my friends, to know that we will see you again in Beroea and in Philippi when Timothy and I set out upon our third journey, next year or the year after! God is good! God is good!"